GIVE IT TO ME

GIVE IT TO ME

A NOVEL BY

ANA CASTILLO

THE FEMINIST PRESS
AT THE CITY UNIVERSITY OF NEW YORK
NEW YORK CITY

Published in 2014 by the Feminist Press
at the City University of New York
The Graduate Center
365 Fifth Avenue, Suite 5406
New York, NY 10016

feministpress.org

This project is supported in part by an award from the National
Endowment for the Arts.

First printing May 2014

Cover design by Herb Thornby
Text design by Drew Stevens

Library of Congress Cataloging-in-Publication Data
Castillo, Ana.
 Give it to me : a novel / by Ana Castillo.
  pages ; cm
 ISBN 978-1-55861-850-3 (pbk. : alk. paper) — ISBN 978-1-55861-863-3
(hardcover : alk. paper) — ISBN 978-1-55861-851-0 (ebook)
1. Mexican American women—Fiction. 2. Self-actualization (Psychology) in
women—Fiction. 3. Divorced women—Fiction. 4. Family secrets—Fiction.
I. Title.
 PS3553.A8135G58 2014
 813'.54—dc23

2014003221

Acknowledgements and Disclaimer

I would like to thank the friends and colleagues
who read the first draft of this story and generously
lent their comments. Also, many thanks to Amy Scholder.

All characters and accounts here are fictional.
Any resemblance to actual persons is purely coincidental.

For the sake of sobriety,
not necessarily my own.

and

For San Antonio de Padua
who helped me
in Kazakhstan.

★ PART ONE ★

1 Mucho traffic and a stampede of plebes down below. Above all, Mulch. Mulch was what Palma Piedras called the wide and astonishingly ordinary middle class at the start of the twenty-first century. Horns blasting, cops' whistles blowing, and an ambulance stuck and siren ignored. She watched them hurry against changing traffic lights in their khaki shorts, flip-flops or sports shoes, and T-shirts or cheap polos. Big, fat men dressed like five-year-olds in baseball caps. Americans were the worst dressers in the world. She was in her hometown.

A year in Colombia.

A letter from Pepito brought her back to Chicago. He was out of prison by the time she got the letter that said he was getting out and could she meet him? A decade locked up. *Ten years, nineteen days*, he wrote. Before he did what he did to get himself locked up about five minutes after he did it—the gun was still warm—she hadn't seen him for a couple of years. During all that time she had stayed in Buenos Aires, Madrid, El De Efe, and Medellín, Colombia briefly—her ex's native tierra, her brief husband. The woman, who'd readily admit she did life better on her own, was attracted to places where Spanish was spoken because it was her other strong language. (In Italy she understood everyone but couldn't put a sentence together.)

Palma changed out of shorts she'd slipped into on that humid day and tried on a summer dress from the mall back in New Mexico. She was broke but didn't want to look broke so she hooked on her best gold hoop earrings and a gold bangle. Accessorizing her mall dress made her look more broke. She changed twice before she was back in the plaid Bermudas purchased at the Sam's Club where Palma was buying a twenty-pound bag of dog food for her forty-pound mutt back home. Home was now Albuquerque. She had returned to Chicago, among other reasons, to meet Pepito.

Pepito was her lil cous', raised by their grandmother. (Little was an expression.) She and him, together. Abuela told her way long ago that Palma's mother, the grandmother's daughter, had been born under a bad star. That bad star led her to follow a worse guy. Not Palma's father, the old woman assured her, although she never said who he might have been. One day Palma came to the conclusion that her grandmother hadn't withheld her father's true identity out of spite for her mother who dumped the girl on her after she was born, but that her abuela truly had not known who he was.

Abuela preferred her own one and only son and treated him like a baby, still cutting meat for him at the table, useless piece of shit that he was, and that never changed even after one day while in the seventh grade Palma came home from school and there was a toddler. A duffle bag the girl didn't recognize was by the door. Pepito is going to stay with us a while, Palma, Abuela said. He's taking your room. My room? The girl said. Where am I going to sleep? With me in my bed, Abuela said. Palma loved Abuela but she found the idea of sleeping with a woman who left her teeth in a glass by the side of the bed a very unattractive proposition.

THEN AGAIN, her lame uncle Jim-bo (or Jim-Boy or Jimmy or Yimmy, depending on who was talking about him or to him) had started making stops at the bedroom doorway with no door late at night when he'd come home smelling like a tavern urinal. The girl had sensed the soused louse lingering and then move on. Even at twelve, and during the unenlightened days in the country's health education history when such things like sex were not considered appropriate to discuss with kids, she knew about *sexish* things.

One day Giovanni, handsome as the devil's own and dumb as dental floss, and she were in the coat closet while the other kids were at recess. He had his fingers way up there like tiny miners lost in the catacombs when they realized the teacher had stayed at her desk during recess. They peeked out and saw her trying to readjust her tights, one leg had been noticeably twisted around the ankle. The teacher had two rods for ankles but football-player calves. Mrs. Preston had taken the hose off at her chair and was now pulling them up straight, the dress up near the bra line. It made Palma and Giovanni hot, and when he stuck his fingers up the girl again she thought he busted her hymen since he'd gone up like an electric screw gun.

Giovanni had been held back because first he was from Italy and didn't speak English very well, and second, because, in any case, it wasn't a language problem why he did so badly in school. By the time they reached eighth grade Giovanni was turning sixteen that summer, and he dropped out. He went to work at his family's deli business on Harlem Avenue. Palma often thought of Giovanni during those long dry spells when she had to rely on her own fingers. She'd recall Giovanni reaching up there and them both thinking of Mrs. Preston's pillow ass with stretch marks and flesh dark as a roasted chestnut with no panties as she gave her tights a clever snap around the flap-over waist.

NOW, GETTING ready for Palma's reunion with Pepito, she slipped on Michael Kors loafers that matched the bag (near-Alta-Mulch-level birthday gifts from a woman left behind) and the bi (buy?) everything woman expelled herself from the hotel room. She didn't know what it was about hotel rooms, but they had the genuine power to suck you in and make you want to stay in them until you died. You became an instant porn addict, threw cochon to the wind and ordered room service late for an overpriced burger that you'd never have ordered except that you suddenly felt like committing suicide and therefore, it was not a problem (another thought you didn't have until you were stuck in that room with a Gideons Bible and nothing to do). You masturbated like a fourteen-year-old boy with a bad case of acne and no social life or later hit the minibar, got loaded, and started texting people who didn't want to hear from you.

The one thing you wouldn't do was pick anyone up. You'd seen enough *Dateline* mysteries. (There was that pretty Russian blond who got into a hotel elevator with a big dude. Cyclops huge. It was caught on camera. Later, you saw him casually leaving the building pulling a large suitcase on wheels. The victim was in that suitcase folded up like a rag doll. Incredibly, she survived.) As for God's hand in the matters of Palma's life, she was dealt the revengeful, wrathful Lord of the Old Testament. If he even ever bothered with a gentile, he had no reason to be any more compassionate with her religion-free existence than he was to Job, Adam, or Moses, who he was constantly testing and they were his favorites.

Palma Piedras had survived thus far. She'd survived

Abuela's house and tío Jim-Bo and Pepito's whininess during his childhood (spoiled from her grandmother's preferring anything with a penis. That's why he got Palma's room). Pepito was a terrible two when he came to their household. The kid got into everything, drank toilet water with the cat. The tomcat, good for killing rats, taught the new household member a few survival tricks of his own. It was as ugly as a boil on your ass, but Pepito was all the opposite. Whose looks he had inherited she didn't know because Palma never met his mother. She suspected he was Jim-Bo's kid and that one of the skanks he went out with on Saturday nights brought Pepito over to Abuela's, once the baby could walk and had stopped sucking titty. He didn't look like Jim-Bo; he looked like the Angel Gabriel.

When he was seventeen Pepito got a girl in the neighborhood pregnant or so the girl claimed when she came over with her mother and father to force Pepito to do the right thing. Now you see what you did? Abuela said, probably imagining the horrors of having the girl move in, drop a kid, and then leave it there for her to raise at eighty-something. She slapped Pepito. He was taller than the shrunken grandma, of course. Taller than Jim-Bo. A boxer, in fact. Only Abuela could touch him and get away with it. Pepito decided the right thing was to leave home.

Palma was done with her first marriage and, by then, living on her own. It took her eight years to get her bachelor's degree. During the day she worked as a docent at the Art Institute. Tour guides normally had their degrees in fine arts. Palma Piedras, lone satellite orbiting in space, had her ways.

NOW PEPITO was out and they decided to meet after all those years. She concluded he wouldn't care that she was forty-plus (to his thirty-two) because he was like a brother to her.

Palma had sent him money now and then. Who else thought of him? A pining ex-girlfriend looking up old boyfriends when finalizing a divorce or drunk with her girls when one would say, Whatever happened to that melt-in-your-mouth caramel, what was his name? Pepito, she'd say. It came right to her lips as if he were waiting for the return of his tongue. She looked him up or asked around and got his address. They'd started writing and she'd send money. Palma figured there were ex-girlfriends because there was one true fact, besides his nature, the Mexican killer instinct, and that was his being a lover. Or so she imagined.

One time when she was living on her own, and Pepito was all of fourteen, he cut school and had the nerve to go to her flat. She was home with a cold that day, studying in bed. He bought a can of Campbell's chicken noodle soup and a small jar of Vicks VapoRub. She thought he was el Niño Fidencio with a buzz cut. Palma felt like the loneliest woman in the world when she was sick like that. He left them on the kitchen table and followed her to the broom-closet-size bedroom where the sick woman climbed back into bed. He looked at her hard, smiling. Fourteen and already cocky. A man with secrets. Fucking, no doubt, not jacking off like a choir boy.

She was all snot and puffy eyed. Her long hair was pulled up in a bun with stray hairs stuck to her sweaty neck. His big cousin stared back at him. Are you in a gang? She asked him. What? Me? Naw, man. I ain't stupid. She wanted him to fuck her but all she said was, That's good. You're a good kid. Abuela would kill you, if you did join a gang. Jim-Bo . . . Aw, he said, waving a hand, meaning he didn't give a flying fig about their uncle. He called him tío, like she did, when he was little, but as soon as he passed Jim-Bo in height he referred to him by name—if he felt like being polite. He was right. If he had been

8

Jim-Bo's son, as the primitos were both led to believe while Abuela never came out and said it, why hadn't Jim-Bo stepped up to the plate? Too late by the time Pepito was in her micropad, three stories up in the big apartment building she lived in then. Palma remembered Giovanni and his *Magic Flute* fingers and looked at her little cousin's. They were nothing like the boy's in the classroom coatroom. Pepito's were powerful. He was already boxing. Maybe he did it to keep himself out of a gang. Maybe he was lying to her and had already gotten into one.

Well, I best be going, prima, he said. Grin. Secrets. My girl's waiting downstairs for me, he said, hand on the front doorknob. You have a girl? Palma asked. Yeah, of course, I got a girl, man, he said. It was about twenty-two degrees out that day. She wrapped a blanket over her shoulders, went to the window, and watched him exit downstairs. A waif in a heavy coat, mittens, ski cap, and long, black hair waited out there. He took her hand and they trudged off in the snow. The girl slipped on a patch of ice and he quickly grabbed hold and steadied her.

Palma didn't see Pepito for a long time after he left Abuela's. Or at least, she couldn't remember. Abuela caught her up on him. He was living for a while with a girl a little older than himself who had two little kids. She came over one time and complained that he had not come home all night. Another time, she came by, crying because he had left her. What do you want me to do to him? Abuela said to the girlfriend each time. He's a grown man, now. He don't listen to nobody, anyway. The third time the girlfriend came by, before she could state her complaint Abuela stopped her, didn't even invite her in. You want to be with a man like that then be woman enough to accept how he treats you, she said. But I love him, the girlfriend said. Abuela closed the door in her face. Pero, lo quiero, Abuela mimicked in Spanish. Bah, Abuela said.

PALMA PIEDRAS never went to her grandmother with complaints about the men in her life. She never went to the viejita during the good times, either. The granddaughter knew well enough that the old woman would cast her pessimist spell on her new love and kill it. Abuela didn't trust men. She loved only Jim-Bo. She didn't trust women, either. When Palma was fifteen, her equivalent of the quinceañera, the fifteen-year-old princess party given to most girls, was a short speech. Remember, if you get yourself pregnant and have to drop out of school, you'd better not come to me. I'm not raising any more hüerquillos. (Punks. She and Pepito.) A few months after Palma's fifteenth birthday, when she got pregnant that winter, her best friend's mother took her on three bus rides out of the city to a private doctor's office in Lincolnwood. They worried that public-funded clinics might require her guardian's consent. The lady fronted the three hundred smackaroos the private doctor charged, a fortune for the girl.

She stayed in bed for a few days complaining of the cramps, which often had her bedridden back then, so her abuela may have not suspected anything. If she did, she didn't say. After that Palma's boyfriend and she had anal sex, their idea of contraception. Her boyfriend dropped out of school, joined the Army, and she soon forgot him and his pulsating dick that sought every orifice of her body. It was easy to forget him because she soon heard he had another girlfriend all that time and she was pregnant with his kid. The dick was killed when home on furlough before the baby was born. A drive-by, they said.

With all due respect, he wouldn't have kept her attention long; by then, what she wanted was to be the next Picasso. Since the girl learned to hold a crayon, she made art. On the white, bloodied butcher paper Abuela discarded, brown carton flaps, and backsides of junk mail. Whatever the girl found to color on became her media. Abuela wasn't big on buying supplies for Palma's "fooling around." In college, svelte and with a passion for dressing up—with or without much of a wardrobe—she designed clothes. They stayed mostly on paper. Art was an expensive enterprise. Somewhere along the line Palma took a turn and instead became an admirer of fine arts and fashion, a coveting aficionado as a tour guide and translator.

She also (and maybe for reasons unrelated to the progenitor of her eliminated embryo) began to see herself as the heroine of the tragedy that was her life. Palma pretended they'd had a great love and that he died a war hero. She never told this story to anyone, just to herself until she started believing it. Palma never took drugs and couldn't hold her liquor. It was all a good thing because the girl's rich imagination had her deluded enough. She liked watercolors, and painted a picture of the dog the Army boyfriend gave her for Christmas as a puppy. Then one day the dog disappeared and she framed the painting and hung it in the living room as an homage. The girl liked her dog well enough but she *loved* him when he was gone. At least that was the impression she gave anyone who'd ask about the picture, Whose dog was that? (Or, What's that?) Palma would say, It's Snowball. It doesn't look like Snowball, the person would say. Not long after that Palma quit painting.

It was hard to believe, but when Palma painted Snowball, Pepito was six years old. His first grade teacher was in love with him. His "big cousin" had taught him to read at four, and the teacher thought he was a prodigy. Palma wanted Abuela to put him in a good school or at least try to get him in a gifted class. Abuela la Evangélica spent a lot of time in her church. She didn't have patience for such nonsense. Anyway, Pepito was not a genius except at seduction. He fooled his teachers but he never fooled his prima. He could get passed on to the next grade if the teacher was a female. And one year, a male teacher. Usually male teachers and he did not get along. It was a mental macho standoff to the end of the school year. Palma was long gone out of Abuela's home when all that was going on. The old woman kept her up on things.

Another chance encounter came to mind. It was the summer before Pepito went to prison. She was coming up the steps to Abuela's and he was rushing out. Hey! He said, and gave her a hug and a kiss on the cheek. Hey, she said. He made her nervous. Palma already sensed danger in him, the danger that perhaps came with a sociopath in the making. His body was solid. If she were a porn star she would have picked him to co-star with her without hesitation. That one with the shaved chest and the thick indio hair. Take off your clothes. Let's see what you got. Oh yeah. He'll do. Palma Piedras wasn't a porn star, and this was long before porn, considered the epitome of seedy, became a household word, before poles were set up in bedrooms to spark up Mulch marriages and Mulch fiancées were allowing strippers to give them lap dances at the request of future husbands to turn them on with girl-on-girl power.

She was going on thirty, single, and overall not feeling that eye-catching on her grandmother's front porch that day, except as the proud bearer of a Bachelor's degree. She was going to show it to Abuela that day. (Abuela was not impressed, given the fact that Palma had no job, and what good was education, much less education for a woman, if not to help her provide for her family.)

Hey, she said again to Pepito and held out the envelope

mailed to her with the degree. I just finished college. A Bachelor's in Fine Arts. Even as she said it she knew it didn't mean jack shit to him. He didn't give a damn about finishing high school but he flashed his Pepsodent smile, Oh yeah? Congratulations, Prima, he said, and took off. She watched him cross the street to his vehicle. It was new. How had he managed to get a brand new Land Rover? He turned and saw her staring. Palma's face went red. He threw his gym bag in the back seat and waved before getting into his ride. The man with secrets. He knew she had been watching his ass.

PEPITO'S PRIMA was outside now, teeming with Mulch as the streets were throughout Chicago's summers, wondering if he had ever watched her ass. There wasn't much of one to watch. She was still the thin-bone woman much like the one he saw on the porch that day over a decade earlier. Now Palma had the finest of crow's feet. Her boobs were not as well positioned as they had been then. She'd had a hysterectomy the year before. Instead of standing on the corner where they agreed to meet, she went across the street. Palma wanted the first-glimpse advantage.

She didn't even see Pepito until his arms were around her and his mouth on her own. She was holding a Starbucks cup to keep her skinny bod steady, and it nearly went flying when he grabbed hold of her. Palma felt nothing from the kiss that was meant to sweep her off her feet and part with all her sense and money, she was sure. You knew from a kiss and Palma suspected he had the same reaction but more than anything, he acted nervous about seeing her.

They walked along the avenue holding hands. Actually, he gripped hers, like Palma might run off, which in fact did cross her mind. She was embarrassed to be walking with a thug. He could have been in an orange jumpsuit wearing his prison numbers, she felt it was that obvious. The strut. The posturing. Want a piece of this? each step spoke. And she, in her plaid, synthetic Bermudas from Sam's and puny arms swinging in the early summer air, like a pet on a leash. Once upon a time she wanted to be an artist. Short of that, a fashion designer, except that it was all about connections. Either way, she never would have pictured herself walking along the Magnificent Mile of Michigan Avenue when she was past forty in sweatshop clothes with a not-so-much-too-cool but too-old-for-school former gangbanger.

A street musician playing sax (two bucks in his open case on the sidewalk to give passersby a clue) hit the first notes of "Let's Get It On" when they sat on a bench nearby. Are you kidding me? Palma gestured to the guy. He stopped, nodded, dried off the mouthpiece, and switched to Aretha. "R-E-S-P-E-C-T." Pepito and she each wanted the other and each didn't want to be wanted. That day Pepito was taking her down. She was taking him down, too. He looked out of breath. It's too much, he said. What? She asked. Seeing you, again. Being here. *Pepito vulnerable?* That could work for me, Palma thought. (Women stuck on stupid had those thoughts all the time, didn't they? Maybe he'll see how much he needs me, they told themselves.)

Pepito got hold of himself, stood up, and took her hand. Dead woman walking, Palma thought, as she saw they were headed in the direction of her hotel. Hey, how 'bout we get something to eat? She asked. He wasn't hungry, he said, although by the size of the man he could obviously pack it in. Their inevitable getting together, when it finally came down to it, frightened the living scampi out of her. They stopped at a place with tables outside. All he ordered was coffee. Sign of a cheap man. And not so bright, since she was treating. She ordered an egg and toast. Palma hated eggs. (Who came up with the idea of eating an animal's preborn?)

You could always order a bloody mary or a mimosa at nine a.m. and not sound off the AA alarm, but right out of the gate she asked for a double shot of tequila. The egg was a ruse. Pepito ate up everything on the plate, so no waste there. Palma swigged down the tequila like it was her last wish. She didn't want Pepito to know she was seeing dos of him so she put her Tom Ford shades back on. Let's go to your hotel, he said again. After Palma paid the bill they got up, and he gave his older cousin a French kiss. She bit his bottom lip hard. He ran an index finger over it. Okay, he said. I can bite, too. Her Day-of-the-Dead skeleton body let him take her hand and lead Palma rattling in the direction of the hotel. She wanted banter. Smooches. A prayer. They marched in silence.

In the elevator he predictably came toward her. The mirrors and unpardonable lighting in the elevator . . . Color me freaked out, she thought, seeing her two dots for eyes in the reflection as they hit fourteen. (Really thirteen but hotels skipped that number for the sake of the superstitious.) She took his baseball-mitt hand, and led him to room 1413.

Palma left her room more or less made up and crime safe by putting away her jewelry just in case she didn't come back alone. (What did she know about Pepito anymore?) They ended up not fucking. He came out of the bathroom fully dressed and her, now in leopard-print Victoria's Secret crap.

I know somebody who owes me forty grand, he said. (But of course, he did.) Maybe you can contact him for me. (Wait for it . . .) I'll give you half. He laughed to himself a little, Okay, not half. But I'll give you ten. *Ten what? Ten knocks upside her head? Get the fuck out of here*, all of which Palma did not say, but thought. She was getting the Bermudas back on. Forget it. I'll find him, he said, obviously aware of his error in judgment. Don't worry. I'll take care of you, anyway, prima, he said, meaning a share out of the fantasy $40K. Yeah, don't do me no favors, she said, and pointed with her chin to the door. He could hardly get a word out when Palma let it close in his face.

2 Jim-Bo stayed in Abuela's house after she died. He had lived there his whole life. He brought a skank to live with him and make his tortillas. Abuela had made him fresh flour tortillas every morning of his life. His skanks could hardly keep themselves clean so Abuela's house must have become a percolating petri dish. He always got into the mowing and trimming so outside the place looked good when Palma Piedras walked up the familiar steps of the modest bungalow on the South Side. The windows were mucky from winter grime and that was the first sign that Abuela was gone. Her Generala Abuela had the granddaughter clean the windows while growing up. Come spring, it was newspapers and vinegar buckets every Saturday.

Jim-Bo had wanted to fuck his niece since puberty, and when he opened the door his gaze feigning indifference was nothing more than a cover-up of the fact. He was in a T-shirt like he always was when not on the street. When stepping out, he put on a shirt, even to mow the lawn. He was wearing khaki pants with the belt buckle lost under his gross panzota. When Skank of Choice came out her panza was bigger than Jim-Bo's, and like his, her ass was lost in her jeans, and thick chin hairs popped out like pay parking-lot spikes. The rest of her face was gray.

Jim-Bo would not like it, Palma knew, but the bottom line was that her grandmother had gone downtown to a lawyer on the last days of her life. Everything she had to leave in the world was left to the granddaughter and Jim-Bo. The way Palma figured it Abuela had known he had a woman who might just try to take over the "estate" and turn it into Casa Pestilencia. Palma owed Abuela little beyond the tacos and tolerance she showed the girl until she moved out, but that was enough to go back there to see her wishes respected.

The place smelled of burned beans or maybe farts and she looked around for a window to open. Three TVs were on. Maybe two and a radio. Skank had a mop dog that started yapping the minute she walked up to the front door and wouldn't stop after she got inside. Palma kicked at it. Don't kick my dog, the woman said, her head of long, nappy hair partly covered with a rag. I didn't kick it, Palma said. Go inside, Jim-Bo told his old lady, meaning the kitchen, bedroom, or hole she had crawled out of. She waddled off with the yapping shit in her arms and Palma thought the second she had the opportunity she was going to knock her out.

She went straight to Abuela's room. It was all as Palma last saw it: bed, dresser, and everything, even the old woman's clothes in the closet, but now piled high with new junk all over like an episode of *Hoarders*. Veronica's just moving in, Jim-Bo said behind her. Skank a.k.a Veronica. Yeah, just moving in. Surely, she'd been there since Abuela's passing while Palma was in Colombia. They went back to the living room. Maury Povich was trying to figure out who was the baby daddy. He was competing with a two-for-one-chef-master-contraption infomercial in the kitchen, and through the floor you heard Chuck Mangione's flügelhorn sounding out "Land of Make Believe." It was coming from the basement. Who lives down there? Palma asked. It was a guess. Her son, Jim-Bo said. The woman came out of the kitchen with a spatula, You want something to eat? Palma shook her head. I was talking to him, the nasty woman said.

I came to give you this, she said, handing over the lawyer's card. Abuela left this house to both of us. What? He said, scarcely looking at the card, which she was sure he couldn't read without glasses. This was my mother's house, he said. I've lived here all my life . . . He stopped. Palma looked at him. She could feel the woman's possom eyes drilling into the side of her head. Most skanks were just skanks. They didn't have paranormal powers. She still felt a headache coming on. It was probably the sulfur smell in the air. Jim-Bo was very wrong. Her grandmother, having stoically mourned the loss of a wayward daughter, kept Palma in mind at the end. Palma also believed that Abuela was privately proud that she sought a profession—instead of leading a life that came off to the mainstream as living la vida loca but in truth was the slow and treacherous rock wall climb of a disenfranchised Latina out of the mire in which she'd been born.

You don't want this house, anyway, Jim-Bo said. You traipse all over the world. You never called my ma. You don't even live in Chicago. He looked around, and smiling, he showed rotted teeth. Palma turned away. Jim-Bo's old lady, sensing herself one foot back on the street with her Quasimodo down there, held the spatula up like a fly swatter. Palma couldn't wait to settle things, throw his ass out, open the windows, clean up and paint the place, and put up a for-sale sign. Abuela had wanted to move out for a long time but never had the nerve. Jim-Bo was like having a dead son laid out in state, which she couldn't bring herself to leave behind. Palma had no issues with giving him his half after the sale, but if he thought he was going to fart his way to China from his lounge chair in the living room, he was dead wrong. Dead. The word of the day. Synonym for her past. Muerto. It was my grandmother's wishes, she said, pushing open the storm door. Throughout the neighborhood she detested all her life, birds were chirping. It was a gorgeous June day.

3 The Art Institute had a new wing. It cost eighteen dollars for nonmembers to view. Whatever happened to art for the people? Most of it was from the twentieth-century collection they'd had for years and that Palma Piedras had long ago memorized. Some new. Ana Mendieta was exhibited there now. Palma was happy for the artist although she had flung herself (or was flung) from a window long ago. Mendieta couldn't have been very happy for the failed pintora having to pay the equivalent of a meal downtown to see the work. Maybe she wasn't a loser as much as a quitter. Anything worthwhile takes conviction, one of her instructors told Palma once. But how did one know she had the talent to "make it," the "it factor"? And what of the rich kids in her classes whose privilege would open doors regardless of whether they worked at it or not? Barred from her, it seemed, were the gallery contacts, not glass ceilings but real glass doors. Eventually it seemed practical to take a straight job.

Palma skipped lunch and treated herself to the exhibit. She walked out high on art and made her way back down Michigan Avenue where she saw Pepito waiting. He had an ankle monitor, which allowed him out for a few hours a day to look for employment. He was wearing a tight, plaid shirt and sweating from the humidity. They made eye contact as if he thought only she could see him. Maybe it was an ex-con thing, thinking they were invisible—or hoping. Most were invisible to everyone except to their target. The fact that he *saw* her told Palma that he was ready for her. Or he thought he was. She was ready for him, too. The night of the day that she threw Pepito out of her room there were about twelve texts and voicemails on her cell phone. Basic message: please, please, please, Prima. He couldn't let her go just yet, Palma was sure, because he had a live one on the hook. He wiped his brow with a cloth hanky and shoved it in his back pocket, his black, long hair tied back. When he walked he had a slight pimp gait. She hated everything about his gangster style. Palma thought for a moment about whether or not she hated him, too. Hey, he said.

Her small hand in Pepito's grip, they headed straight to her hotel. As far as her little cousin was concerned, they were consenting adults. Let's make up for lost time. We'll recapture that day I went to see you when you were sick and I was cutting school, he said. Me, fourteen and you, twenty-four.

Palma left on her bra. She had this idea that if he truly desired her he would take it off. He never did. He was a big man, twice her size and weight. He laid on his back and propped the woman on his face. He was going to ring Palma's chimes, float her boat and send her to paradise, he said. Cliché his way to her heart was how she took it. He knew she was with a woman so the intent was to show her he could do with his tongue whatever a female could do. She came so hard they may have heard her elephant mating calls in the next room. I've gotta go, he said, after getting washed and dressed. He glanced down at his ankle with the monitor. I've got a job interview tomorrow, he said. What time you leave for the airport?

What? Palma said, half believing what she was seeing and hearing. He'd wasted no time getting out of bed. Men were said not to like to cuddle, but as far as she knew this one had not been held for over diez años. He acted like a fugitive on the run. I saw Jim-Bo yesterday, Palma said. Pepito's left eyebrow went up. He looked only mildly interested. Jim-Bo, you know? Your uncle? Most likely your father? Pepito made a get-out-of-here face, put on his cheap watch, and patted down his hair. I'm making him accountable about Abuela's house, she said. It was the house we grew up in, man! Don't you care? She pelted out questions, one after the other, with no response. Then he was out the door.

4 Two days later she was back in her stucco house in Albuquerque, her cat gone, and the dog still at Ursula's. Ursula worked nights and hadn't gotten around to bringing Dog back. Palma could get him but was too worn out from her trip down memory lane. The cat would come around and the dog was fine wherever he was as long as you let him out twice a day and kept him fed. As pets went, hers were loyal only to meals. That made them ideal for Palma because it was about as far as her commitment went. Pepito had bitten her tongue and it blistered. It was the one undeniable sign that she had not imagined their shenanigans in the hotel. There was more evidence about the trip. When Palma went into Abuela's closet she got out the suitcase her grandmother had carried from Mexico as a young bride. Among other Abuela-deemed tesoros it held were the letters and postcards Palma sent from her own travels. She confiscated them, stashing them inside her bag. Back in Albuquerque, they went in the top bureau drawer. One day the ramblin' granddaughter would tell her life story.

Ursula called. She was coming over later with Dog. I'm bringing some Chinese, Ursula said. Okay, Palma said. Do they have papers? Pause. You are most hilarious, the other woman said. Why don't you audition at the comedy club and stop wasting your talents on a tired-ass dancer like me? Her ass was hardly tired but yes, she really was stripping her way through nursing school. It was Ursula's night off and she came over with takeout and the dog. What's that? Palma noticed something different about the mongrel rescue right away. Oh, I took him for his shots, she said. He's got tags. No, that other tag, Palma said. Yeah, she said. I named him. *Romeo?* Palma said fingering the brass, bone-shaped tag. Yes, she said. He's our loverboy, is he not? Why someone would adopt a dog and refuse to name it I haven't figured out, hon', Ursula said. She was in a tight exercise top and Spandex shorts. It was hot in the desert. Palma's lover was slim and well formed with reddish brown hair all gathered up on top of her head. She looked like she had been out on a run, sunburned and sweaty, and pulling off her top she started making her way to the shower. Her boobs were pale compared to the rest, and while Palma was old school and did not approve, the implants looked good. Almost real. Not *too* big. Palma didn't mind them small or hothouse tomatoes like her own. Ursula's were a business investment for the time being, she said. Once she had her nursing degree she'd have them removed.

Palma caught up to her. She kissed her mouth, moved down to her neck and then each nipple. Her lover had large areolas. They showered together and made love. (Two women making love required a whole lot of patience. More when they were standing up.) Afterward, the couple took their Chinese to bed and watched the latest broadcast of 48 Hours on the laptop. Why do you like to watch that morbid stuff? Ursula said, sleepily. Palma didn't know. Those murder investigations fed the latent state prosecutor inside her, maybe. Half the time she'd get freaked out and couldn't stop thinking about how many shows centered on wives who had been killed by their prominent doctor husbands or ministers, proverbial pillars of the community, telling herself that Abuela was right, you couldn't trust nobody. Especially not among los gringos. Yankees. Gabachos. Gachupines. Güeros. Palma turned off the light.

I've got something to tell you, Ursula whispered. There's good news and bad news, actually. Which do you want first?

I could use good news. Palma opted.

I'm quitting my job, Ursula said.

Dancing? Palma said, as if her lover had another job.

Uh-huh, she gave an earlobe nibble and stretched her taut body against Palma's. That was in fact, super news. Then she said what sounded at first like details about the good news. My mom has offered to pay for my schooling.

Your mom in Houston? Palma said. It was unlikely that Ursula was talking about any other mom so the fact that she said where Ursula's mom was revealed that her subconscious guessed the bad news. Her lover was lost without family in Albuquerque. Yes, that mom, Ursula said, the one who said she'd pay for my schooling if I came home. Palma rolled over and Ursula hugged her back, I'll miss you, she said. Palma patted the other's hands at her belly, I'll miss you, too. The truth was she liked Ursula a lot, but unlike Snowball, Palma knew that when she was gone Palma would not love her.

5 The letters and postcards that Palma Piedras sent to Abuela over the years from her adventures were spread out on the bed. Without thinking about it she had brought them out. She told herself she couldn't sleep because she'd drunk coffee too late in the day. The fact was that it was going to take time to get used to Ursula's absence. Getting unused to someone around, Palma thought, was not the same as missing them. She noticed there were a few envelopes held together with a rubber band. They weren't in her handwriting but addressed to Abuela. She picked the bundle up and turned it around a few times. The return address was in LA. Who did her grandmother know in LA? Well, the answer could be anybody. Most likely a relocated pastor from her church or former church member.

Out of curiosity as to why the old woman would keep those letters, eight with her own correspondence, Palma pulled off the rubber band. It was so brittle it snapped. They dated back to when Palma was a mere Tater Tot. Included were two business envelopes with government return addresses: The Department of Human Services. The others were in letter-size envelopes. Large, loopy handwriting. She opened one randomly. *Mami.* It was addressed to someone's mother. Palma skimmed to the end and the signature, in round letters was, *your dauhter, Angela.* (Daughter was spelled "dauhter.") Her abuela's daughter, a.k.a, Palma's biological mother. *Dear Mami, How are you? I hope well. How is our baby Palma? We miss her!* Her gaze ran frantically over the page. *Her tiny toes with teeny toenails. I love her so much,* she read . . . about her. *She's such a good baby* (i.e., said baby never cried). She put the letters in order chronologically and began reading about Angela and her boyfriend, Mariano, Jr.

Apparently, they had Palma when they were both around fifteen. Kids. (So *he* was Palma's biological father—not a rogue as Abuela insinuated.) Mariano, Jr.'s family were migrant workers, the letters revealed. Abuela was opposed to the pregnancy, the couple getting married, and most def did not want her daughter to go on the migrant trail picking onions, tomatoes, and fleas off their necks and ankles at bedtime. But Angela went anyway. (It explained why Palma's birth certificate read that she was born in Indiana.) Angela and Mariano, Jr. left her with her abuela over summer when they were working the fields with his family in that nearby state. When they came back Abuela had begun the process of taking full custody. Those kids had little wherewithal to understand what was going on. They appealed to Abuela's compassion, which only existed for Christ on the Cross, Jim-Bo, and the Holy Spirit—nothing left for bad girl Angela, who'd gone against her mother's wishes.

If only my father were still alive, Angela wrote in her last letter, *he would never have taken my dauhter away from me.* As far as Palma could tell, her parents married, stayed together, and eventually settled down in Los Angeles. *You are heartless,* Angela had written to her mother from there. Not exactly a news flash. What Palma didn't know was how had Mariano, Jr. felt about it all that time. Leaving his baby behind, and with Angela's "heartless" mother?

Everything Palma had taken for truth was rearranged.

If she'd felt sorry for herself her whole life because she believed she had parents who hadn't loved her, Palma now felt worse discovering that they had. Knowing she was possibly wanted, every corpuscle, capillary, and nerve ending started to quake. She gulped down a glass of ice water and then put the glass against her forehead. Palma's brain went rat-a-tat-tat with one doubt after the next. Had they tried hard enough to get her back? A Rubik's Cube of scenes from her entire upbringing shifted around in her head. The day-by-day blows of her upbringing. The kids in grammar school who mocked her for not having a mom and dad. Arrimada, the Mexican kids called her. It meant an orphan freeloader. What would have getting her menses been like had her mother been there, and not an old woman from a village who believed it was one more shameful aspect of femaleness? Silly things came to mind too: the mother-and-daughter tea as a senior in high school with their pretty hats and dainty gloves, going to the salon together beforehand for manicures. Palma never knew if her grandmother would have come, but as a teenager she was ashamed of the old woman—the scant English, the wrinkles, and the tote bag she used as a purse. The fact that around her own—other poor Mexicans—she was a tyrant, but with Alta Mulch or even regular Mulch, Abuela shrank until she became an India watermark on the wall. Totonaca de pata rajada she called herself.

Would someone have asked the girl to the prom if she'd had a dad willing to lend him the car and made sure the boy got her home at a decent hour instead of the word around the school being that she could be had for a song? When Palma got called dirty Mexican in the neighborhood, what if her hard-working father came out and pounded them with his farmworker fists? Would she have worked evenings waiting tables at the diner if she had parents to insist that homework came first? Did Palma have her mother's eyebrows that at fourteen she started plucking, then shaving, and then had to draw back in as slim flapper's lines? Was her humor that people called sardonic her mother's—a distilled version passed on from Abuela's acidity or from the Y-chromosome? Or instead, just an urban Darwinianesque trait adapted for survival in the South Side of Chicago?

Most of all, what Palma Piedras wondered that night was, would those anonymous parents have loved her for the girl she was, had they come back when she was eight? Sixteen? At forty-plus it was too late for a mommy and daddy, but could she ever set her heart straight?

6 *I miss you, baby.* Most of his texts were like that, short and sweet and possibly sincere. She didn't know what to make of them. Palma would have preferred that her lil cous' pick up the phone and make an old fashion call, although obviously, he already had his cell in his hand when texting. Why was he calling her baby? She didn't text back. The current object of his affections figured he was sending texts out like e-blasts to every female who gave him her digits. One day he sent a picture of himself. A kind of man-on-the-street pose. No message. He was fine, no lie, but Palma already knew that. What conceit. She saved it to her phone. Another day she got an animation of two kids on a park bench. The boy slid over and kissed the girl on the cheek. Hearts appeared like bubbles. That did it.

Palma called. Why did you send me this? She pretended to be irritated. What? He said. It's cute. It's to let you know I'm thinking of you. Palma considered the thought. Maybe time had stopped when he was in the joint and he thought he was still twenty-two, the age when he got arrested. It's fucking childish, Palma said. She used the F-word for emphasis.

Another thing he did to let her know he was thinking of her was send cold, hard cash. Not literally. It came in a cashier's check. Apparently the forty grand he mentioned that first time they met again had come through. The Post-it

31

attached read, *Your share*. Palma deposited the eight grand into her account. Pepito called and asked, Did you get my gift? She understood. Yeah, she said, it fit beautifully. (Thanks to the Patriot Act you never knew who might be listening in on your cell phone.) What did I do to deserve it? She asked. Whoa, he said. Whoa yourself.

Ain't that what family is for? He replied.

How would I know? She asked. What should I do with it? Why don't you use it to take an art class? He suggested. No time, she lied.

Buy yourself that Chanel suit you always wanted, he said. (He remembered. When she was in high school she tried to sew one from a pattern on Abuela's Singer. Sewing, as it turned out, was not her thing, and the discarded fabric in Abuela's hands made expensive seat covers). Depending on how thrifty she'd be (and taking any page out of the Abuela Book of Ultimate Frugality—from buying day-old bread to getting the kids' socks and underwear at the flea market), he'd set her up for six months. We'll see, Pepito, she mumbled.

I don't go by Pepito, anymore, He-Who-Reinvented-Himself reminded his older cous'. That was a child's name. He was grown. I go by Joe now, he said. In prison they called me Chi-Town José to distinguish me from all the other Josés. But you can call me Pepito, Prima, he said. She imagined the smile of white, even teeth, made whiter against a reddish dark hue. He had a smooth face. Palma began to trace it with her mind's eye. The square jaw and even hairline. Tell me you love me, she heard herself say. It wasn't something she had ever told any-one herself, maybe not even him as kids. Maybe she had. Was there a pause? A nano-second hesitation?

I love you, Pepito said, with a voice that nearly sounded as if he had left his body. A macho had to be the loneliest creature on earth. He never let anyone in. Women mistook the aloofness as the result of a man being wounded. Pobrecito, they said. And like the snake the old lady cared for, which once it was healed . . . people were surprised when they got hurt by such a man. Pepito's upbringing was no better or worse than anyone else's, but the macho could not let people get close because he perceived himself at war with the world.

Go to hell, she said. They hung up. Palma was at war, too. Possibly MIA. Saving Private Piedras. She went to the stereo and put on an old CD. Whitney belted *I'll be your baby tonight.*

7 Ursula had been gone a month. She took Romeo with her as Palma's going away present. (Once the dog had a name it felt too personal.) The cat had no trouble with its owner's noncommittal issues and hardly ever came around anymore. Palma discovered the neighbors were feeding it. She was left on her own in the desert. If you had a job or a relationship, a place made some sense. If you had a sick mother or a kid in school to look after. Things that nailed people down. She stopped answering Ursula's "miss you" texts.

Pepito's texts, however, were heating up, even after, or maybe because, she had initially ignored them. He had gotten a part-time job working the floor in a men's suit store and furrier managed by an "old friend." The second Palma read the text she imagined her tall, dark cousin in a three-piece suit. Something Wall Street. Distance made the libido grow fonder and she masturbated that evening in a hot bath. There were things you might imagine a thirteen-year-old girl doing, a young coed doing, young being the operative term. Most people didn't fantasize about a forty-two-year-old woman in a small bathtub fondling herself while thinking about her cousin. The truth was all over the world, women, single and married, pleasured themselves in the shadows, made ashamed of the desire they felt. They used casual encounters—the brother-in-law, cousin, pool boy, delivery boy, student, postman, UPS guy, accountant (just kidding), divorce attorney, taxi driver, school bus driver—to propel their sabotaged imaginations. Ladies now also had a ton of anonymous disembodied sources added by the Internet.

Men used porn sites, too, of course and still resorted to old-school *Playboy* issues kept behind their toilets, and maybe any woman on the street. Middle-aged guys were notoriously horny, and despite having erectile dysfunction, baldness, paunches, gastritis, colitis, no money except that which they could steal from obligations to family, bad taste in humor, boring stories to go with the lack of character, and being void of any personal sense of dress style, they managed to get some woman's attention. And society thought it okay. Men were men, the universal adage went.

Then, one ordinary evening Pepito busted all her notions about unrequited female desires across the globe and throughout the generations wide open, like a lit firecracker inside a cantaloupe.

Pow.

Her cous' called and asked, Do you remember that picture you sent when I was locked up where you had on white slacks and sandals?

Yes, she said, although she didn't.

Your hair was kind of blowing in the wind and you were standing in front of a statue. (Palma remembered. She was in Medellín. Her ex took the picture. Her head all over the place. Colombia. Rodrigo. The unprecedented sense of alienation she felt in his mother's home and in a foreign country. The letters to and from Pepito.) You looked so good, prima, Pepito said. I can't tell you how many times I got off with that picture.

What? She asked. Nothing, man, he said. You looked great. You were *thick*.

She was. A healthy woman in her prime. (That was before the hysterectomy. When he first saw her again in Chicago, Pepito said, You look frail. You need to put on some weight, girl.) She imagined him rubbing himself. That ain't me no more, Palma said. (Who was she then, between scars you saw and couldn't see?) Your hair was blowing in the wind, he repeated, and some strands fell across your face. He gave a moan. Ay, flaquita, you have no idea . . .

Palma Piedras did have an idea. Tell me, she said.

First, we have a nice dinner together. We order whatever we want. Then we go up to our room. In the elevator I am kissing you, all over, just loving you up. I have ordered champagne and a platter of goodies—chocolate, caviar, and exotic cheeses . . . (Exotic cheeses? She wondered what that meant for him. White cheddar?) *We have a glass of champagne* (Read: Andre) *and toast to our love.* (?!) *We're playing Barry White and you do a slow strip tease for me* . . .

She wanted to interrupt and ask why *he* couldn't do a strip tease for *her* but held out to see where they were going on the good-libidinous-ship lollipop.

You straddle my lap, he said, *and I put my penis inside you. I get it in way deep in that wet pussy of yours, like I always knew it was. You're wet for me now, right, baby?*

Holy cow. Heavens to Murgatroyd. Silly Rabbit, tricks were for kids. Uh, yeah.

8 One evening Palma's gay friend Randall called her to go to his bar. Why do you have to say he is gay? A woman who was no longer Palma's friend asked when she said, Randall, my gay friend . . . It was called putting it into context. What she was going to say about him would not have meant at all the same thing if you didn't know he was gay. Being gay wasn't incidental. Randall was in her bedroom, patting her off after their shower with no hard-on, maybe a slight salute to be a good sport. I am a man, after all, honey, he said. But just 'cause it goes up it don't mean it wants to go in. He gave a slight shudder for effect. Theoretically, they each had at least some of the equipment the other needed to get off. So what's the problem? Palma Piedras asked. It was mere curiosity. Okay, a little turned on. She wasn't in love with Randall. If they never fucked it was okay. I'm doing research for the Kinsey Report sequel, she said, and gave his ding-dong a tug. (He actually pushed her hand away.) But you like those effeminate types, she said. The cross-dressers with Posturepedic posteriors, implants here, there, and everywhere, and daily hormone shots. Palma cupped her olive-toned hands first over her breasts and then the butt cheeks.

I don't like *women*, Randall stated the obvious. Not that way. He elaborated to enlighten her: I like the *idea* of a woman in a hard body with a dick. Sometimes, he said, I'll dress like a bitch and let a tranny have her way with me. She nodded. Sex was very complicated and with the strict exception in any shape, form, or fashion of taking advantage of a child or a mentally incompetent adult, or any unwilling participant, for that matter, who could judge what got your rocks off? Randall pushed her gently down on the bed and started to jack off. His eyes were closed and she pulled him down next to her and started her own thing on herself. It was a true bonding experience. When she quivered after making herself come, Randall leaned over. He put his mouth on one of her nipples and gave it those little bites you felt from small fish when snorkeling. He bit the other one harder and she lifted herself up to go down on him. His dick and balls were the freshest Palma had ever smelled on a man. Or not smelled. He took impeccable care of himself. Don't do it, if you don't want, girl, he said, but he was already hard. Her clit and nipples were stiff as she sucked him off like she was lost at sea with no food or drink. Fucking bitch, he said when he started to come, pushing Palma's head into him. Fucking mamacita. Hija de su puta madre. She hadn't known that Randall spoke Sex Spanish. Dámelo, papi negro lindo, Palma muttered and he did and afterward the would-be Kinsey researcher knew that if she ever mentioned what had transpired, most likely, he'd land her in a hospital.

PALMA WENT to see Randall. He and the Chicago transplant hit it off years before because they both hailed from the Midwest as he put it. He said Chicago. He was from Milwaukee but she let him feel that was close enough. There were no female customers, and while that didn't bother Palma since she was there to visit with Randall, get a buzz with a free cocktail, and let off some steam, sometimes the men in there didn't like the presence of pheromones. Or naturally harvested tits or twat. One gay told her he thought "bitches smelled like bad fish." Oh? she said, kinda like your balls? In women's bars sometimes she'd fared no better. Palma once got blindsided with a left hook after taking a stool in a lesbian bar in Mexico City that she didn't know was being reserved for somebody's "vieja." It perplexed her as to why straight-up gays and lesbians sometimes hated on each other. At least the old-school ones did in bars in Mexico and South America and along the back roads of San Antonio and Tijuana. And if the truth were told, even in gay-activated places like San Francisco and Madrid.

She waited for Randall to catch a sec to come talk to his gal pal from behind the bar. So, what's going on with you and Ursula, lady? He asked. He already knew she was gone. Why? Palma, who liked being thought of as a lady (although she fit in a post-modern Gaga definition of it at best), asked. He explained that his cousin Ed was coming to Albuquerque to attend a seminar at the med school. Oh, he is a big, good-look-ing, successful man, Randall said. He used to work for a phar-maceutical company but has started his own, selling holistic supplements. (Palma's friend went to take a couple of drink orders and eventually was back and continued.) I know you like it both ways, he said; his waxed eyebrows went up.

I heard the same about you, Palma said.

Whatever, Randall said. After a moment, he resumed the topic: You are the only woman I know to fix up with Ed. Who am I, anyway? Randall pretended certain self-importance over the matter while he busied himself drying a glass. The mil-lionaire matchmaker? he said. He was pale like a lot of white people were in New Mexico, which was stupefying to Palma because the one thing that the state guaranteed was sunshine.

Ed goes by don Ed now, Randall laughed. He followed that don Miguel to Mexico, came back all spiritualized, looking like a born-again Buddha, quit his job, left his wife . . . oh, honey. Randall fanned himself with a cluster of cocktail napkins.

Wife?

Divorced, honey, Randall said, I never could stand that pretentious beyotch with her Beamer and plaid Ann Taylor capris and equestrian lessons. Puh-lease, girlfriend. Don Ed looks like a white Shaquille O'Neal. Go get you some while you can. Plenty for everybody.

Big. Palma Piedras liked that. She hadn't had sex in over a month. It was time to go back out on the playing field. Give don Ed my email, she said. Her cell phone was for lovers, past and present. The landline, for the current amore. And email, the application form.

9 How Palma Piedras got to Albuquerque was via Rodrigo's career. Her Colombian ex-husband was not in a cartel. He was a school administrator. They met in Chicago when he was looking for a new job. A few months later he landed one in Albuquerque. They married in Reno, and not long after settling down, they bought the house that was now her home sans Rodrigo. He was at his job about a year when his brother, who she had laid odds on then was in a cartel, contacted him. He said that their mother was ailing and that Rodrigo had to go back to Medellín, or actually, the outskirts of that mad city. The couple went, pretending it was their idea and not a brother's who was suspected of disappearing people as casually as flushing his turds down the toilet. The house in Albuquerque went up for sale, didn't sell, went up again, didn't sell, while renters through a property manager came and went. In the end they hung on to it. "Hanging on," an operative term that seemed to have hit Mulchdom like a sudden cloud of tear gas released for maximum crowd control and had otherwise been known worldwide as The Recession.

In Colombia, their Mulch marriage broke down. She wasn't able to prove it, but Palma Piedras, who'd kept her maiden name (having scarcely been a maiden at the wedding chapel), had the distinct feeling her husband's Sundays, which he spent at his ex-wife's home, had as much to do with re-kindling the flame with the ex as it did with their kid he left behind when he immigrated. That wasn't what ended it. (It only helped.) Rodrigo told Palma that in Medllín it wasn't proper or right for a wife to go anywhere without her husband. He meant an-y-where. And guess who got to care for the bedridden mother? (Why anyone would leave Palma in charge of his mother left even her to wonder.) Rodrigo deferred to the patrimony of the household. Rodrigo's older brother didn't exactly give anyone a choice when he told you what to do.

You've changed, Palma told Rodrigo, who refused to do anything together and was out a lot. *You* have to change, he said. We're not in your women's lib country anymore. Besides, here you could be killed and nobody would care.

Not long after that remark Palma did go somewhere. With one carry-on and her passport she made her way to the airport and never looked back. When the runaway wife returned to Albuquerque and filed for divorce, he did not contest. As long as she kept up with payments, he said Palma should keep the house. Now *that* was not like Rodrigo. The suggestion that he was not planning on returning to the States led her to think she might have escaped "the family business" but her marido had not. She had miraculously managed a clean break. Palma's ex, formerly a middle school vice principal, was now likely toting a machine gun and supervising a private landing strip in the middle of a cocoa plant field.

There was one thing that earned Rodrigo Reyes more than an honorable mention ribbon at the science fair. He was the only man who ever found Palma's G-spot. She knew that some men thought the G-spot a myth, feminist propaganda. She'd had true faith that it existed but no man had found it. Rodrigo did so by accident. They had a high four-poster bed and one time when they were having sex, he pulled his lover toward the edge, her legs hung over and he, standing up, entered her; it turned out to be the perfect angle for anatomical starbursts. God was good. He and Palma were going at it when the fluid spurt out and ran down. Ha, he said. Golden showers, eh? He acted as if he was cool with the unannounced program but he had struck gold all right. Palma wasn't sure at first what had happened. She just knew that she wanted it to happen again.

10 One day she got a call from an editor at Greene & Gaye Scholarly Publishing in London. They knew Palma Piedras from having translated a few César Vallejo poems for an anthology on twentieth-century Latin American poets. Would she be willing to translate the text in a coffee-table book on new Spanish artists? Spanish to English? Sí, que yes. You had to go with the flow as a Recessionista. Hopefully you weren't being pulled down the river but upstream and one day you'd wake up from the nightmare and tell yourself it was okay to make plans for your life again. They paid decent. It was a start back to financial independence or at least paying a few bills. A week later la Miss Resourceful, practical when she wasn't being extravagant, had a copy of the Spanish version of the book along with other materials. She usually worked on the translations at night when the heat went down and she could think.

Early one Saturday morning the obnoxious racket of a chainsaw and a lot of male yelling back and forth woke her. It came from next door. She knew her neighbors, avid golfers, were always gone on Saturdays. Palma threw on the flimsy, thigh-high, cheetah-print robe she'd bought for Chicago and went to the backyard. (She had thought leopard before but Palma wasn't a zoologist. It could go either way.) Pulling over a short ladder she peeked over the six-foot-high adobe wall. Two small men were up in her neighbor's mulberry like a pair of spider monkeys. One was holding a power saw as they prepared to knock off a big branch. The jefe below gave directions. A couple of others were carting wheelbarrows of gravel to lay out and flagstones for steps. One lugged a huge sack of what else? Mulch. Someone might've been planting corn while another hammered out the calendar. It was a scene out of *Apocalypto*. Does the owner know you're doing that? Palma called out. Female sighting. Production halted. Yes, el Jefe said, or rather, jeah. El Sr. Armijo fue a jugar el golf, one in the tree shouted.

Come by, a couple of you, she said, when you are done. If you want to earn a few extra today. I have work for you, she said. Palma got off the ladder and went back to bed. Late that afternoon when two showed up through the backyard gate, el jefe and Talking Spider Monkey, the sun was still high and aching for a sacrifice. She was lying on a lawn chair sunbathing in a bikini. Her top was off. All the tools are there, she said, indicating with her nose toward the shed. The hedges need trimming. Ursula had kept up with the rose bushes. Palma loved roses but not when still alive. Thorns, pruning, watering. That was what FTD was for.

The two spoke low as they picked up the clippers and sheers. Do you want us to mow? The chief said. Palma lifted the towel that was over her face covered with SPF-50 sunscreen lotion and shook her head as if annoyed. (Actually they did annoy her but there were some things one had to put up with to get certain things done.) More low talk and then Chief said, I'll go, señora. He can take care of whatever you need. He left and she lay there listening to a plane go by overhead and the decisive snip-snip of the spider monkey at work on the hedges trying to think if she ever saw a *Dateline* mystery about

45

a woman being mutilated in her backyard by a dehydrated Mayan. She was baked on one side and as she turned herself over, she slipped out of the bottom. Her booty was almost white since it hadn't seen sun since the summer before. It was as ripe and fuzzy as two peach halves. Palma stretched out her legs so that her feet hung over each end of the lawn chair.

Spider Monkey hauled off all the cut leaves and branches and took them to the trash. They did a thorough job those Mesoamericans, she thought. They had built Tikal. Some believed they'd come to earth on spaceships. Rodrigo and Palma once took a trip to Ecuador to see the Nasca Lines. They boarded an eggbeater and were taken over a large expanse of desert or semi-desert, which everyone knew was one of the aliens' favorite places to land, and saw their humungous drawings. One, in fact, was of a spider monkey.

The sunbather was dozing off with depleted ozonosphere deadly rays roasting her flip side when she felt a pair of coarse paws slowly moving over her back in a pretense of a massage. Foreplay. They were rougher than bark, and along with the hurt the sun was doing to her skin, Palma cringed. The massage stopped and she heard sneaky activity like a zipper going down and pants being dropped.

The neighbors on the other side were out, hickory smoke and kids splashing in the kiddy pool. If they heard Palma, they would surely pop their bobble heads over the wall to invite her over. She didn't know why Ursula had made friends with them, most supreme of Mulchdom. Turkey patties from Sam's that came in a lifetime supply and box wine.

He lifted his random employer by her hips, straddled the chair, and stuck his weenie in from that slant where she could feel it. Sonofaprimate, it felt magically delicioso, wiggling around in there like a leprechaun at the end of a rainbow. The most earnest of elvin topping the morning to you. The heat on Palma, her ass in the air, Hank from next door yelling at his kids, birds chirping (she liked birds, just not eating their embryos), it was a good time. Slowly, slowly, sweet peloncillo going in, out, wiggle-wiggle. His cell phone rang, killing Palma's concentration. Her interior gallery show was featuring an ivory cameo with a silhouette profile of Pepito, which had her about ready to come. The monkey's cell had a loud banda ringtone. Hay viene la migra . . . The breakfast sausage removed from the warm oven, she covered her head with the towel. Even Palma's scalp felt sunburned. Sí, sí, ya voy pa'lla, Spider Monkey said to his monkey lady. She could hear her screeches, irate over the fact that he had not shown up with the rest on the truck. He clicked off and stuck in the Bob Evans link to finish up. It had gone south from talking to his wife. His naked lunch gave a low phony moan to encourage him and it grew hard. She did not count on the monkey giving out a victorious yelp and then a whimper as he pulled out and came on her butt. Ew. Take that home to your wife and propagate, chango cholo. Silence next door. Then whispering or maybe it was patties sizzling on the grill. Palma Piedras was getting hungry. The spider monkey scrambled back into his scruffy jeans and mumbled something. If he thought he was getting paid for trimming her hedges he was mucho mistaken. No, he was apologizing for having fucked her. As if he had been a guest and dropped his pupusa on the carpet, he gently took the towel off Palma's head and wiped off her warm ass. She looked up and told him as softly as she could to scram. What? He said, putting his diminutive monkey ear to her lips. Vete, cabrón, she said, before my husband gets home and catches you. Mi marido te mata.

11 Pepito and his ever-willing cousin were sexting. He asked if she'd send a picture au naturel of herself and Palma cut to the chase and clicked a picture of her twat. She was about to send it when on second consideration thought it not the best representation of herself (bedazzled as her sweet va-j-j was. A former "colleague" of Ursula's, needing the practice, had decorated Palma's pubic area with rhinestones for free.) Palma called her lil' cous' on his cell; he was at work and with a customer. If I send you a picture of my pussy, would you think any less of me? she asked. Heh, he said. On the contrary, I'll think of you a lot more.

Abuela always told her granddaughter that men didn't like women who gave it all away. Cell phone image transmission of one's genitalia was not what the old woman born a century before had in mind, but Palma knew her grandmother would def have given her a wallop upside the head for it. She saved the picture and decided to wait.

RANDALL'S COUSIN Ed wrote emails in fluent Spanish. This was extremely off-putting. White men talking to Palma Piedras in Spanish always was. Not whites in Mexico or anywhere else in the world where Spanish might be the common language for two people, but in the States where speaking to her in Spanish made her feel like a foreigner. Don Ed emailed Palma about his new calling as a Gaia-style guru and invited her to his home in Baltimore to meet his sixteen-year-old son and their dog, Chip. (He never said the dog's name but once she named it in her head and it became real, an object potentially requiring true love and devotion she knew she wanted nothing to do with it.) It was always a positive sign when a man was prepared to invite you to where he lived. (Sometimes not so much after you saw it.) It indicated he had nothing to hide and that you were not going to be hidden from his life. She had no plans to go to Baltimore (ever).

One night as Palma was turning in after a dreary night of translating, having finally finished the ten-page foreword, he called and serenaded her. It was on her cell phone, the number of which she had recently emailed for when he came to town. He was on his guitar and had, in fact, a superb tenor voice. He sang, "¿Cómo Fue?" It was a bolero and, like all boleros, romantic ad nauseam. In the song the crooner (don Ed) asked how it was that he fell in love with the person he was singing to (her?). Maybe she was tired and without the usual armored response but Palma dripped an Aw, how sweet. After that he started calling every night after midnight. At first it was enjoyable to hear a human voice after hours concentrating on her work, and when he called really late and caught her sleeping, the chats even felt sexy. They didn't do any kind of sex talk but it was like the old days, when hearing a lover or would-be lover's drowsy voice at the other end, miles away, was by itself a mood enhancer.

Finally came the day of don Ed's arrival in Albuquerque. Palma asked him to meet at a franchise that opened up in the ever-growing business side of town. He didn't seem happy about it. Not a fan of the American-invented, Pan-Asian cuisine? Could he smell the pricey menu or the fake froufrou ambience all the way over to his room at the Sheraton in Old Town? Or maybe, don Ed preferred to dine at a green-or-red-chili-enchilada diner? All of the above, as it turned out.

When Palma Piedras walked in, dressed in a little black crepe number to play it safe, she was still willing to give him the benefit of the doubt. Holy Moby Dick, she thought at first glance. Obviously the photo attachment he sent was a lot more hair and a lot less weight back in time. (It explained the Destiny Child's tour T-shirt.) Not losing what she hoped was an effervescent smile, she approached the age-appropriate date and held out her hand. He somehow freed himself from the stool his derriere had crushed, and as the host led the way to a table, Palma kept just ahead of don Ed, feeling a little like Jonah before the big swallow. They got through the meal with a lot less to say than on the phone or email but for reasons she couldn't explain at the moment, Palma was unable to bring herself to end the date, go home, get into pjs, get out the Haagen-Dazs, and call Randall to tell him where he could shove his big-ass cousin. Instead, as if a ventriloquist had his hand up her back to move her mouth, she heard herself suggest they step into the restaurant's humidor room. Don Ed considered the thought and then said, Okay, we could do that.

A combination musk-sage smell filled the air and they found a couple of cushiony seats. Someone came right over to offer cigars out of a large, cedar-lined box. To her surprise (then, but not in retrospect), don Ed, who didn't smoke, picked out the biggest one. The waiter helped him get the small bonfire going while she sat, back straight, ankles crossed with a stiff pageant smile, looking like a housewife turned escort. Don Ed was pulling hard on the cigar like he was giving it a blow job when he stopped and asked, Do you know how I came to be called a "don?"

Randall had told her about the Chichen Itza ritual but she said, Let me guess. Back in 1922 you started this little "thing of ours?" Like any native Chicagoan she knew her *Godfather Trilogy* and *The Sopranos*, but it went over don Ed's head—a close-cropped-hair head. Don Ed (and this was not the only discovery she was to make that evening) was not white, as it happened. At least not by half. He was, as her abuela would have called mulatto, in the States was known as *mixed race* and soon in the world, *just like everybody else*. His skin and eyes were lighter than hers and lips fuller and nose wider. Her fated lover didn't get her kidding. She pulled on the string of cultured pearls she wore that evening (erroneously chosen, since don Ed was hoping for a Toltec queen, not Princess Grace). For his part, he had not worn a sport coat (with his jeans) for dinner, but instead had on an off-the-charts size guayabera in tribute to his first expedition to New Mexico, which after a hundred years of statehood was still thought by some (like don Ed apparently) as belonging to old Mexico. While Palma got the lowdown of don Ed's knighting by the author of *The Four Agreements,* his most favorite book in the world, Palma threw back three appletinis. Shooting herself in the head would have been another way to obliterate her consciousness. (There was no explaining to herself later how she managed to leave the restaurant unless don Ed had carried her out in his pocket.) The next thing she knew they were at the Sheraton.

In his room with a king-size bed, the flickering lights of Albuquerque below served to flummox her further, while a drunken Palma fluttered around like Breakfast at Tinkerbell's, trying to take off her itty dress and bitty shoes with finesse.

She had thrown out any notion of herself as a seductress, and by then, aspired only that don Ed not roll over her in his sleep. Once she was naked and he in his natural wildlife state lying flat on the bed, she began her arduous climb, something for which she had not trained.

NASA had directed her to blow in his ear while yanking the moon where she found no life and which, as it turned out, was much smaller than it appeared from orbit. Playing back later what she did recall and skipping the pre-broadcast, she'd gone straight to the landing of Apollo 11. While Palma was certain she would return a national hero, the universe went black right about then.

12 When Randall came over with his new boy toy, Palma gave them her version of *Gulliver's Travels*. Vladimir said, Oh, I should fix you up with my brother.

Vladimir was the prettiest chicanito she had ever seen. His hostess couldn't place her finger on why she thought that, but Palma did believe in the eye of the beholder being a truism, plus the way he brought his cigarette up to his Sal Mineo mouth and half-closed eyes, the smoke creating a halo around his tragically curly head, was the stuff of gay legends for generations to come. Vladimir from the Lower Valley barrio.

Your brother? Randall said, pouring the Shiraz he brought. She hated red wine. Everyone knew that. He did it so as not to have to share. Pour me a glass, she said, and then left it there. What's wrong with his brother? Palma asked.

Nothing, Randall said, pursing his mouth.

My brother is younger than me, Vladimir said. Hector is the brain in the family. He practically runs the Apple Store, he added. He's a poet. (See, right there, she thought, was reason to call out Vladimir, sitting on her white couch, in Randall's best shirt, holding the Nambe wineglass with a pinky out like he was on a reality housewives reunion show. A poet couldn't run an electric pencil sharpener much less a store that sold the very definition of high tech.)

He's twelve! Randall said. He went to the kitchen and came back with the multivitamin bottle that don Ed gave Palma in lieu of a bouquet on their first and last date. It was from don Entrepreneur's product line and all she had that Randall found to snack on. Palma looked at the boyfriend. He's not twelve, he said. He's going on thirty.

Yeah, Randall said. In about five years.

Listen, Mishu, darlin', Palma said, renaming He-Who-Named-Himself. As Russian names went Palma liked Mishu better. I'll meet your carnalito, she said, but first I'm on my way to Chicago. I have some unfinished business there.

13 It was September, but global warming brought heat to the Windy City as murderous as Albuquerque's desert. Palma Piedras was waiting in front of Abuela's grave at the Calvary Cemetery north of the city. A warm wind picked up, coming in from Lake Michigan, and she pushed down her size-two printed frock. It was just above the knee, this side of bad taste for a forty-plus-year-old. (Whatever side the open-toed, red-soled, patent-leather stilettos were on hardly mattered as long as Chi-Town Joe appreciated them.) She bought Abuela flowers from the Jewel's market. When alive, Abuela would have scolded her for wasting money. There were blessings from her grandmother being dead. One was the silence.

Mexican workers were mowing nearby and one brought over a holder he pulled up from another grave with a thick wire you could stick in the ground. Tenga, señorita, he said. (Señorita. Right.) Señorita Palma caught sight of Pepito, now Joe-the-suit salesman, coming toward her. In dress slacks he acquired a kind of Denzel Washington stride. He was wearing a cashmere, short-sleeved shirt. The Silverman Brothers Suits for Men Store, established 1943, had given the lil ex-con cous' a makeover. As he grew near she saw he wore a better watch, a gold chain, and what looked like diamond-post earrings. He also cut his hair. He could have been walking out of an *Esquire* photo shoot. The Native American special issue. Good Lord, where were her vapors? Pepito was swinging a garment suit box in one hand, the way she might have carried a Whitman's Sampler box. He kissed her right on the mouth, running a tongue oh-so-briefly over her lips. Palma let go of his neck and collected herself, knowing six landscapers' eyes and a whole lot of dead were watching. I like them shoes, Pepito whispered.

What's that? Palma asked, smoothing out her dress crunched by the thug hug. It's for you, he said. Don't open it 'til Christmas. He laughed a low heh-heh and handed it to her. In silver, swirly letters the top read: Silverman Brothers. It was weighty. Is it a suit for me? Palma joked. Yeah, I got us matching double-breasted tuxes, he smiled.

Pepito reached into his pocket and pulled something out. It was a lock of hair. His ponytail. The Silverman Brothers' best salesman looked over his shades, and the landscapers pushing equipment in the heat, tongues dragging, lumbered away. The pair walked over to Abuela's grave holding hands. She could hardly walk on the misogynous spikes as they sunk into the soft graveyard grass. (If she ever became a fashion designer Palma Piedras would start a stiletto line for men called Vendettas.) They scooted down, said an Our Father, and made a sign of the cross. Then Pepito reached into his back pocket and pulled out a Swiss Army knife. He started digging in the dirt until he made a hole deep enough to bury his chongo, which he'd let grow while in prison. It was for Abuela. She used to come visit me, her lil cous' said. Dabbing the inside corner of one eye, he then readjusted his glasses. Down state? Palma asked. How'd that old woman get there?

Abuela took the bus, Pepito said. The idea of their grandmother going that far from her neighborhood was as unlikely as Palma flying a plane. Abuela went to places besides church, sure. She headed downtown now and then. Sears on special occasions. The lawyer's office that one time. When did she come see you? Palma asked, as they made their way out slowly toward the street where she left the rental. The old woman had never even visited any of Palma's apartments in Chicago over the years. She'd never met Rodrigo. She wouldn't have liked him, in any case, but the point was she didn't bother. Bother? Yeah, bother was the right word.

When they got to the economy car from Avis parked right outside the ironwork gates, she asked, Can I drop you back at work? He nodded, opened the back door, tossed the garment box in the backseat, and then got in the passenger side. Palma was about to go around when he caught her wrist and drew her to him. You've lost more weight, he said, arranging her on his lap and pulling the door closed. *You don't weigh nothing. Are you even here?* His voice was heavy in her ear, like the smell in the humidor with don Ed. Pepito was not don Ed, or anyone else before or after, as he gave such wet besos all over she thought he'd suck up her labia through the inside, all the way up and right into his mouth.

Are you even here? Had spoken to her slight frame, but also to the ten years—a lifetime—of his longing for her. Palma's thong, barely there anyway, was pushed aside and he was in. For a second Palma thought she had a silent stroke. Pepito's penis had made its way up to her ghost ovaries. The two remained still—very. Abuela, forgive me, she thought. Palma felt his mouth on her neck. He was actually giving a grown woman a hickey. Send us a baby, Abuela, she said. Palma didn't like babies. She'd hardly liked her abuela. She had no uterus but she might have gotten pregnant then and there. Pepito's hands were clutching her peach halves and after a few throbbing thrusts she knew he had sent his troops off to infertile territory. She started to come when a cop siren went off, and the squad car pulled up and stopped next to the car. The rest, as they said in Chi-Town, was brown history. Or if they didn't, then someone should.

14 That night back at the hotel room there was no reply to her texts or voicemails. Palma Piedras had been detained at the station in the spirit of being further embarrassed. She hadn't been harassed by the city's finest for such public displays since her high school days at the pier on summer nights. Kids parked their cars and steamed up windows all the time and if they didn't have a car and were adventurous enough they went down to the beach. It closed at 11:00 p.m. and by 11:05 the cops were patrolling the area.

That day in front of the cemetery there was no proof of any lewd public display. Sitting in a parked car, a rental, Pepito, who even in a Silverman Brothers cashmere shirt looked like the last Aztec warrior with Ray-Bans, undoubtedly sent off the chota alert. Bingo. The cops found out he was on parole. She wasn't putting it all on her gangsta cousin. A brown woman in the compromising position that Palma was found in spelled puta for pay. It wasn't just the white conservative neighborhood. She had been propositioned, harassed, and even manhandled from Paris to Ibiza, fancy beaches, promenades with expensive shops and tourist night hot spots, taken for a prostitute, for no other reason that Palma could think of except for her so-called exotic features among Eurotrash Mulches. She always thought such sordid affronts occurred because she had been unescorted, but apparently being escorted by an "exotic" man cancelled it out.

WHEN PALMA didn't hear from him after returning to Albuquerque, his prima worried that the incident had been enough to send Pepito back to prison. She'd forgotten about the box until at the airport the kid who took the keys at the rental found it and came after her. Not until Palma was home did she start getting itchy to open it before Christmas, but in the end she put it away unopened. Palma got back to her translations, went to a Zumba fitness class, and started telling herself that she was pregnant. Pepito's prima was in love. It had been a long time, but the symptoms were there. Each hour of every day that went by with no word from him was like being hung by her heels. A week went by and then another. She didn't answer calls or emails.

The editor from Greene & Gaye skyped. Palma took the video call. Well done! the woman said about the work. When Palma was finished with the project, her publisher had a novel to translate by a new English writer. The story is reminiscent of *Chéri*, the editor said. You know Colette? Yes, Palma knew who the French writer was, and she knew the story of the young man who was ruined by an older woman. It was scandalous writing back then, even in Paris. Sex was the forte of the French. Along with Bourdeax and chocolate croissants. Those people had produced the Marquis de Sade. Palma said she'd do it.

SHE'D GONE to Chicago to put Abuela's house up for sale. The lawyer reported that Jim-Bo said he was not in a position to buy out her half. She was not prepared to buy out his ass, either. He has a right to stay, the lawyer told her, although you can ask him for rent. Good luck to me with that, Palma told herself, and decided the only way to get things moving was to go there in person, thus, the main purpose for her recent visit. (The morning she went by was the same day when she met Pepito later at the cemetery.) Jim-Bo was at work, but the squatters were there. When Veronica opened the door she immediately grabbed up her dust mop on four legs as if Palma was the dogcatcher. She didn't exactly invite her in and the uninvited guest didn't exactly give a rat's ass.

Palma shouldered the woman out of the way and went straight to Abuela's room to start collecting her grandmother's personal possessions. In all frankness, most of it would end up at the Salvation Army, too worn or worthless, but Palma took photo albums with sticky, clear pull-back sheets and random family pictures back with her to Albuquerque for when she sat down to write the cautionary tale that had been the Life and Times of Palma la Piedra. The house was going up for sale, but the lawyer warned her that Jim-Bo didn't have to take the first offer. Eventually, he'll have to accept a reasonable one, the attorney said, but with this economy it might take a while, you know.

She wasn't in the mood to look at pictures of her pubescent self before her hair thickened. Or of Pepito with a missing-front-teeth grin over the Lego Space Center his big cousin bought him for Christmas. Jim-Bo bought nothing for anyone, and except for carrying Abuela's fake Christmas-tree-in-a box and ornaments up from the basement, he did nothing to mark the occasion. Abuela, at her church most of the time, did little more. The tree was for Pepito. Before he came to the house to live, the old woman had already determined the girl had grown out of childhood and had no right to indulge in such notions as Santa Claus or los Reyes Magos who were said to bring children treats, left in their huaraches on the Epiphany. It might have been the old woman's religion behind the lack of Christmas spirit toward the children, but the granddaughter was of the mind that being a soldier of the Lord just gave her Grandma Scrooge the excuse.

One day Palma finally heard from Pepito. They hadn't sent him back to the joint. What law did I break, man? He said defensively when she asked. The detachment she'd felt from the duration of silence was confirmed by the sparse conversation. His call almost seemed like a perfunctory check-in. It was hardly what a woman expected after a consummation that broke the sound barrier.

Look, Palma, he said (finally, speaking his mind), you're the most special person in my life, but I'm not in love with you. Right after the whack on the back that knocked her breath out, he added, And you're not in love with me. We are in love with the notion of being in love. What you and me have is an infatuation.

It was like being stunned with a Taser. All they had was a foolish crush? She'd come to pine, cry, made her stomach bloat with a psychological pregnancy, prayed like a soldier's wife "return him safe to me," in other words did all the things that any sonsa did over any sonso—how did a woman exit gracefully from that?

Then he eased her out. I gotta get back to the floor. Love you, prima.

15 Palma Piedras cut the broccoli out of her diet, and presto, la tummy went flat. Having received an advance from Greene & Gaye for the next project she decided to put it to good use on a new laptop and drove over to the Apple Store.

A girl with braces and a clipboard and earpiece came up. How may I assist you? She was New Mexican hispana and whiter than most whites. Actually, Palma said, do you have any poets here who could help me? The girl looked as if the customer had just asked her to explain string theory and maybe was about to when another employee stepped over and said, Yeah. You mean Hector. I'll get him for you.

Palma wandered around the celebratory wedding of technology and capitalism when a kid walked over wearing his polo with the genius logo (in case you didn't guess, his strong suit was not his looks—a black loofah beard and a McNuggets-with-special-sauce-diet complexion. The startling good looks apparently did not run in Mishu's family). I'm shopping for a new laptop, Palma told him. Hector gave the air of not being up for working with the generation whose minds could not grasp anything after the VCR, and silently led her to the display. He lifted an arm to indicate the latest models and then dropped it like he'd lost his will to live.

With that kind of sales drive, Palma said, you should be soaring up the ranks in no time.

I don't care if they fire me, he said. I'm a poet.

With a trust fund? She asked.

Money's not everything, he shrugged his droopy shoulders.

Aw. Our first fight.

(Wince.)

Look—she started getting to the real point of her Apple drive-by—your brother Vladimir said we should meet. The guy adjusted his black horn-rimmed glasses. Vladimir? He asked, and then, cracked a smile. Oh, you mean, Vincent. Something clicked in his hard drive and the poet started nodding, oh yeah, yeah. Then he looked at her directly for the first time.

Call me a cougar, Palma thought, but unless he got himself into a gym and did something about the Amber Rose buzz cut, he'd be one little cub left out in the woods. She started to walk off when he said, wait. I get off at five. If you want, we could go for coffee. Palma stopped. Or, I mean, we could have tea, he added.

INSIDE HECTOR'S messenger bag were journals and yellow legal pads with a cargo of handwritten pages he called poems. He was no César Vallejo. Or Dr. Seuss, for that matter. Palma showed him the anthology in which her translations appeared, and he stared at the book like she had handed him an unidentified relic.

Well, who *do* you read? Palma asked, sipping her chai (which they had in her home and not at a café that would have charged the equivalent of two hours of genius labor at the Apple Store). Hector and she were both hungry and she warmed up leftover take-out pad thai. Cheap first date.

I like Dead Prez, Talib Kweli, Kanye, Mos, Hector said. (*Rappers.* Not exactly reading material, Palma thought.) Nas, he continued and then jumped up and broke out into break-ing, scrawny legs suddenly going sideways in the air, Hector ready to do a headstand.

Hey, B-Boy, she said, moving fast to get her glass coffee table out of the way, calm down. That is, unless you want to break *nakid.* Hector stood up, processed the proposal, took a forkful of Thai noodles, shoved them in his mouth like a can of spinach to Popeye, and nodding with new vigor said, Yeah, I could do that—if you get *nakid*, first.

Her new playmate was showing a whole new side. Palma had guessed he was a virgin. Minutes later, up against her he weighed no more than she did and was not any taller, but men having the muscular advantage (even when one couldn't see muscles), he lifted her and leaned in. Palma Piedras could almost hear a bad rap song being composed in his head with each thump of her body against the wall.

16 A new restaurant serving Sicilian opened not far from the Pan-Asian spot. It was his night off and Randall, who had just broken up with his latest petite amour, invited Palma out to dinner. It wasn't Mishu, who was a couple of petty lovers ago. It made it easy not to mention the nerd rapper brother. She didn't bring up the spider monkey incident either. Palma had the feeling that talking about her sexcapades would remind Randall of their infelicitous fellatio fiasco. While the thought of having traumatized someone by going down on him was disturbing, talking about sex would only remind her of Pepito anyway. Palma Piedras's current mission in life was to never think of him again.

They were studying their menus when Randall reached over and patted his gal pal's hand. I've got to tell you about the guy I met last night, he said. Oh, honey . . . Just then the chef was at their table. "Chef Chana" embroidered on her white coat. She had the whole rock star chef thing going—a bandana tied around her head like the pirate of Penzance and in a pair of classic Crocs, green like her eyes. The chef of Babbaluci looked like she'd done some serious taste testing, but Palma would have called her pleasantly plump. Def not fat. *Date night?* The woman asked them.

Yes, it is, Randall said, somewhat surprised, as if she were psychic. I'm meeting him later.

The woman gave the slightest wince, recovered, and turned to Palma. I don't think I've seen *you* here before, she said. (Had the chef given her a wink or was it a tic?)

No, no, Palma said, our first time, well, my first time here. Palma's tongue was tripping over itself and the room had just gotten warm.

Well, enjoy, the chef said, and moved on.

Before they ordered, a complimentary platter of oysters was brought to the table. Well, if this ain't a hint that the dyke wants you, dear, Randall said, grabbing up the first oyster.

Don't call Chef Chana that, she said. Palma liked saying Chef Chana. Hannah, Hannah, Hannah, she sang, in a low sweet voice. *My honey Hannah gave me a gift of oysters.*

Normally, she didn't think seafood in the desert was a good idea, even if it was said to be flown in the same day, but Palma already trusted Chef Chana. Babbaluci meant snails, and seafood was the house's forte. This is Chana, thinking of you, Randall said, picking up an oyster and slurping it. *Chana and Palma sitting in a tree. K-i-s-s-i-n-g* . . . He could be obnoxious without trying, although he was trying that night, licking his fingers after each swallow. When dinner was over, the friends had cappuccinos and an assortment of cookies. They were about to ask for the bill when the waitperson brought dessert. The chef sent her a special on the house. A large slice of amaretto almond cake with two forks. Randall gave Palma an I-rest-my-case look. They were waddling out when Chef Chana caught up to the pair. Was everything all right?

Oh, we'll come again, Randall said.

Good, Chana said, then—hold on. She returned and

handed Palma her card. We're having a private party here Tuesday for a film crew. Tommy Lee Jones is in town. Palma took the card while Randall studied it over her shoulder like she'd just been given a backstage pass to Barry Manilow. (Randall seriously liked Barry Manilow.) Chana took down their names for the guest list and told Palma to bring the card in case there was any problem at the door. The other woman looked at the plain business card and turned it over. The chef and restaurateur had scribbled her cell number on the back, and underneath, *Anytime*.

ON TUESDAY night Randall couldn't join Palma because it was the night he closed the bar. After eight, she walked into Babbaluci alone. Tables were rearranged and there were a lot of people there that she would have said were from LA, Hollywood types, in the biz, if Palma talked that way and if she had any pre-formulated ideas of what such people would look like. All in all, they were mostly white, casually dressed, and came off like they had put in a hard day's work and were grateful to have free goodies and vino, while acting glib about it—because that's what you did in the biz.

Palma Piedras knew no one there except Tommy Lee Jones and Palma didn't even know him except to say that she might recognize him in the crowd if he showed up, which she doubted he would. The party seemed to be for something related to the movie but not its beginning or its end (which she guessed those in the "industry" called a wrap). Palma went to the small bar and a cute guy offered her his stool. Thank you, she said, taking the seat. You're welcome, ma'am, he said, not looking at her or missing a beat in his conversation with his buddies who were standing nearby. It led her to think that it wasn't flirtation or chivalry but a be-kind-to-the-middle-aged consideration. Well, I'll take it, she thought. A seat was a seat. Way in the midst of the crowd, Palma caught a glimpse of Chana. She was in civilian clothes and saw Palma but didn't come over. She ordered the bianco secco they were serving gratis, and when she spun her stool back around to keep an eye on Chef Chana, Palma bumped a guy reaching over to get a drink. Whoa. Whoa, he said back good humoredly, and then apologized. That was segue enough for Austin White to stick around after he got his scotch, neat. It was all he drank, when he drank. I get up too damn early to be out late when I'm working like this, Palma's new acquaintance said.

Austin lived in LA and was in town for the film. Are you an actress? He asked. She thought it was his idea of a line and rolled her eyes, then remembered he came from a world where they churned out actresses. Austin White was thirtyish, well groomed, and in a black shirt with tiny white dots. Folded-up cuffs revealed an apple green lining. Palma had never seen anything like it, def not in Albuquerque, but also not on the streets of Chicago, or Mexico City where she'd most recently been when out of the country. She brushed her slender hand over his biceps. Moschino, she uttered.

Yes, it is, he said. So, let me guess, you're in the fashion industry?

Unaccustomed as she was to admitting to life's disappointments, nevertheless, for some reason Palma admitted: a long time ago I studied dress design.

One of his faint eyebrows went up.

Translating pays the bills, she said. Austin's brow went up again with an approving nod. Not bad, he said. You must be pretty smart. Pretty AND smart.

Well, I ain't a tack, she said—to the head of wardrobe on the movie set or so he claimed. How is Tommy Lee Jones to work with? Palma asked. It was conversation. (She saw Tommy Lee Jones in one movie, the one with Javier Bardem, who was the reason Palma saw the film. Weird as he was in the role, she still would have done him. She was loyal that way.)

He's off for a few days, Austin said. He's got a polo match. We don't need him right now anyway.

Most of the food gone, the crowd was thinning out fast. Austin took out a pack of Dunhills and was about to step outside. Palma figured it would be an opportune moment for her to leave since by then she'd lost sight of Chana.

It was a chilly night and her new acquaintance put his sports jacket around her shoulders. (Chivalry was back with a vroom, vroom.) Austin was about to light his cigarette when Palma said, Stop. She put her hand on the lighter and drew close with a pucker, planting a kiss on the generous lips. What was that for? He asked, lighting his cigarette.

It was for me, she said. Having been looking at the man's sculpted face all evening she knew she would not have forgiven herself if she had not kissed those Luciferliscious lips before going on her way. Austin White was black, and in the palette of humanity's skin tones his was Shade No. Wesley Snipes with a smoldering-Seal soulfulness. He took her hand and spun Palma around to check her out. Then he tapped his chin with the cigarette hand as if he had something to say. What? She said. It's the shoes, right? (She was wearing the heels she'd worn to see Abuela at the cemetery).

No, no, that's not it, Austin said.

Is it the dress? (The same she'd worn on her whale expedition. Maybe her whole look screamed so last decade to the discerning eye.)

What size you wear? Austin asked. Palma told him. No, I don't think so, he said. That's a nice dress, all right, but it fits you like a sack, baby. She looked down. He was right. Where were her hips? Austin flicked his Dunhill and said, I got an idea. Men always did, she thought. Let's go. No, Palma said, I'll follow you. (Not that she wouldn't have preferred to ride in his Porsche Boxster with the Golden State plates instead of her box-on-wheels, but she'd already gone through her mental Rolodex of crime episodes and came up with one that might ring familiar with the current situation: a smooth professional gambler in Las Vegas, who, it was later found, not only had a wife and child in another state, but stabbed both of his parents in cold blood for the life insurance with a collector's sword they kept in their closet. His Vegas girlfriend never had a clue.)

They drove to the movie lot and when Palma caught up to him, Austin was chatting with one of the night guards. Come on, he said, a jailer's size ring of keys in hand. When he opened a mid-size trailer, she peeked in. It was dark and Austin got by Palma, hopped in, and turned on the lights. Don't worry, he said, I ain't gonna bite you.

Another guard in a golf cart went by and Austin leaned out to wave at him. Hey, Mr. White, the guard said. See? Austin said. The guards know me.

Inside there were a lot of clothes and shoe boxes, and the eating table was covered with makeup supplies. There were wigs on stands for all seasons. Here's where we create some of our magic, the stylist said. He looked around, dug through some dresses piled on the cot. You like Moschino. Here, he said, handing Palma a black leather dress. What size shoes you wear? He guessed right when he turned over a pair of black Cavalli, high-heeled dress shoe boots. She ran her hand over their texture. Ooh-la-la, she said. Rah, rah, rah, he said. Roma, roma, ma. Keep the bad romance, gimme a pair of Manolos,

71

anytime, hombre. Manolos? Oh, yes, after tonight we be on first name basis.

There were several other items he thought would look good on her, and then they left the trailer, her arms full. I have to get up in a few hours, he said, and yawned as he walked her back to her car. Am I stealing these things? Palma asked. No, he laughed as if she didn't know nothin' about nothin' and he would have to explain it all. Palma Piedras carried off a starter wardrobe easily worth several grand. We bring all kinds of things to see what'll fit and what'll work, he said when they got to her car and placed the collective haul in the trunk. (She was most def going on YouTube the next day to show it off to the unwashed masses of shopaholics. She might start her own channel.)

Austin went over and opened the door. When she got in, he said, Well, Miss Palma, it has been a pleasure meeting you. (*What? That was it?*) The window was down and he reached in and gave her a peck on the lips. I still think you'd make a smokin' actress. He bit his bottom lip. Mm-mm-mm. Her face went hot. He stopped and looked like he was having a thought. Another one. (She liked his thoughts.) Why don't you go to Babbaluci Friday morning? He said. We're filming a scene there. We could use some extras. Just give them my name. Be there at five a.m. Don't be late.

Can I bring someone? She asked. Yeah, sure, he said, straightening up, patting the window ledge, just as long as they're as gorgeous as you, baby. Stepping back, he pointed. I'll make sure we have you someplace where you'll be seen.

17 The next night, Palma Piedras, proud owner of a new star-studded wardrobe was going through her closet sorting out her rags. Most of it was in a pile going to Goodwill. She was taking the Silverman Brother's box on the top shelf, along with all her old sketchbooks from her past life, out to the garage when the ding on her cell indicated an incoming text. The nerd rapper. *Can I come over?* When had everyone become so busy and self-important that they couldn't be bothered to call someone and ask how they were before getting to their agenda? Y? She texted back.

I wrote something for you, Hector messaged. Whatever else it was, she was glad he didn't call it a poem. Palma put the cell down on the nightstand and went back to her solitary Wednesday night. If on any night people should find themselves alone it should be midweek, she thought, so they could get some of their shit done between weekends.

The cell rang next. Hector. His persistence paid off and a little while later, his bike parked in the front entranceway, they were sitting on her back patio. He bounced around with an invisible mic in hand as he rapped.

Hey, lady with the cool eyes and fresh smile,
best of all, a wild style,

You walked into the Genius bar
like everyone knew you a star.
Girl, you dope, you sick, you the bomb
Cocoa Puff of my heart.
How'd you do it? How'd you do it?
You dope, you sick,
you the slick chick who stole my heart.

He rhymed for about ten minutes or what felt that long. It's for you, he said when he finally stopped. I had this major writer's block before we met. You're my muse, girl, he said.

Oh, Palma said, In other words, you wrote it *for* me the way you might write something *for* a class? Yeah, he said. You are my muse, he said again. Hector yanked up his baggy pants and went in the house. Palma sat and waited. A few minutes later the kid came out with a throw she kept over the easy chair in the living room. Spreading it out on the grass, he called her over. Now I am going to teach *you* something, he said.

Did you bring a condom? she asked. He shook his head, waving her over. They lay down together and were immediately accosted by the plethora of lights that shone in the desert skies. Hector put an arm under her head for a pillow. You see there? He said, pointing up. That's Ursa Major—the Big Bear. Where? She said. There. That's the constellation that houses the Big Dipper. Next, he pointed to the Ursa Minor, the Little Bear. Cassiopeia was the Queen of Ethiopia. Cepheus, her king. There's Draco the Dragon. Hector was pointing as if Palma were following along. You can't see the Little Dipper in big cities but we're lucky here. The Little Dipper is where the most famous star in the sky (after the sun) is—The North Star or Polaris. Hector must've noticed Palma's eyes were closed and he stopped talking. He brought her head to his chest and she fell asleep. Hours later they woke to the chit-chit-chit sound of the automatic sprinkler going on at six a.m. Both wet, they ran inside.

18 Palma Piedras wore the Moschino leather dress and Cavalli shoe boots because she knew that was what the wardrobe director would want. She also cut bangs and gave the rest of her hair a trim. As a recessionista, she never went to beauty shops anymore. Palma gave herself mani-pedis, and with a gray hair or twenty coming in, she was coloring at home.

The sun wasn't out yet, but all the windows of Babbaluci were covered outside with black paper to keep it looking like night on the inside. Many of the people she saw at the party were rushing around getting things set up. Palma and Mishu went in, and Austin, who was in the midst of making a bamboo-shoot blond into perfection, waved them over. He and Palma exchanged kisses on each cheek, which she gathered was what show business people did. And the French. (Another thing they were known for.) This is Mishu, she said.

Mishu was a hustler vision in one of Randall's tailored shirts and a sport coat he got from the guy he spent the night with—or most of the night since he had gotten up at two in the morning to get ready for what he considered would be his legendary discovery by Hollywood. (The way Austin looked at Mishu, she got the idea the hustler might just get there). Come, Austin said. He was wearing Burberry jeans with a boot cut and brand-new Western boots. On top he had a V-neck, long-sleeved tee. His hand behind him, he kept making a come-on gesture as they made their way with people hurrying all about. Austin put Mishu and Palma at the bar. Here's where we're going to shoot. That's if Miranda shows up. Who's Miranda? she asked. She's the leading love interest, Austin said.

I never heard of her, Mishu said with a fluttering of eyelashes, already working it. (And again, the lustful look from Austin at Mishu. *Oy Vey.*) No one else is ever gonna hear of Miranda either, if that chick doesn't get her act together, he said. Drugs? Palma said, feigning alarm. *Everything?* Mishu said, immediately drawn in. Whatever you both do, when she sits down here, do not speak to her, Austin said. Miranda doesn't like it.

He went off and they were left to wait. Afraid to lose their places, the pair took root over the following hours. No Miranda. No Tommy Lee Jones. Then Mishu asked a kid who was setting up lights and he told them that the celebrity would show up when they were ready for him. He's not gonna be hanging out *here*, the kid said. Yeah, not like us, Palma whispered to Mishu, her makeup wilted. Mishu's too. She pulled out her compact to re-touch them both. Something just then started happening. The bar area was crowded with extras and the bamboo-shoot blond playing the bartender got behind the bar to start mixing fake drinks. Palma got a flute glass with sparkling apple cider. The starlet came in, makeup people trying to keep up with her, Austin yelling at someone who wasn't moving fast enough to bring him a lint roller, cameras, lights were in place, and after Miranda sat down and got into character, she snuck a sideways glance at Mishu. Double oy vey, Palma thought. The kid was a sex magnet. Turning to look in the other direction, she saw Chef Chana. In character *as herself?* Chana was wearing her white coat and pretending to be chatting with the customers. Her chestnut hair was done in a pageboy. (Not the best look after forty.) She saw Palma eyeing her and came over. They were supposed to be engaging in lively conversation so it was okay that they were filming. The cameras were on Miranda, anyway. Sorry I missed you the other night, Chana said. I wish you'd stayed. I was taking care of the VIP room.

VIP room? The chef was referring to a section of the restaurant that Palma figured was normally only opened when the rest of the place filled. Palma nodded. She understood the gangsterlike pretentiousness of the restauranteur. These days you could be invited to an event but it was no biggie if you didn't get into the VIP area. Even so, who cared if you got in but weren't lavished on? Chana knew the game. And she had deliberately left Palma Nobody out. Palma knew the game, too. In Colombia, when Rodrigo and she went out with her brother-in-law and his people, it was a scene out of *Carlito's Way*. Her cuñado played Pacino to the T, short legs and all. (Rodrigo was Sean Penn, always bragging at the wrong time and wrong places.)

For the moment Palma didn't feel much like talking with Chana and turned back to the bar. Miranda was chatting up Mishu. He was smiling, eyes half closed, holding the rim of his glass to his mouth and not drinking but holding it there. Funny, how you could read seduction in things like that. Well, that hookup hadn't taken long. Next stop Hollywood.

Then lo and behold! The near-septuagenarian star of the hour actually appeared. Tommy Lee Jones materialized in a sheriff's getup, hat and holster, and stuck himself between Mishu and Miranda. Palma couldn't catch a word of dialogue, even when leaning in. Then, he was gone. Stillness. Suddenly shouts all around and a lot of everyone rushing. It was over.

Mishu and Miranda pulled out mobiles and exchanged digits. She gave Palma a once-over, patted her platinum coif, stood up, and shook her anorexic ass out the door. Ha! Palma scoffed. Instead of a smile or grin, Mishu cut his eyes at her. It wasn't the first indication of how full of himself he was, but it was the first hint that he might not like Palma much.

EVENTUALLY AUSTIN retrieved them like his two puppies. T.L. is amazing, isn't he? One take, Austin said. They both agreed. The word amazing could mean anything those days, and what did they know? Both tried to step down from the bar stools with legs that had fallen asleep hours before. You guys hungry? Austin asked. Let's get a real drink. How's that sound? He was hyper. I'm free the rest of the day, he said.

The rest of the day meant from happy hour on by the time they got to the Hard Rock Hotel where Austin was staying. Mishu was in his element. He wasted no time in the suite calling down for a margarita on the rocks (for Palma), a bottle of champagne (for himself) and, reading off the menu, ordering an array of overpriced dishes. Austin's scotch was already in the room and he too, fixed up a drink right quick for himself.

Here, he said to Mishu, and stretched out a long-fingered hand. Pills a la paella. The kid lapped them right up and swigged them down with a Red Bull he'd grabbed out of the minibar. *Well, let's get the party started, why don't we?* Palma thought, as if she had walked on to another movie set. Two Boys + One Reluctant Lady. Austin offered her prescription pildoras, too, but she stuck to Rule #1 in the Palma Piedras Single Gal's Survival Handbook. Chapter one, under: Hotels. Stay alert. *(Or risk being carried out in a suitcase.)*

Along with the drinks arrived Southwestern quesadillas

with slices of colorful sweet peppers on the side and a spoonful of pico de gallo and Kobe sliders with small bottles of condiments. After she threw back the margarita and they had the food down to the last grilled onion, she was relaxed. It had been a long day just to film ten minutes. Apparently, however, she wasn't as relaxed as Mishu and Austin, who by then were making out on the bed. Come here, baby girl, Austin called.

Palma got up and went over. She might've been pouting because when she reached the bed they pulled her between them and were giving her feel-better pecks on the face, hair, and shoulders. Aww, Austin said. Hey, didn't you say you're bi? he whispered. (She might have mentioned it, she thought, but it wasn't the equation Palma had in mind.) He started making out with her, hands all over the place. When she heard the distinct sound of cellophane tearing she guessed Mishu was putting on a condom. Things were looking up for her, Palma Piedras thought, just as he made a ninja move, jumped over her, grabbed hold of Austin and attached to his ass.

Austin's tongue down her throat froze.

Palma was in her beloved Moschino leather dress (having not been invited out of it). Austin began peeling it up to her waist. Mishu was on him like they were a pair of mating dragonflies as the sandwiched Austin mounted her and brusquely dug in his penis. Palma was almost forty-three and, feeling her heartbeat accelerate, had the fleeting thought that maybe she wasn't up for the *Realm of the Senses* anymore. Austin's muscle-tight body pressed into her soft one beneath, while Mishu hooked into him—the three were a chorus of grunts, mmms, and eghs (the last from Palma praying her crushed lungs wouldn't collapse) when a soft knock on the door broke the triple-decker wave. *Can I turn down your bed, Sr. White?*

19 It was Palma's forty-third birthday. Four + three = seven. Seven was the symbol of the chakras and truth seeking. It was going to be a good year. Ursula sent flowers—tuberoses, her favorite. Chef Chana invited Palma Piedras out and she said no. The chef had sent over a special delivery of escargot, the house specialty, the Sicilian version, and the birthday girl threw it all out in the backyard where dead snails belonged.

It was a weeknight in October, her favorite month, even if it hadn't been her birthday. When she was a child, before global warming and when seasons were identifiable, the air changed quality in Chicago in October. The season of the witch. It didn't matter if you smelled burning piles of leaves in the burbs or trash burned in alley garbage cans in the city. Something was different in the air. If you were smart, if you were wise, if you paid attention, October was the month that you could turn the planet on its axis and make it spin the other way. Palma Piedras was doing none of that on her birthday night, but translating a chapter in the book by the English woman who was the most recent European writer to discover the libido for the Mulches.

She popped open the bottle of Dom sent by Austin who was back in LA. (Apparently she was the first woman whose clock he cleaned since his divorce six years before.) One day Austin and she were going to see each other again, "baby girl" was certain of that on her witching-hour birthday night. Randall called her from the bar and said he could stop by late with Mishu, the Comeback Kid.

His little brother Hector (now going by Fierce H), had come over in the morning with two guitarists, dos tíos, Drowsy and Drunky. They all sang "Las Mañanitas" outside her house. She watched from the window, gave them a nod, and went back to bed. Fierce H left a poem. *It's in iambic tetrameter*, he wrote. He was still no poet. Punk Pepito hadn't sent a card or called, tweeted or trended. A year had not gone by during his whole bit in the joint without him remembering her big day and now, nada. Zilch.

When Palma was tired of working that night, she set the bath, poured in jasmine oil and Mr. Bubbles. Her neck ached. Hiney, too, from sitting on the floor using the coffee table as a desk. Ursula had left a message on the landline and her ex-lover called her back. How was your birthday? Ursula's voice sounded far, far away. Great. Fantastic, Palma said. She never told Ursula anything anymore. The women hadn't been together long enough to share one of Palma's birthdays. They met, in fact, on Ursula's birthday the previous spring. Palma was coming out of the Motor Vehicle Division in a strip mall after trying to renew her driver's license that expired while she was in Colombia. They said she needed glasses. Ursula was sitting at a small, wrought-iron table outside the Baskin Robbins near the bus stop. The young woman was wearing cut-off jeans with the pockets exposed like a pair of white tongues on her runner's thighs and treating herself to a pistachio ice cream cone. That looks good, Palma said, and decided to drown her troubles in one, too. She went in and got it. When she came out, Ice Cream Girl was still there licking away. Palma took the table next to hers.

They said what they had to say or felt like saying, including that it was Ursula's birthday and she was alone, away from home, and in Albuquerque to get into nursing school. She had also just been hired at a strip club. Her father was a neurosurgeon who had worked in Houston, but was back in his native Deutschland. He was divorced from her mom. Palma guessed she found out a lot about Ursula in an hour, enough to be invited to the dinner that the German-Texan was going to treat herself to at Little Anita's in Old Town. I'm too old to be making a fuss over my birthdays, Ursula had said. No matter how old Ursula felt, twenty-nine wasn't old, Palma had thought then. Twenty-nine was being on the precipice of the end-of-the-last-decade of real youth. It made people feel their chances at success in life were running out. Maybe they had.

Palma Piedras went home with her. The two fucked for three days. It was that basic. Day. Night. Mini-blinds closed. Pizza Hut deliveries. Runs to the 7-Eleven for Ursula's Coronas. When you were having sex with a stranger it was fucking. A month later they thought of it as making love, but chose not to move in together although they were both as single as that lone sock that came out of the dryer.

Ursula was with her when the divorce papers came through and they messed around all night to celebrate. When she laid herself on top of Palma, parted her outer lips and then her own, as much as the first would always love men (alien-looking external genitalia and all), the lovers cut to the quick and connected to 220 volts. She let Ursula do everything to her and Palma did everything to her lover. Some of it was highly classified female information, top secret and without a need to be revealed to those who believed sex was not sex without

83

penis interruptus. Ursula and she were society's worst nightmare, a two-witch coven, a primal matriarchy with no desire to let in a male for the sake of perpetuating the species. They were fine just as they were those three days. Then Ursula got an asthma attack. After four thousand orgasms and counting, and a near death experience, they were practically joined at the clit. And they knew no more about each other than what they learned at the Baskin Robbins. The sex faded out as it had to over the months or they would have laid each other to waste. What was left was the kind of intimacy you couldn't get without emotional contact—when you held tight, pushed away, and came back together, brief tidal waves of heart-wrenching feelings. It was like a gestalt retreat. It was always like that with women.

Palma intermittently took emotional respites with men whose needs were clearly defined and did not include artery-slitting discussions at three a.m. Sex, food, don't mess with their routines—that was men, not always in that order and not always in equal portions. It depended on the man, but you could count on it like the Big Ben: sex, food, don't mess with their routines, and everyone will get along just fine until you die.

Eventually the couple got a grip and settled into each other's daily rhythms. One didn't mind picking the pepperoni off the pizza and putting it on the other's side of the pie, or throwing an extra cover on her side of the bed because the other had hot flashes. Your girl knew when you'd had a bad day just by the look on your face, so she steered clear; and you knew if a piece of shit at the club stuck his fat finger up her while she was giving him a lap dance because she insisted on showering alone that night, and later all she wanted in bed was to be held by your stick arms.

Then one day she was gone and you were talking long distance on your birthday night. Why was Ursula crying? (*Was she crying?*) Oh, I just miss us, she said, when you asked again. (Was there ever an *us*? It would be nice to finally clear that up.) Silence followed by what felt suspiciously like regret on both ends and that was precisely not what you wanted at 10:30 p.m. on your birthday when you lived alone at forty plus and counting.

Palma got off the phone and was about to get in the bath when she noticed there was a text on her cell phone. Pepito. *Look outside*. She grabbed hold of the first thing handy, a housedress like the ones Abuela wore. (An impulse buy at the Dollar Tree for her penniless old age.) It was mint green with sunflowers. Palma went down and opened the front door. Nothing. And no one. She walked around to the back. Nada y a nadie.

When she returned to the front, there were some roses wrapped in green tissue lying on the ground. Not long stemmed, elegant and costly, but the last minute gas station kind with no smell. Palma picked them up and looked around. Who had Pepito paid to deliver them? And not a minute too soon since her birthday would be over in less than an hour. She went in the house, closed the door, and locked it. The atmosphere was altered. Palma opened the lock. (Now and then survival instinct kicked in that way.)

Sure enough.

A lit candle on the coffee table, an opened bottle of red wine and two glasses. Palma realized someone was on the couch, lying across it, long legs and dark arms. A big head of hair. Pepito stretched out like an odalisque, but fully dressed. He looked up smiling, and in the candlelight all his prima could see were his white teeth and the whites of his eyes. She flicked on the sconces on each side of the kiva fireplace.

Come here, flaca, he said, his arms stretched. The house-dress flew off. Palma lay herself right over Pepito's hard-on. His hands gripped her narrow hips while her tongue went down his throat. When she tried to undo his trousers, he lifted her upright like a barbell and sat up. Chi-Town Joe wiped her saliva from his lips and poured the wine. How was your birthday? He asked.

She told herself that they had all night and he was right to slow things down. Although she was much less in the mood for a glass of red wine than for him. Palma took it and they clinked the glasses he brought along for the occasion. She pretended to drink while he gulped down the contents of his. He got up and went over to the chair where he had left his jacket. Her lil cous' was in D&G: trousers, a casual shirt, and sleek loafers. I'm here on business, primita, he said. My boss just invested in a new fighter in Albuquerque. A middleweight. Jay "El Toro" Ramos. Ever heard of him?

Palma shook her head—her reeling head. (So, they really were *not* in love with each other?) She felt a headache coming on.

Since I am, was, am a fighter, he continued, my boss thought I should come and check him out. The kid fought tonight. He's good, man, Pepito said, and threw a few short jabs in the air.

The Silverman brothers' boss? Palma wondered aloud.

The son—John Silverman, Pepito said. The Silverman brothers retired in Florida a long time ago. One of them already died, Pepito said. He threw on his jacket. Something hit the rug with a thud. He picked up the revolver and stuck it inside his pants in the back.

Did you just put away what I thought you did? Palma asked. He pulled it out, looked at it as he was checking to make sure before he answered, then handed it over to her, handle first. You want it? You might need a little protection, Palma, living alone in this cul-de-sac.

What's wrong with a cul-de-sac? She asked. (He pronounced it the way he might have said cod sac.) He shrugged and put it away. Palma took a sip of wine, holding the glass by the stem, trying her best to look couth under the circumstances, butt naked and about to watch him walk out again.

Pepito had hastily thrown all of her translation work, books, dictionaries, and the laptop on the carpet while she had been outside. He now picked up her work tools like they were drug paraphernalia. Look, she said, it's a clean living.

I'll help you out, girl, Pepito said. You know you can count on me. He lifted the bottle and took a chug. She watched his Adam's apple go up and down. Then her tentative lover came over, bent down to kiss her, and poured the wine in his mouth into hers. He took the glass from her hand and dropped some of it over Palma's chest, it ran around her breasts and down to the couch. She was about to jump up when he stopped her. Stay there. Hand up like a stop sign, he stepped back and took out his mobile. He clicked a few photos, flash stinging her eyes. Putting it into his jacket pocket, he readied to leave. I'll always look out for you, he called over his shoulder. I told you that, man. By the time she recovered and went after him, he was gone.

Palma's neighbor Hank was outside smoking a cigarette. They looked at each other. What? she said, went back in, and slammed the door. The last thing she wanted to see was the ruins of another rendezvous; she picked up the Abuela garment and went upstairs. Instead of a bath, she showered to scrape off any trace of Pepito. She was mad at herself too. Scarcely drying off, she powdered herself, went back downstairs, and was about to dump the bottle of red vinegar her cousin considered wine down the drain when she heard a car pull up. I will kill him, she thought. Lo mato. Palma took out a kitchen knife from the drawer and went straight for the door.

There were Randall, Mishu, and who the hell would have ever guessed why, but Chana. She was in a pair of jeans, a polo shirt, and Coach sports shoes with Velcro straps. Even in the vague light Palma picked up things like that. Like Randall's dilating pupils. Mishu, fractured angel, was out of it, too. The trio hesitated, seeing her condition, and then came inside. Oh that's a shame, Mishu said, spotting the red stains on her white couch with the instinct for being drawn to disaster she suspected he had. Randall went to the kitchen to get some glasses for the Veuve Clicquot he brought. You all right? Chana asked her. Palma was in a grandma dress looking like chicken ready for frying. Clearly she was not all right.

We went to pick Chana up after she closed her restaurant, Randall said when he was back. Mishu, on the other hand, was all warped wings of desire, sipping the champagne before anyone; meanwhile Chef Chana's expression said she made a quick assessment of the modest homestead and wasn't impressed but still game. The chef came over with an extra glass for her, and when Palma took it, she put an arm around her waist, clinked her glass, and said, Here's to us.

They didn't want to keep her from anything she was in the middle of (wine-stained couch, roses flung against a wall now lying in shambles on the floor, the scent of *Kill Bill* aftermath permeating the air), and as soon as the champagne was done the three left. I'll call you, Chana promised. For a real birthday celebration, she said.

20 Pepito called forty-three + one day the next morning, at six a.m. to be exact: Wanna come watch me spar with our boy? He asked. She was up drinking a Coke to cure her birthday hangover. All her lil cous' managed to do since their first encounter in Chicago was walk out and leave her stupefied. She played out in her head how different things would be in a world without clauses. For example: What *if* Pepito had not left her that first time in the hotel? What *if* he had not left the night before? And *if* he had not called the next morning and found Palma yearning for him like the last survivor on *Star War's Slave 1*? She would not be there.

¿Dónde?

Loretta and Pedro's Gym and Club an hour after he called. Pepito came out in black trunks and tank and fully equipped: headgear, chest protector, groin guard, and fist and arm protection. He was sparring the champion of Burque who was a good half-foot shorter than Chi-Town Joe. Palma went to cheer for Jay "El Toro" Ramos and took a bag of caramel corn. In the middle of one of the boxer's waves at his chola girlfriend, Pepito socked him. Ramos fell flat. Fight over. Show off. Palma should have guessed her lil cous' was good at sucker punching.

She went out to the parking lot and waited in her car.

Eventually, Pepito was there, tapping on the window. He was in the jacket from the night before. Thanks for coming, prima, he said. She nodded. A drizzle had started and he hunched over. It was cold out. Pepito looked around and without glancing back he said, Let's get some chow, flaca. Sorry, champ, she said. If he was disappointed he didn't say it. Bueno, I'm taking off. Back to Chi-Town, man. He made a plane motion with his hand. Pepito walked back to his rental, got in, turned on the ignition, and didn't move. A thunderstorm rolled in at Biblical proportions. Palma started driving and saw his headlights following. They went to her home. He missed his flight and the one after that. Way after the two ran out of condoms, anything edible in her fridge and pantry to sustain them, talking or not talking, they were armlocked in bed.

It was way past midnight. Pepito switched on the TV. She was beginning to recognize the look—the traveling back to where he had spent the last decade. I had a cell-y once, Pepito said. He was doing thirty years. Thirty years man, with no parole. This guy did everything to preserve himself—ate low carbs, exercised, kept out of everybody's way to stay stress-free. He kept pulling out his white hairs as they came in. He planned on coming out the joint looking exactly like when he went in. The fact is you can't stop time, man.

Pepito had a point, Palma thought. No one could stop time and all too soon Chi-Town Joe would be walking out again.

This guy, you know the one who tried to stop time? (Pepito was off and running down ex-con lane.) He used to wake up screaming from nightmares with cockroaches.

Were there cockroaches in your cell? Palma shuddered. She hated cockroaches.

Some, Pepito said. His nightmares came from childhood,

Pepito said. His brother used to make my cell-y eat them, you know, when they were kids.

Did your cellmate go to prison for killing that brother? (She started feeling itchy.) Pepito shook his head, Naw. He killed the man he found in bed with his wife. Palma's cousin came back to the present and looked at her. Convicts ain't much different than civilians, prima. They just done some things everyone else thinks about doing.

Look, Palma said, taking out her mother's letters from the drawer in the nightstand. Cockroaches and the letters had no connection except that they both made her sick. She *and* my father wanted me but Abuela refused, she said. Pepito picked up one of the letters and smiled. Abuela wrote to me a lot. He smiled. *What?* (It occurred to Palma that her abuela and his abuela might not be the same cantankerous old lady.) What do you know about this? Palma demanded, waving an envelope in front of him. Pepito pointed the remote at the TV and clicked it off. Abuela told me a lot about her life when she'd come see me, he said.

Like what? Palma asked.

Like when and how she came up from her village in Mexico, Pepito said. Palma felt annoyed by his nonchalance. He adjusted a couple of pillows against the headboard and leaned back. Palma leaned back too. She tried to imagine Abuela traveling alone down state to visit him in prison. She visualized the viejita going through security: being busted with the aluminum-wrapped tacos she would have tried to sneak through, bending over to pull off the thick-soled, orthopedic zapatos, then hardly being able to stand back up, finally having to raise her bursitis-stricken arms for the metal detector device. The old woman was one of those people you could never imagine young. Like Morgan Freeman.

What *was* Abuela's story? Palma asked. Tell me, she urged her cousin.

Okay. Okay. Pepito pat her on the bare knee. He ran his fingers through his hair. Well, it's like this, prima. He smiled. It seems the abuelos came up north as newlyweds, he said. Abuela rode a burro part of the way. (Pepito's gaze landed on a painting of palominos on the far wall and stayed there. Palma had found it at an estate sale, i.e., garage sale in Rio Rancho. The horses' legs were out of proportion.) Abuela rode a burro to Chicago? she asked.

I said *part* of the way, he replied. It was during the Second World War when Mexican labor was being recruited. Mexicans came up north however they could.

Palma gave him a look of disbelief, which he ignored, and continued with his narrative: The husband found factory work. Abuela worked at a slaughterhouse. She had some miscarriages, Pepito said, before she had Jim-Bo. Palma nodded. That explains Jim-Bo, she said, developing in a womb taking in the reek of slaughtered animals. Pepito nodded in agreement. Something had to explain their knucklehead tío. Abuela's husband eventually died of lung cancer—Pepito said—from all the years he inhaled asbestos at his work.

And what about Angela? Palma asked.

Angela came along a few miscarriages after Jim-Bo, Pepito seemed to recall. His grandmother came to the prison and talked all the while they sat together, Pepito said. By the time Abuela had her daughter, she was working at a cleaner job, not easier, not better paying—an assembly line building auto parts.

Did she love her daughter ever? Palma asked.

Abuela didn't talk much about her daughter, per se, he said. *Per se?* Palma knew what it meant, she just didn't know if he knew. He said it a lot. As in, We're not in love, per se. They both became quiet. It was time to change the subject.

Have you ever heard the joke about the Tiger's Leap? Palma asked. El salto de tigre. She heard it years before in Mexico. Pepito shook his head and made a gesture with his chin as if to say, go for it. She did. Palma threw back the sheets and began. It was her turn to tell a story: An old woman complains to a young wife about how things had gotten boring in the bedroom with her longtime husband, Palma said. (Old, like her age now?) Well—the young woman said—you've got to try new things to keep the excitement going. Oh? the old lady said. Like what, for instance? Well, the young one said, have you ever heard of the tiger's leap? The old woman hadn't, so the young one explained. Have him get on the bureau and make a mighty tiger leap onto the bed on top of you. It's very invigorating. Sounds good, the old woman said. A few days later, they ran into each other. The young woman was shocked. The other one was in a neck brace, a cast on an arm, and using a crutch. What happened? The young woman asked. The old woman waved the crutch. The old geezer, she croaked. He came down on me bureau and all!

Pepito laughed even though his prima wasn't the best joke teller. Palma told it in Spanish as well as she remembered. Then she got an idea and went over to the bureau. Give me a hand, she said. He got up and lifted her up. Just don't fall with the whole thing on top of me, he said and went back to the bed to lie down and wait for the leap of the tigress. Palma moved aside the items there, a lit Virgin of Guadalupe candle among them, which she blew out first and before propping herself up, in an indio squat. Pepito had a once-in-a-lifetime vantage point. He was taking it in. When he was hard she stretched out her arms. Her hunk got up, carried her off the bureau, arranged them both, and they went around the room connected, out into the hall, down the stairs, and ended up on the wine-stained couch. She dozed off and went straight to REM sleep. Palma was riding across a *Mad Max* terrain on a dune buggy with Abuela next to her on a burro, waving her fists. Or maybe it wasn't Abuela. And there was no burro. She only knew that after Pepito kissed her neck goodbye he walked out on her again.

★ **PART TWO** ★

1 On Saturday Palma drove to Chana's country club. Do you play golf? The chef asked when she called to make the invitation. Sports and Palma were like texting and driving—a bad combination. They decided to meet after Chana's golf game and have brunch there. Palma gave her name to the guard at the gate and found her way to guest parking. Chana was waiting in the dining room chatting up club members, passing her card around, and inviting them to Babbaluci. The women were soon given a table by a window. It was bright out, a shimmering, man-made pond in view. In a few minutes a bottle of Moët was brought out on ice. They were officially celebrating her birthday, Palma figured, when instead Chana toasted, Here's to finally getting together.

I've taken the liberty of ordering for us, Chana added, her male energy at full throttle. She had an accent. She was from Southern California but there was the teeniest hint of Spanish. Her parents were from Costa Rica, she said. Chana's mother relocated to Central America from Israel with her family as a girl. They'd gone to study horticulture and never went back. The girl married a Costa Rican, and later the two moved to Los Angeles, where with some family money, they opened up a bread shop. Then, Chana said, they got smart and went into the panadería business selling Mexican bread in Huntington Park. Pan dulce? You know? Chana said.

Yes, Palma knew. Conchas, empanadas de camote y piña. Pan de ceniza. Püerquitos. Churros con cholocate. Yum. Palma said, remembering breakfast after Sunday Mass as a kid.

Chana and her folks lived in Brentwood. She had tutors and home schooling until a place opened up for her at Ohr Haemet Institute for Girls. When I was little I spent almost all my time with Mami and Papá in their bakeries, Chana said, showing off her dimples. Talking about bread, or maybe food in general, lit her up. She stretched out her arms to show her generous panza. Or big bosom. Chana's life and upbringing were as different from Palma's with Abuela and Jim-Bo as a bagel from a bolillo. Only in Palma's case, instead of the bolillo being warm and soft, it was so stale you'd have to stomp on it to pound it into crumbs for the pigeons.

The salads came out and Palma was lost thinking of the recent revelation of having parents. My mom and dad are in Los Angeles, she said to Chana, words as foreign as Sanskrit caught in her throat.

Oh yeah? the other said. Understandably, Chana was oblivious to her date's upbringing in stark contrast to how Palma imagined hers. She'd grown up with a mother and father who, Palma was sure, had always taken their precious girl's chubby, little hands as they crossed streets and read bedtime stories to her at night. (Abuela's idea of a bedtime story was La Llorona, the phantom who was said to have drowned her children so as to go off with a lover. La Llorona has fangs and claws, Abuela would finish up the story: *And she's coming through the window to drag you out one of these nights for being so malcriada*. To date, Palma still slept with windows closed.)

Chana's father baked each of her birthday cakes. Her mother, a seamstress, had made all her dresses, as Chana said, modeled after child stars. I hated all those petticoats and tulle, the chef said. Mami wanted a girly girl and she got me instead. I much preferred being out with my dad working on his car. Chana laughed. Palma liked the woman's laugh and reached over and lightly touched her face. Chana caught her breath and moved her salad plate aside to start on the beef bourguignon she ordered for each. Palma hated red meat. (Couldn't Chana have asked?) She considered herself a vegetarian with exceptions. They had nothing to do with spiritual or dietary considerations. Menudo after a major cruda, for example. Meat tamales at Christmastime. Italian beef sandwiches in Chicago. When it came to comfort foods (or anything else that comforted her), political correctness (and good taste) was flicked off like a dead bug.

As Shirley Temple went on about her charmed child-hood, Palma recalled the slips Abuela made for her when she was around five and six years old. The grandmother cut them out of flour sacks. The center of the slip read "US FLOUR" with a circle of blue stars around it. Crafty Abuela embroidered the arms, neck, and hem with colorful trim. There was no way lit-tle Palma could run in the school playground or climb monkey bars in those things. One time the public school children were all sent to the nurse to get lice treatment. The woman thought the child's slip was hilarious. Palma Piedras was mortified.

Excuse me, Chana, Palma said, dabbing her mouth with the cloth napkin and getting up to find the ladies' room. She was coming out of the stall when the chef came into the restroom. You all right, sunshine? Chana asked. (Sunshine? What was next—Pumpkin?) Palma washed her hands, rinsed her mouth, and splashed her face with warm water. I had an allergic reaction to something, she said. Chana took a few deliberate steps and cupped Sunshine's chin with her Pillsbury Doughboy hand, feigning concern about Palma's health. Palma knew her super-sized, alpha-female suitor wanted to kiss her and therefore did not help Chana out. She let herself go limp and Chana put an arm around her as if she were trying to steady Palma, but in fact, she made her move. It was the Chana show. Chana's country club. Chana's restaurant. Chana's fat hands and dimpled smile. Chana was footing the bill. She wanted it that way and Palma would let her have it.

The first kiss was juicy and long as she maneuvered Palma back into the stall and closed the door. Normally by then Palma would have the other's shirt off or her own blouse but there was nothing to be gained by taking initiative. There were butches who, like scratch-and-win cards, revealed girl, girl, girl. They cried easier than you. They adored animals and babies and couldn't have enough of either. They were clumsy, and no matter how buff they got, you could knock them out just like that because in the end they were all heart. Or they were excellent athletes and lacked the competitive gene. Straights got confused about couples where one cross-dressed because they assumed she was the "boy," the "man," then found out she was the one who had birthed your babies or stayed home and took care of your children while you went out to fight dragons. Maybe all she wanted ever was to be a boy and remain forever fourteen and in love with her beautiful, feminine mother.

Or at least these were among Palma Piedras's conclusions, especially after the Mexico City girlfriend, Danorhrial. (It sounded like a prescription for constipation. Her parents put the name together from their mothers' names. She went by Dani.) In all her posturing and make-believe bullying, Dani tried to punch Palma out one night when she was drunk. Palma caught the fist in mid-air, twisted Dani's arm behind her back until she was on the floor, and dug her knee in her back.

Palma reached over, got one of her cigarettes, lit it, smoked it, gave her a drag or two, and when she finished, as the story went, so were they. That was the woman who gave Palma the Michael Kors bag.

Chana had just given Palma a Gucci gift certificate as a belated birthday gift and she planned on replacing Dani's memento. The thought of that Gucci certificate brought out the ho-for-hire and Palma started sucking on one of Chana's big boobs that popped out like a helium-filled balloon. She let Palma do that for about ten seconds then Chana pushed the other woman's face away, her weight on Palma as she pressed her against the toilet. Palma was panicking, but she'd have been a liar if she claimed no freakish part of her responded, *give it to me, girl.* Then Palma's head started to hurt and not only because it hit the wall. Bang, bang, bang. Chana pulled her out of the stall, where Palma flew out like a Jack-in-the-Box, stumbled, and fell. The other pounced and in a flash was down at her rear entrance all over the place, hands, mouth. What a freak. And like all freaks, it was about herself getting off. Whenever Palma tried to move, Chana pushed her head back down. Her purse with the Swiss Army knife that Pepito had passed on that day back at the cemetery when the cops had pulled up next to the car was on the sink and out of reach. I'll never forgive her for this, Palma thought, feeling the tongue in her ass. The rules had been broken. You asked first, cabrona. Chana turned Palma on her back; her fingers went in the front, one, two, three, four. Look how wet you are, mami, she whispered. Finally, her fat fist slid in. Palma held her breath. Her back hurt on the tile floor. It was like having a baby in reverse seeing Chana's arm sticking out from her pussy. She could see by Chana's face that she wasn't present. Palma would make her pay, she kept saying to herself, her fingers with nothing to grip. She would take her restaurant. She'd send her to Costa Rica in huaraches.

Knocking on the door. *Are you okay, in there?* Chana had locked it. Always somebody on the other side of a door, a wall, a fence. Freaks listening in. She saw Chana's other hand, down her pants, working hard on herself. I don't want you to have a baby, she remembered Pepito saying the other night. Palma's womb was gone. Chana's fist was all the way up there. Palma came through tears, spread eagle. Chana straightened up. Happy Birthday, darlin', she said. Palma began to plot revenge.

2 Right after the Kali stampede, as Palma Piedras called it, she got a cashier's check from Pepito for thirty two hundred dollars. In the left hand corner he scribbled *4 ur fotos*. She called. He'd sold the couch pictures. Don't worry, prima, he said. They went to a private collector. They're not going on the Internet. I got a good price. Took my cut, naturally. She considered catching a plane and shooting Pepito with his own gun. Instead, Palma deposited the money. Call her 1-800-PUTA. As she saw it, some sex, if not all, was sheer performance. Puro teatro. And she gave as good as she got.

Every night, some time after midnight, Palma drove to Chana's restaurant or home. They would either re-enact some of what happened that first time on the Lysol floor of the clean, empty restaurant kitchen, or they'd do it somewhere in Chana's house. Outside by the pool, in the closet of Chana's guestroom, kitchen, bathroom. All the places back in Brentwood where her father had been molesting his little girl from ages nine to eighteen. He'd take her with him to the bakery to start the bread making, letting the mom sleep in an extra hour or two. The child began to associate the smell of bread with her father's dick and his love enmeshed in all her senses. Whenever he could—sealed both in a bond against the mother, who was distracted by such things as giving her child a moral upbringing—he messed with the girl. When Chana turned eighteen and graduated from the girls' Jewish institute, he gave his daughter the money for culinary school. She left for Italy.

Despite giving away shellfish and snails, the chef wasn't the most generous of persons. Palma Piedras went back to the country club and found out from security that there was actually a camera in the bathroom. She didn't ask to review the tape or even mention it. There was no doubt in her mind that her limpid posturing and slight frame next to Chana's bench-pressing body would stand up to a Supreme Court ruling. They had a sit-down. She replaced Palma's jalopy with a Mercedes. It wasn't off the showroom, but something Chana agreed to. Being around a woman like Chana made Palma wish Ursula was still in her life, Ramen-noodle-making Ursula. Life seemed clear as a drop of saline on a contact lens with her.

One evening, Palma was on the cell phone with her ex, sitting on Chana's patio by the pool, for once saying back to her, I miss you too, hon', when Kali the Killjoy came out and overheard. Who were you talking to?

As usual, Palma's timing had been off. She should have waited to return Ursula's call. No question Chana was pissed. Not out of love or hurt feelings. Chana was a dry block of yang ice, lost on the Ego Planet. Chana had brought out a platter with hummus and carrot salad, and before Palma could answer, she got up, and it was thrown in her face.

The Mercedes had not been the revenge or even a semi-payoff. Palma had been waiting for the precise opportunity to give Chana a piece of her mind about dyke decorum. No matter how many times she had taken Chana's directions in bed (even while they never did it in bed) there was still that first time. Nobody had said it aloud. Nobody was going to name it. But it was there between them.

Now, carrot and hummus on her face, she jumped to her feet and, like a Chihuahua on steroids, grabbed hold of Chana's Nike-shape-long bra straps from the back to get a good grip as she angled the stealthy woman toward the edge of the pool and pushed her in. HALP! HALP! DON'T LEA . . . gurgle, gurgle, ME HERE! *SPLASH.* PALMA, PALMA! The last thing Palma Piedras heard as she gathered her things and left was her name. Chana, California girl, born and bred, had learned a lot of things along the way. Not among them was how to overcome her fear of water.

3 The galleys for the Spanish artist's book were being prepared and Palma la Rocky started translating the British novel. La Rocky was how she was called during her teen years. She never joined a gang, not that she hadn't tried. The girls in her neighborhood rejected her request. I'll kick anybody's ass you want, she volunteered. No, they said. Something about her they didn't like. Brains, maybe.

One night she went to Randall's bar. Are you kidding me? He said, acting scandalized, picking up her car key on the Mercedes-Benz key chain that she'd dropped on the bar. Before Palma could say anything or snatch it back from his hand, he said, What's wrong with you, Miss Thing? You tried to drown that woman? After she bought you a fucking Mercedes? I know *I* have commitment issues but you've taken yours to new heights. He didn't wait for an answer but went to serve drinks to a couple of guys at the other end of the bar. It was a slow night.

Nothing sadder than a grumpy gay, Palma thought. Randall looked worse than how she'd seen him on her birthday two weeks before. Palma figured that his business partner (and former lover), was stealing from the till, cooking the books, Enroning the business in other words. Randall said he couldn't prove it yet, but as soon as he had concrete evidence he was going to sue the guy. He'll probably go to jail instead, the bar owner said about his partner, he's so fucking broke it's pathetic.

Palma waited, staring straight ahead. She could see part of her face in the mirrored wall between the Grey Goose and Johnnie Walker. She could also see the reflection of the person on the stool next to her. Bad wig. A mask of makeup. Her neighbor reached over for the bowl of mixed nuts. How you doin'? she asked.

All right, Palma said with a nod, looking straight ahead.

Is that true you tried to drown somebody? Mask-face asked.

Palma turned. The person next to her was a hundred years old. Maybe two. Arthritic knuckles like ping-pong balls. Yeah, Palma said. After she bought you a Mercedes? Methuselah asked. One of her false eyelashes was ungluing and when Palma reached over to fix it, the other backed away. (Palma stood corrected. Sadder than a grumpy gay? A traumatized drag queen.)

Randall returned. Girl, you are too much!

Never too much, she said. In point of fact, Palma thought he might be a little jealous of the whole Chana affair. Sex for a Mercedes. He did it for free. Yeah, it was all glam and games until someone got thrown in a pool. He didn't have the lurid details. Apparently, Chana was keeping them to herself while giving a whole new, self-serving version to people. With the pageboy, dimpled cheeks, and the localized glitz lent by her upscale snail trattoria with the back-tables-VIP section, she had Randall fooled. Chana was his type, too, Palma knew. He liked (as in empathized with) masculine broads: feminine guys and macha women. God bless her friend behind the bar, where he'd been almost every night for the last twenty years. He was shaved and his dirty blond hair thinned to its lowest common denominator, spritzed, and sprayed. He was in a tight, tie-dyed, long-sleeved shirt that showed off a man who kept himself, above all things, fit at fifty. Randall grit his teeth. Since when have you and Chef Boyardee become pals? Palma wondered. She gave a party at her place the other night, out by the pool, he said. Catered.

Of course, from her own restaurant, Palma said, unimpressed.

Tiki lights, the works, girl. It was fabulous, Randall said. (His first fabulous of the night; his mood must have been improving.) She was telling *everybody* there, like we were the CSI unit. Pointing at the pool. Candles all lit up drifting on the water like it was the Ganges River and we were imagining her ghost floating in the water.

The Ganges River is polluted, Palma interrupted.

Everybody was asking if you were drunk when you tried to drown her. I said, I'd known you for years and I had *never* seen you drunk.

Thanks, Palma said. And by chance, when you were giving that vote of confidence on my sobriety—and therefore, implying that I was fully conscious of my supposed psycho acts—might *you* have been on one of *your* cocktails of Xanax, Oxycodone, and Flexeril? Or maybe Fentanyl chased down with your favorite Shiraz? Palma felt her face turn red. Methuselah let out a gasp. When Randall and Palma gave her nasty looks she gave them a nastier one back. I just know that I've done some abhorrent things . . . he told Palma.

Yes, you have, she said.

But what could have Chana done to you to make you push her into her own pool knowing she couldn't swim? He made Palma feel guilty for about five minutes, then she said, See you later.

One thing she knew was that when gossip benefited people, they perpetuated it. There was a time when Randall would have thrown Chana back in that Ganges pool for talking smack about her. In those days Palma could have called him her best friend, she remembered that night, driving around with the top down in the Mercedes convertible, despite the cold November air. Randall was the first friend the Chicagoan made when she moved to Albuquerque with Rodrigo. Her husband didn't mind that she spent so much time with a gay man any more than she did; unless the two were traveling, Rodrigo was as boring as a restaurant that gave a calorie count on the menu. When she first met him she thought a man who wore cuff links must be fascinating. How wrong she was.

Fierce H's muse decided to respond to his last text and she went from the bar to find him. He was at a poetry slam/rap/open mic at a grungy beer hole near the university. When she arrived, there were a lot of kids. Who else? Palma was standing by the door looking around when she spotted him. He came right over. You wanna beer? Sure, she said. Palma didn't drink beer. Everyone knew that. Maybe not. (*He* didn't and he was actually pretty smart.) Hector returned and handed her a cold bottle. To my muse, he toasted. To my amusement, she toasted back. They wriggled their way to his friends' booth and somebody gave up his seat. The guy "whispered" in Fierce H's ear over the loud DJ music or whatever the sound was splitting her skull. *She's smokin', man. You actually hit that?* Fierce H took a pull from his beer and nodded all sappy faced. They were staring at Palma Piedras like they had 3-D glasses on. Palma pulled her sweater tight around her front and turned to the girl sitting next to her. She looked ten. Is that your boyfriend? Palma—two decades past that scene—asked about the guy next to Fierce H. Both guys were grinning, staring, and clutching their beer bottles like they were holding their dicks. The girl glanced over as if she had not noticed who was sitting by her. We go out, she shout-whispered. Then she gave Palma the evil eye. Maybe it wasn't the evil eye, but she turned back to her friends and cut her off. Fierce H leaned over and said, I'm going up to perform right after the break. Okay, Palma said, as if she gave a damn. She had made the detour to the place only because of all the nonsense Randall had been saying regarding Chana, and Palma didn't want to go directly back to her catless home.

She had never thought of her home or life as being catless except for all the recent social assumptions or the pharmaceutical party line portrayals of middle-aged women as lonely cat women and small-dog women and going-to-bed-with-everything-but-a-man women—parrots, ferrets, and inanimate laptops, but let's not talk about sleeping-together women. Heaven forbid women should find comfort with each other, if not full-on lust. Love! It could happen and it happened often. Palma was reminded of it when she'd gone to a women's bar after she left Chana to sink or swim, imagining the next day's headlines. They couldn't prove anything, Palma was convinced while nursing a ginger ale and watching some ladies play billiards. Ladies was a stretch. No one had caught up with William Shatner yet, who found his wife dead in the pool and claimed she was a drunk. (It was one way to avoid a costly divorce with someone you wanted to dump a month into the marriage.) Why would they think that Palma, of all the good and kind people in the world, would want to hurt Chana? They always looked for motives. And there weren't any, were there? (Not if they didn't look at the Country Club tapes. Eventually they would and the next thing you'd be watching Palma on *Primetime* just as she always suspected.)

The DJ stopped spinning and an MC jumped up on the stage and introduced Fierce H, who hurried up there. A beat started over the speakers. Heads were bopping. The rapper grabbed the mic. *Like rum and like Coke,* he started bouncing on one leg, then the other. *Like weed she all smoke./This ain't no joke she my Queen/Bee and then some./Yeah./Bring out the rum./Bring out the Coke./Didn't I say this was no joke?/Come on, girl./Come watch the stars./They shine for you and me./Yeah./ They shine for you and me./Don't trip, don't slip, don't leave your lipstick./I got someone I can't kick./Gonna be kickin it with.*

Right then Miss Nickelodeon started pushing to get out of the booth. Palma stood, managing to keep the Gucci bag on her lap from dropping to the floor. Why don't you go be with people your own age? The girl spat beer saliva at Palma as soon as she stood up. Cougar bitch. (Right. Like *that* was going to hurt Palma's feelings.) Then the chick made her way through the crowd in the direction of the unisex toilet. Palma realized that when she asked if the guy next to Fierce H was her beau (cougarspeak for fuckmate), the girl must have looked at Fierce H.

Palma seemed to recall there was a time when she had girlfriends. On second thought, that wasn't true. Why re-write history? She'd never been tight with other women. Abuela was right. They turned on each other over men. Could Palma have straight friends? Probably. But who had the time?

4 Fierce H had apparently become a forty-watt star shining dimly in the Burque hip-hop scene, and after that the reluctant source of his inspiration only heard from him on those sporadic occasions when he needed recharging.

Who Palma did start hearing from again was don Ed. After their one rendezvous that went retrograde she continued to get midnight calls, which Palma did not answer. One day there was an email. He was coming back to attend a sweat lodge near Española. He invited her to the spiritual ceremony that was being conducted by folks he knew. They are Chicanos and Pueblo Indians, he said. She replied and thanked him. However, Palma said, she was behind on her work, and in addition, very anxious about her lost cat and busy passing around flyers to get it back. She was offering a reward. It was a fib she figured don Evolved would understand.

The afternoon don Ed rang the bell, Palma was in the kitchen making flour tortillas. One thing Abuela taught her granddaughter that had never steered her wrong was how to cook Mexican. There was Mexican as in Abuela's sopes from her pueblo in Puebla. There were tortas from LA and burritos from the Bay Area, breakfast tacos in San Antonio and Laredo, and then there was everything in green or red chili

Nuevo Méjico. Perfectly round tortillas, the basis of a cuisine that went back to pre-Aztec, came to Palma as easy as corn pie, thanks to a knock or two on the head from Abuela with her rolling pin. The now all-too-grown granddaughter decided to make New Mexican-style burritos from scratch for the big guy. It wasn't hard to decide to invite him for lunch as much as it was trying to figure out how much flour she was going to need to fill him up. She made Sonoran-style tortillas, except not light as a crêpe but hubcap weight filled with pork in red chili. She used lard. Abuela would have been proud. (Potential diabetes be damned.) Palma would feed the Beluga and send him on his way. She couldn't say why she considered seeing him again, but his voice had almost come to a whimper when they spoke on the phone. Palma said she'd put off the cat posse for a couple of hours if he wanted to come feed.

When she opened the door and looked way up, Palma's neck cracked. Sonofabitch, she muttered. I can help you with that, don Ed said, stepping in with a Sasquatch-size foot. She heard the faintest of squeaks. He was holding something in his bear claws. He put it in her hands. Holy minutia, Palma said. It was practically new born. Miu, miu, it cried, looking up at Palma, hungry, eyes half shut. It was on your walkway, don Ed said. I think it wandered from its litter. That's probably what's happened to your cat. She went to have her babies.

They searched outside and found three more babies in the hedges. *Thanks, cat*, she thought, who could very well have had her litter next door where she freeloaded, were the animal not out to make Palma look bad. Don Ed found a crate in the garage, packed it with some rags, and placed the kitties there. Later, he said, when the mother shows up, we will move them to a safer place where she'll find them. *We?* (Was this the royal we, or the Book of Genesis we-are-the-gods we, or was by chance Belugaman trying to tell her he wasn't just passing through that afternoon?)

Come with me to the sweat tonight, he said, after chowing down two blown-out burritos. I've never been to a sweat lodge before. It's not gonna hurt, is it? Palma asked don Ed. He chuckled and she considered for the first time that more than any kind of don he was just an average guy with a soft heart (and a softer penis). They didn't have to screw or die trying. Not that it had technically happened in the first place. But just be nice to each other.

Another knock on the door. A somewhat familiar face. The neighbor Hank's wife. It's me, Patricia, she smiled, seeing Palma's blank expression. She held out a hand. Palma shook it and invited her in. So, did Ursula really go back to Houston? Patricia asked. What a shame. What a nice girl, she said. Then added, how are *you*? Palma took it to mean Hank's wife knew about Ursula's and her relationship. Because of the open space, Patricia noticed don Ed at the table (not that there wouldn't have been a sighting wherever he was in the house). Oh, I didn't mean to interrupt, she said. We have your cat, Patricia said. We have the kittens! Don Ed said. Yes, that's right, Palma said. Mystery solved.

5 With basic instructions from don Ed about how to prepare for the sweat ceremony Palma gave in, and the two got in his SUV rental and drove to Española after sunset. She was equipped for the cold night ahead in fleece-lined sweats, but underneath had on a pair of Bermudas. El Beluga had his own insulation and didn't wear a coat. It's gonna get hot in there, he warned. They found the sweat lodge that night along with about five people waiting to go in, including the leader or Giver, whose lodge it was in his backyard. Except for a couple of sturdy pine trees, it was dirt and gravel. The lodge was a domed hut made of saplings and covered with sleeping blankets and tarps. You'd have to crawl in on your knees. Inside there was a pit in which volcanic rocks were placed.

The Giver was a wiry vato around Palma's age, wearing cut-off jeans, a T-shirt, and a hoodie. It's gonna get hot in there, he warned.

I can take it, she said.

No, the Giver said, whose name was Pancho, I mean, it's gonna get HOT. Caliente. You speak Spanish? She nodded. He seemed one peyote button short of flying without feathers. A long time ago, women gave the sweat lodge to the men, Pancho said. It represents the womb of mother earth.

Palma nodded. Interesting. It was very cold out that night and don Ed had brought over his sleeping bag and put it around her as she bunched herself up on a foldout lawn chair.

That's because the women already had their moon time, don Ed said. Palma nodded. You on your moon time? Pancho asked. That's a mighty personal question, pardna, she said. She could hardly see Pancho's face. He probably couldn't see hers either. You can't do a sweat if you are on your moon time, Pancho said. Okay, Palma said. Women didn't used to participate, he said. She looked around; there were two other women present. Oh, they can *now*, he said. We've changed a lot of the rules in modern times.

Don Ed was to be the fire keeper. Traditionally, throughout the ceremony a fire keeper stayed out and brought water to pour on the broiling rocks inside to steam up the womb space. Finally they were invited in. All the participants sat in the pitch-dark on the dirt floor. You could see the narrowest sliver of light by the flap. Pancho beat the drum and began to pray: *Grandfather, we thank you for your blessings, and we ask you to help us here tonight to stay on the Red Road. Teach us, Oh Grandfather, and give us strength to heal ourselves.*

Don Ed reached in and handed Pancho a bucket of water with a ladle that he used to pour water over the rocks. One ladle after another, then more, and the place turned into a killer steam bath. A couple of people coughed and others took deep breaths. Palma was woozy but promised herself that she would not die like those victims of the vainglorious James Arthur Ray that Pancho and don Ed had talked about earlier. Ray was doing too little time too late for stealing the rites and customs of a culture he obviously understood nothing about, they said. Far from a womblike ambience, Ray's *The Secret* enterprise was a circus tent. A clown car that fit fifty people. (*The Secret* was a cotton-candy book spun not for dreamers but schemers.) The lodge Palma found herself in was cozy in a claustrophobic, buried alive way.

Throughout that long, steamy night there were four cycles or rounds. Each round signified one of the four worlds according to native peoples' beliefs. (The fifth world, don Ed told Palma, started on the winter solstice of 2012.) After each round, the flap of the lodge was opened and those who wanted to could step out. She did each time, her eyes popping out like a Gila monster on peyote. (For the record, peyote wasn't used in the sweat lodge, although she had a feeling that don Ed and Pancho had VIP privileges.)

In the sweat, Pancho beat a water drum, directed the prayers, and sang what (despite her lack of experience, Palma guessed) were not entirely traditional ceremonial songs. (Her favorite of his that night, dedicated to the Great Spirit, was to the tune of "Black Magic Woman.") Pancho started out with prayers to the four directions; the next round, prayers to the universe and humankind; third, to those in the lodge, and by the fourth, they were all praying for vim and vigor. After his chants, remarks, and songs, Pancho said: All My Relations. Ho. And everyone repeated: All My Relations. Ho!

Relations, dead or alive—Palma found herself dwelling on Abuela and wondered if the old woman had joined her husband in purgatory. Where else would she be? Her husband had been Catholic and the Catholic Church kept all the souls in detention until Judgment Day. I bet it's as hot where you are as it is where I am now, Palma spoke to Abuela in her thoughts. It's not too bad, then, she decided, bringing her knees up to her chin. In her memory's ear she could almost hear Abuela's tambourine hard against her cracking knee, everyone in her iglesia shouting *Amen, Señor! Aleluya!* People swooned and spoke in tongues in Abuela's church, meanwhile Palma read *True Confessions* stories about adulterous wives and Lolita babysitters, the magazine hidden inside her open missal.

In the sweat tent there was silence. Wind. A neighbor's dog barking.

We are here to pray and give thanks and ask for forgiveness and courage, Pancho said. But you must also listen to what the Great Spirit is trying to say to you. Listen to his instructions as to how to stay on the path, on the Red Road. (Ho—a few people called out, less enthusiastically as the heat went up.) People around the circle began taking turns making admissions in the safety of the dark, throwing out prayers or calling words of thanks. One or two sang short songs of praise to life or the Great Spirit with warble-y voices. By the last round everyone had spoken, except her. Feeling obliged to contribute, Palma finally said, Thank you for having me. A disembodied voice said, ho. Then Pancho said, We pray with our hearts. If you don't know how to say what you feel, the Great Spirit knows.

When the ceremony was over, Palma Piedras promised the Great Spirit of the Sweat Lodge of Española that if she did not suffer cardiac arrest on the way home after so much heat exposure, she'd stop being selfish, and as proof would keep the kitty don Ed put in her hands. (Okay, well, maybe not keep so much as take responsibility for in her own way.) To stay on the Red Road I'll have to be realistic, she told don Ed as he drove her home at two a.m. I'm fairly certain, she said, that the Great Spirit wouldn't take kindly to grandiose promises made by first timers under duress. Don Ed made no comment and they listened to talk radio the rest of the way. At her door he declined the invitation to come in. I'm heading back to Española, he said, pointing a big thumb over his shoulder. Call me, Palma Piedras said with that pinky and thumb gesture that people gave, although she didn't know what made her do that. They were both soul-searching that night, but it was clear beneath a silvery moon they had not found their soul mates.

6 Patricia would find homes for the kitties as soon as they were weaned, she told Palma. The helpful neighbor also said she was from Gallup and part Zuñi. Palma wasn't taken by surprise about the woman's Indian blood. She and Hank looked all-Native, as did the children. She was in fact pleasing to the eye, Palma decided, the day after the sweat, if anyone could shut her up. You could leave the room and come back and Patricia'd be carrying on about very little that seemed like more because she kept repeating herself. Don't worry, we'll keep the cat. We don't mind feeding all the neighborhood cats, so don't worry. She said inane things like that over and again until you wanted to fold her up like origami and stick her on a branch.

Palma felt her neighbor's eyes as she brought in laundry stiff from the outside line (since the dryer had drawn its last warm breath). Palma said she hoped Patricia didn't mind if she folded while they "visited." (The neighbor had dropped by unannounced.) Her skin was dark and she had stringy hair. She wore no makeup, not even eyeliner to bring out her light eyes. She liked the jeans Palma wore, and from how the neighbor's gaze kept going back to them, her boobs, too. Then Patricia said, Are those real? The other looked down at her breasts in a tank top. Yes, she said, folding towels. I mean, I know they're real, Patricia said. Palma knew what the neighbor meant. She nodded. I mean, the neighbor said, because Ursula—a beautiful girl, don't get me wrong—told me hers weren't.

Palma's once-girlfriend talking to the woman next door about her breasts sounded like curious conversation. She stopped folding. Patricia wrinkled her nose. We were just talking, she said. It was meant to assure her nothing happened between them. Well, that little vixen, Palma thought about Ursula. She took the laundry basket off the couch (the new, red leather couch) and sat down.

Nothing happened, Patricia said. Palma closed her eyes and gave a sigh. The woman came and sat next to her. Nothing happened, she said again. Chingao. Vieja necia, Palma thought. She gave the neighbor a come-off-it look. It didn't matter if anything happened or not. It was over with Ursula. Does your hubby know about your inclinations? Palma asked. For a moment she thought Patricia was going to say nothing happened again, after which she swore to herself that she would not be accountable for her actions. Instead the woman shook her head. Then she nodded.

Which is it? Palma asked.

I don't know, she said. I think he suspects. But Hank would consider it cheating no matter who it was. (Well of course her husband should consider her betraying their vows if she was having sex with women, Palma thought.) He suspects, the other repeated.

You seem to be carrying around some weight on your shoulders, Palma said. The other nodded. Ever try going to a sweat? Palma asked. The neighbor nodded again. It worked wonders for me, Palma said. I lost about five pounds. She was trying to lighten the mood, since obviously that wasn't the point of a sweat. (Anyway, Palma hadn't lost five pounds but more like 305 with the final retreat of Big Ed.)

Is that what you got out of it? Patricia asked. It's a sacred ceremony.

Well, Palma said, I don't know what I got out of it. Going over to a bookshelf, she pulled out a new drawing pad. In an effort to sketch what images came to her that night in the tarp womb, Palma ended up instead doing a series of women's pantsuits. Back at the Art Institute where she'd gone to school years before, Palma had won a prize for one such outfit in the annual student fashion show. She now flipped through the pages quickly. The neighbor couldn't care less. What could Palma say? Some got inspired by sacred ceremonies to do pious acts; she got motivated to follow Vera Wang.

Patricia left and the other woman went back to tidying the house, avoiding the translation project. About an hour later, her doorbell rang sharply. (It was hard to explain how a doorbell that played Frère Jacques could ring sharply. Maybe it was a hunch.) There they were. American Gothic. Instead of holding a pitchfork, Hank had a bottle of tequila in hand. He looked like someone had smacked him in the face with one of the burritos Palma made for don Ed the day before. (Maybe she still had food smacking in mind because of her recent altercation-breakup with Chana.)

Now what? she thought. Let me guess, Palma said to both. You've talked it over and you've decided you want catrimony? Back payments in Purina Cat Chow?

No, Hank said, and stepped in without an invitation. His wife followed, looking agonized. He handed Palma the truth serum. Uh, oh, she thought, sensing the potential of a mean drunk ahead. (It sounded racist to say Indians couldn't drink, but not only couldn't they—she—drink, their turkey livers trembled, like the king's tasters, at the first drops they soaked in.)

We just want to talk, Hank said over his shoulder. Palma looked at his wife, who nodded. Palma went to the kitchen to get glasses. (Another thing about Indians—and mestizos— the salt and lemon? Child's play. They went straight for the firewater.) Oh, I like mine in a short glass with ice, Hank called. Palma came back with Hank's glass with ice, a shot glass for Patricia, and an RC Cola for herself. He filled up his drink right away. Then he said, Patricia's told me everything. Everything? Palma said. (She herself didn't know "everything.") She turned to the woman, who poured her own shot and swilled it back like a pro. She held out her shot glass and Hank filled it again.

Palma sipped the RC out of a straw in a can. (Whatever happened in the next thirty minutes, she intended to be sober for it.) Hank stared. AA? He said. Palma shook her head. He shrugged. We came over because there is only one thing we can do now, Hank said. He was maybe mid to late thirties. Forty, tops. He looked younger than his wife. The kids were Patricia's. He had been out raking leaves and was in a dusty hoodie and baggy, gritty jeans. Muddy sports shoes. Uh-oh, Palma said, putting up her hands. (A ménage à trois never ended well in those TV criminal investigations. If Hank had decided that was the way to get even with Patricia's infidelity, they could count her out.)

No! Hank crisscrossed his hands in front of him. I mean my wife is here to apologize. He looked at said spouse, who stayed silent. He turned to Palma. Then at his old lady. He set the glass hard on the coffee table (just to the side of the coaster) and left. When he was gone, Patricia said, I didn't mean to break you two up.

What? Palma said. Well, things happen, she added, underwhelmed by Patricia's mandatory apology. The other plopped down on a cushioned chair. She stayed at the edge with both hands clutched between her knees. She had a hoodie on, too. His and her Mulch outfits. We're going to work on our marriage, she said.

Glad to hear it.

Getting up and treading toward the door, the neighbor stopped. We're making Sunday dinner after church tomorrow. Do you want to come by?

And that was how Palma's first friendship with two straights started. If you could call Patricia straight.

7 Sunday afternoon, Palma had dinner with Oscar Mayer. There were hot dogs and chips at Hank and Patricia's. The kids were happy. There were soya dogs, too, which tasted like dildos. When she threw hers at the cat, she sniffed it and walked away. Palma's hosts and she were getting to know each other—Hank worked at the Boys and Girls Club and Patricia worked full time at Planned Parenthood—when Patricia's doppelgänger appeared.

Palma was coming out of the bathroom and there she was, Patricia's evil twin. (She had no reason to think of the woman as evil except in retrospect.) She was identical to her hostess but with clear distinctions. The twin's hair was lonnnnnnnnnnnn-g. It was not stringy like Patricia's, but somewhere down her back it became wispy until it stopped at her calves. The twin had a softer face but her complexion was sun damaged. (From ceremonial dancing as a girl, she told Palma later.) Patricia and the twin were average weight, except the latter looked bulked up. This is my sister, Patricia said, Lucrecia.

What up? Lucrecia said, moving toward her to offer a vato-style handshake replete with opposite shoulder bumping. Like Patricia, she wore no makeup, and unlike her sister, she had tattoos. The red Zuñi sun symbol on her right hand. Tats went up and down her arms and Palma saw one with fangs on her neck. All kinds of animal medicine. A badger, a bat, a beaver, and bear. The surface of her skin was a zoo. Black and blue ink on her dark, reddish-brown flesh.

My sister just moved to Albuquerque from Gallup, Patricia said. *Like that very minute?* Palma wondered. Lucrecia had materialized out of the not so thin air in Hank and Patricia's home. Patricia went to load the dishwasher and they followed. Her butt was smaller than Lucrecia's, but Lucrecia's butt wasn't big, just firm.

With the arrival of a new guest to take the pressure off the unhappy couple, Palma was quick to announce her departure. I've got to get work done this weekend, she said. I'm behind on my translations.

Take some food home, Hank offered, breaking away from watching a football game on TV. The kids were behind him. The boys, about eight and ten years old, were trying to tackle him. You're going up for your bath! Patricia yelled. Tomorrow is school. Lucrecia smirked, leaning against a counter. Yeah, Hank, she said. Give the kids their bath.

Hank left with the boys, and Lucrecia and Patricia were two heads with one body, a double embryo. It was disorienting around identical twins, like being cross-eyed. One laughed and threw her head back, long hair like rainfall behind her. The other threw her head back, light showers behind her. Ha-ha, one said, ha-ha, the other said. Their breasts were modest beneath loose T-shirts. Not stylish, these twins from the underworld. Something about them made Palma suddenly feel like crying, as if somehow she knew that, like her, all they ever had was a Hansel-and-Gretel abuela deep in a black forest. She had already forgiven Patricia for her tryst with her ex, but now she forgave her doubly. And while Palma was experiencing sadness in her gut (residual effects from the sweat lodge maybe), she forgave Lucrecia. A disconcerted Palma knew, between the two, that girl was capable of resounding betrayals. Betrayals that would take NATO sessions to break down. That was Lucrecia at first sight, Palma thought, finding her chaotic and compelling at the same time.

I'm taking off too, Lucrecia said. She was so close behind Palma she could have given her two rear flat tires. The twin was hot on the trail. Once outside, she stopped in front of Hank and Patricia's and started to give Palma a wave. Have a good evening, Lucrecia called. The other hesitated. Disaster was already in motion. You couldn't stop a piano dropping on your head once the ropes broke, and there you were strolling by, oblivious. (Was she oblivious?) Want to come over for some tea? Palma called.

Okay, Lucrecia said and followed all casual-like, as if the very idea of continuing an acquaintance with the high-falutin' haircut and painted fingernails neighbor had not occured to her. After Palma got the tea together and the women were sitting at the table, her visitor asked if she could use the phone. I want to call Billy, Lucrecia said. Who? Billy, my business partner. They had started a moving business. He owned the truck and lived in Albuquerque, not far, she said, in a trailer park. I'm going to see if I can crash at his place, the Indian woman with the long, long hair said.

Why not stay at your sister's? Palma asked the obvious.

I don't get along too good with her husband, Lucrecia said. She rose and went to the phone and called her associate. No answer and she left a message. Hey, Billy? You around? I'll call you back, awright? Lucrecia started to hang up and then added, I'll see you later, awright? It was dark and cold out. You didn't throw out people, even the relations of Mulch neighbors. (Ho!) You can crash on the couch, Palma said. The women were pretending Lucrecia wouldn't end up in her bed.

She got out the blanket and pillow and moved the books and laptop upstairs. Palma went about nightly routines: took the garbage out, turned on the backlights, and turned off the front ones. Lucrecia acted like crashing at a stranger woman's Mulch house was nothing new to her; as if the night before she hadn't slept on the floor of a trailer while nearby Billy snored loud as a charging moose; and before that, who knew where she had laid her head. Lucrecia slipped into her life by virtue of Palma's petroleum jelly of denial, guaranteed to give a good night's rest while you brought ruin on yourself. I'm going up, Palma said, hoping she wouldn't wake up the next day with her throat slit.

Thanks so much, the guest said, really, man.

Palma, possibly the loneliest woman in the universe, went upstairs slowly, as if in gravitational boots. All the while, love or the hope for it remained a minuscule acorn planted in her prefrontal cortex. It may have once had Pepito's name on it. It did not have Lucrecia's name, that acorn of love-hope, but she did steal it that night. In its place was left a nugget of badger shit.

Later, in her room, Palma heard the stairs creaking as Lucrecia came up. The light was on and the door ajar. (She'd wanted to make sure she could hear Lucrecia moving around.) The woman came in. She had taken off her hoodie but was still in street clothes. I brought you some tea, Lucrecia said. I figured you were working. She stepped slowly in, carrying the hot cup, and placed it on the nightstand. Books and the laptop on the bed. Palma wasn't especially horny. She pulled the woman toward her. She was ready for the tidal wave but Lucrecia was light and careful as she landed. Her hair washed over both. She was bigger than Palma with a flat belly and strong. They kissed a long time, tongues and all, when Palma's landline rang.

She wanted to let it ring and felt the other woman stiffen

up. They could hear the old-fashioned answering machine go off downstairs. Hey, Lucrecia? Lucrecia? It was a man's gruff voice. He sounded like what a badger might sound like if he could talk. Then, sing-songy, LU-CRE-CIA! *How'd he get my number?* Palma whispered as if he could hear. He probably hit redial, Billy's protégé said; scrambling to her feet she ran downstairs.

What came to mind, not then but a long time after, was that there had been a phone by the bed that Lucrecia could have picked up. If she'd done that, however, Palma's guest couldn't have stopped the answering machine from recording their conversation.

The next morning, when Lucrecia left, Palma applied herself to her trade and worked all day on the translation project. When the twin called later she wasn't surprised. Palma was a little surprised, however, that she invited the twin over, and more so to have her in her bed. That night they had sex. Palma Piedras called it sex because while it wasn't fucking, it wasn't making love. Someone was going through the motions and that someone may have been herself. In the middle of it she began to think how she rarely used condoms and never a dental dam. Since Palma's divorce she'd become reckless between the sheets.

In the throes of it a distracting thought hit her. What if Lucrecia were "with" Billy the Badger with whom she supposedly worked? Billy's gone drinkin', Lucrecia said, when she came in and threw her backpack on the floor by the couch. The woman, shabby as she was shady, wasn't hungry, and Palma found that odd for someone who claimed to work all day.

Are you going to your sister's for Thanksgiving? Palma asked in bed. It was an attempt at normality in a situation that was anything but. Patricia and Hank had invited her over. She figured Lucrecia would be there, too, but the other woman shook her head. I don't know, she said. Palma looked at her. Lucrecia didn't look back. Her hair was in a long, long braid but lots of flyaway hairs surrounded her face. The amber light from the bedside lamp created an aura around her head and for a second Palma was almost not afraid of her. (She hadn't even realized she was afraid until that moment.)

I might go home to Gallup, Lucrecia said. My father's been pretty sick. Every word sounded like a lead pellet she had to force off her tongue. Odd, Palma thought, about the incongruity regarding the two sisters' stories. It seemed that Patricia had mentioned her father had passed—crossed over—she'd said. Maybe Lucrecia was referring to a stepfather. (Forcing the square bullshit peg into the round hole of your mind was what you did when you were in trouble.) Oh, Palma said. In fact, she herself hadn't decided if she would go next door yet for Thanksgiving dinner. (They might serve a soya turkey.) To change the subject she said, my new washer and dryer are supposed to be delivered on Friday.

Lucrecia smiled somewhat, nodding, as if a washer and dryer were a prize and not necessities Palma had purchased on credit.

They're charging me a bunch to deliver, Palma added.

Oh, man, Lucrecia said, don't have them deliver. Me and Billy can bring your washer and dryer here. We won't even charge you, dude.

Really? Palma said.

Really.

Oh, but I'd give you both something.

Well, Lucrecia said, whatever.

SHE ALWAYS arrived around dinnertime. Dinner for Palma Piedras could be leftover take out, a smoothie, a TV dinner; in other words, she never cooked for herself. Lucrecia, however, never ate. She didn't drink. Palma's guest seemed to have no notable vices, although she had the distinct impression that noticeable vices were in Lucrecia's not-so-distant past. Have you ever been locked up? Palma brought herself to ask one night. It was Wednesday. They had known each other a total of four days.

Her lover nodded. I got caught up in a Circle K robbery, she said.

Let me guess, Palma said. You were driving the getaway car.

Yeah, she said. Except that I didn't know my friends were in there robbing anything until after we took off and the cops caught us.

Tsk, tsk, Palma said. Don't you just hate it when that happens? The twin nodded, which left her hostess further horrified (a word which meant nothing since instead of throwing Lucrecia-the-getaway-driver out then and there, they cuddled and went to sleep). Palma had fallen to the bottom of a dry well while Lucrecia crashed in her home in crusty clothes.

One morning, Palma's new lover left her hoodie on the bathroom floor after showering. She was downstairs getting her shoes on and Palma picked it up to take it to her. Something dropped on the tile floor with a clink. It was a browned short glass straw. She went downstairs. What's this? Palma asked.

Oh, Lucrecia said, and snatched the crack pipe, quickly sticking it in her backpack. It's Billy's nephew's. He helped us with our moving job yesterday, she said. I caught him smoking, and I took it from him before his uncle found out.

Lucrecia left and Palma went to the kitchen to make tea. She had a temperature and by the time the twin was back that night, Palma was in bed with the flu. Lucrecia fussed. She drove the Mercedes to the Walgreens and came back with a stash of useless over-the-counter medicine. Palma's new sweetheart brought flowers. People also brought flowers to the dead. Lucrecia called Patricia who came over and said she'd take Palma to the emergency clinic. You've got to go! one twin said. Yeah, man, the other said. Finally, everyone calmed down. Patricia left. Lucrecia slept on the couch.

Unable to rest because a trillion invisible needles were piercing her flesh, Palma looked up an old *Dateline* on the laptop. She watched a story about a southern belle who picked up a woman with a hard-luck story on a train. The young socialite introduced the (unbeknownst to her) sociopath to one of her best friends, a man who was not in her social circle, and the two became an item. They ended up murdering the southern belle but not before asking her to see if she fit in a big suitcase. The suitcase theme was starting to get to her.

By Friday morning, Palma was only partially revived. Lucrecia said, Don't argue, man. We're going to the emergency clinic. Since she had no health insurance and therefore no doctor, it was the only option. But my washer and dryer are coming today, Palma said.

Don't worry, Lucrecia said. Billy and his nephew will deliver them and by the time we get back they'll be installed. Palma was dubious about letting badgers into her home, and Lucrecia assured her that Patricia had agreed to come over while they were there. Too weak to argue, she gave Lucrecia the keys to the Mercedes and they went to the nearest clinic.

It was a cold day with viruses and germs taking over Gotham City and the clinic was packed. After signing in on page three, Palma sat down with a clipboard with several forms. Her eyes were blurry. Will you fill these out for me? she asked Lucrecia. Sure, she said, and took the clipboard. Time

slowed

down.

Lucrecia had scarcely printed Palma's name when her cell phone rang. The transient now had a cell phone. She said Billy had insisted because it was important for their business. It had a bling cover. Pink. (Most def not what Palma would have imagined a woman like Lucrecia ever doing—dressing up her mobile.) She got up and walked away to talk, and when she came back the twin said, Stupid Billy can't find the house. I'm going to have to meet them and show them where it is.

Palma started to ask about Patricia. Lucrecia had a quick reply. Her twin was on her way back from an errand, something to do with the kids. By the time they got there Patricia would be there with them. It's gonna be a while before you get called, Lucrecia said. I'll return by then. She left and Palma waited. Time

slowed

further

waiting to hear her name. Her calls to Lucrecia's new cell went directly to voicemail, which wasn't surprising since smart phones worked like that, which, was to say, they didn't. Finally Palma went into the doctor's consultation room and more time passed before she was seen. The visit was over lickety-split with a hasty prescription. When she came out to the waiting room, Lucrecia was still not around. The sick woman walked out into the cold air and her car was nowhere in sight. She went inside and waited. Palma didn't have Hank and Patricia's numbers. She finally called a cab.

Neither the Mercedes nor her neighbors' cars were anywhere in sight when she got home. Everything looked as peaceful and undisturbed as when they left that morning. The door was locked. Palma had given Lucrecia her house key on the same chain with the Mercedes-Benz key. Where the hell was she? Palma wondered, going over to the stone by the side of the house under which she left a spare house key.

How inconsiderate, how rude, Palma said things like that in her head when she heard a car driving up and turned around. It was Patricia with her kids pulling into their driveway. (As Palma thought about it later, it was the usual time the neighbors came home on weekdays. As it turned out, she hadn't taken the day off.) Hey, she said. Palma couldn't wait to give her an earful. Patricia didn't have the cleanest record with her either, come to think of it. Patricia got out, nodded her way, the boys ran toward their house waiting for their mother to open up, and the last hint of day vanished. I need to talk to you! Palma shouted.

Once all she worried about was getting her translation projects done. Now, her head packed with mucus, her mere existence felt pitiable. A minute later, a new word for pitiable would have to be created. Lucrecia's outlaws had moved Palma Piedras out.

8 OHMYGAWD! Randall cried out, his hands on his cheeks like the kid in *Home Alone*. Palma called him that same night after the detectives left. Besides her delirious report, they took fingerprints off doorknobs, which was basically all that was left besides the lead about her stolen car. Nearly everything was gone. Most certainly anything of any value. In other words, the books were still there. Not only had the robbers made off with the old washer and dryer, she found out later, they'd picked up (with her unsuspecting permission at the store) the new ones.

Even the cheap artwork was taken down from the walls. (Five-hundred-dollar originals from Art Walks.) Copper pots and pans. Abuela's rosary collection before she became an evangélica. Only what was in the "office" category was left.

OHMYGAWD! Randall kept saying, walking around the shell of a house. Even Rodrigo's shot glass collection—poof. Palma Piedras' ex liked to pick up shot glass souvenirs wherever he travelled. The collection had stayed on display in a China cabinet. (In fact, all his crap, which she'd put in the attic, was gone, too.) The Badger Moving Company had done a thorough job. The history of a life robbed.

Randall slid against the wall until he was sitting on the carpet. Hands still pressed on his flushed face with a beard shadow at that midnight hour, he looked like a Ralph Lauren celebrity model—sexy and weather-beaten (like the expensive "distressed leather" cushioned chair that used to be in her living room). Oh, girl, he kept muttering. What she-wolf in cheap clothing did you let in your home?

If you say the Mercedes getting stolen by a chick on crack is my payback for Chana I'll . . . Palma started to warn her friend. He put a STOP hand out, Oh no, he said. That bitch was in my bar and pummeled Liza into the ground. Poor ol' catastrophe disintegrated into a pillar of salt. (Randall was talking about the Methuselah.) He continued, I told Chana the Cannibal if she went to anger management therapy we wouldn't press charges. (By "we" he meant he and his partner, with whom he apparently had come to a new understanding, which included Randall getting a bigger share of the business.) Vindication being Palma's gave her little comfort at the moment. She sat next to him, holding back tears. She was still sick and had never gotten the prescription filled. Randall said he'd take her by a twenty-four-hour pharmacy and then they were going to his place until they figured out what next.

The What Next? came the following day. Palma was feeling better with antibiotics demolishing whatever microscopic demons Lucrecia had put in her system (whether through the exchange of bodily fluids or an evil twin curse). Why don't you come spend Thanksgiving with me in Wisconsin this year? Randall asked. They were having coffee and muffins. Her friend didn't go for herbal tea. He had, however, made fresh OJ. Apparently a glass of juice and a minor arsenal of vitamins and supplements to guard against aging and the possible contraction of "certain" diseases was Randall's daily mojo. He put a little pile of such pills in front of Palma to take too. Thanksgiving in Milwaukee? she repeated. Well, she did have to go to Chicago regarding Abuela's last will and testament.

As if reading her foggy mind, Randall said, we could take a train there afterward. I can't wait to meet that luscious cousin of yours. (Palma groaned.) But we have to spend Thanksgiving with my folks, Randall said.

Do you guys serve real turkey? She asked.

What? Yeah, but we have the traditional dinner late because we always go see my sister first.

I didn't know you had a sister, Palma said. He frowned. Was Randall's sister in a hospital, she wondered? Maybe that was why he never mentioned her before. She's not your evil twin, is she? He shook his head, untied his silk bathrobe, adjusted it, and tied it again. Matching PJ bottoms. Palma was in a pair of his sweats and thermal long-sleeved top, sleeves pushed up past elbows. Randall poured coffee, sat down, and gave a great sigh. My sister is a saint, he said.

A saint? she repeated. Palma could def use a saint in her life. A live one even better. What's her name? she asked. I'll start praying to her right now.

Sister Claire, Randall said.

Of the Poor Saint Claires? she asked.

No, Randall said. The Blind Sisters of Saint Lucia. His friend scratched her head. A religious order of blind women? Do they have their eyeballs plucked out in order to join? she asked. It was totally medieval. Palma liked it. Randall gave her a look. She let him explain. You know the Catholic Church, honey, he said. They work all angles. It's an English order, he said. They are women who were mostly born that way but not necessarily. They might have become blind from illness, a barbaric brain operation, or maybe an accident. Anyway, they are amazing, girl. They are cloistered and do everything for themselves. No help from the sighted whatsoever. Garden, can vegetables, milk cows, churn cheese, and of course, what they do

137

best and most, pray and sing in their steeple church. Claire went in when she was sixteen and she is the happiest person I know.

TO BE at peace without possessions, that was a challenge to the American Dream, wasn't it? The physical and spiritual unburdening of greedy human nature. Oh, she had once been a fully bonded member of the Mulch Union. She once had a husband with an upstanding job. She had shoes in their boxes that had never been worn. Palma took piano lessons—the Wurlitzer was gone too—on such afternoons and met a Berlitz teacher at Starbucks for private Turkish lessons. (Rodrigo and she dreamed of going to Istanbul one summer to visit the Hagia Sofia.) She wore only designer clothes (all gone except for the Moschino dress—oh, her Moschino dress!—long out of style.) Palma would never have imagined wearing costume jewelry again in her life, and now, all the real stuff—gone with the wind. (The diamond-drop earrings Rodrigo gave her for their first anniversary came to mind because most possessions didn't mean nothing without sentiment attached.) Days after the theft she would end wakeful nights not counting sheep but stuff.

Randall steadied Palma later that day at the Walmart, where she picked up sweatshop items and a roller carry-on bag for the trip. You can't afford high-end or even near it, girl, he reminded her when he pulled up in the airport-size parking lot rather than the strip mall. Oh no, don't say that! Palma said, shriveling in his passenger seat like the Wicked Witch of the West when she began to melt. You'll be all right, Randall said, now get hold of yourself. I bet you don't talk to Methuselah this way! Palma shouted. Don't call her that, he said, her name is Liza Menealo—a legend in her own mind. Me too, she said. Yeah, we all get that, he said.

When Palma Piedras returned home, Fierce H came over one evening after his muse called to say what she had done to herself. (She refused to think of herself as a victim. And whether it was her refusal to get her nose out of Lucrecia's pussy, or a catless woman's desolation that let her guard down to obvious trouble, the universe had given her a punitive wake-up call.) He brought over a MacBook Pro so she could resume her translation work. You can use it until the insurance check comes in, he said, when you can buy a new one. What insurance? Palma asked. Aw, man, he said, Just keep it. Let me know if I can help you out in any other way . . .

Wow, she said. You're so mature for your age.

Well, I *am* thirty-four, Palma, he said.

But Mishu said . . . She started to say.

My brother, Fierce H cut her off. Let me tell you something about my *older* brother. He relies on his looks, right? So, in order for him to remain forever young he keeps making me out to be even younger. The truth is, Vincent is not twenty-seven, he's thirty-seven.

Furthermore, he made an announcement: Fierce was a man spoken for. Off the market, girls. He was going out with the spit-firing chick from the open-mic night. Palma crossed her arms. She called me a cougar bitch, Palma told him, feeling sorry for herself or wanting him to feel sorry for her.

Well, Palma, he said, let's see. You *are* a cougar and you *are* a bitch, but I do love you. (*He loved her?*) Then he said a very mature thing. I love you but I know it's not realistic to think anything serious could ever happen with us.

That's not true, Palma Piedras protested. She was naked,

halfway looking passable and halfway needing to cover up. When she spoke she could hear her echo in the empty house. Why not? Palma asked, grasping for love straws.

It's true, he said. And the best part about it is that I'm always going to care about you. And you'll always care about me, right? His part-time lover stared at him. Right, she said. He leaned back on his hands, legs stretched out on the floor. Fierce H had a white T-shirt underneath a checkered short-sleeved shirt. The pants were off. His dick lay exhausted. It was loveable in its defenselessness. Hector had hairy legs, like thousands of spider legs smashed against pale skin. (Unlike Mishu's, who, along with his age deception, she realized, must dip himself in paraffin.)

I think the people next door had something to do with my house getting robbed, Palma said. His Cookie Monster eyebrows went up. She continued: In your hip-hop circles, do you know any gangsta rappers? He sat up. Are you talking about retaliation? he asked. She nodded. Do you know for sure that they had something to do with all this? He looked around at the void. No, Palma did not know anything for sure about anything anymore, except for the extreme urge she had to do someone or something some damage. Shortly, she got the chance. When they were at it again, Palma pulled Hector's hair and yanked out a satisfying chunk.

9 On the train, watching Randall polish off a family-size bag of Doritos, and thereby annoying everyone around with his crunching and cellophane racket, Palma obsessed about the Order of the Blind Sisters of Saint Lucia. The eyes of the saint, an early Christian virgin martyr, were taken out by a fork. (She lived at the end of the fourth century, way before forks, so go figure.) Lucia was symbolic of illuminating grace and mercy, and Randall's travel mate couldn't wait to meet Claire. She pictured her and the other nuns radiating a light from within like Chinese lanterns. They would love her and Palma would love them. And if they asked her to join their order, she'd think about it.

Randall's parents picked them up. He looked just like his mother. They even had the same goofy laugh, which sounded like the way people laugh when they were tickled too hard, bordering hysterical, except that Randall and his mom, Mrs. Burk, laughed like that out of nowhere. And just like that they'd stop. They loved each other, you could tell, mother and son. Mr. Burk was so quiet, even when he talked Palma could hardly hear him. He didn't laugh at all. They went straight out to the country to the cloister of the blind nuns. Palma had been praying to them, especially to Claire, since the day after the highway robbery of her worldly belongings. The exceptions were the yet unopened Silverman Brothers box, as with other things bypassed in the garage by the thieves. Palma's desk was gone but they had dumped everything on the floor—staplers, highlighter pens, and paper clips, left behind her flash drives and paper files. Her work. Good for her.

THE MOTHERHOUSE was a scene not out of an old-fashioned Christmas card with glitter and snow. There was snow but right down to the adjacent cemetery filled with the graves of blind nuns and the priests who had served the order, it was a lost Edgar Allen Poe story. It was almost dark when they got there—the Burks, Randall, and she in his parents' Pontiac hatchback. Massive clouds were heavy with a pending storm and flurries were already coming down in every direction. No one was out. Not even a raven. Where's Annabelle Lee? she muttered. What was that? Mrs. Burk asked. Nothing, Palma said. Ignore her, Mother, Randall said. She's still delusional from having been so sick last week. Oh? Mrs. Burk said. You were sick? Yes, she said. Dangerous fevers. Well, let's say a prayer for you, dear, the woman said. The sisters have made this place sacred ground.

Palma nodded, shivering in her new Mulch Burlington Coat Factory faux-shearling coat. (She hated it.) They walked over to the main house, a two-story, red brick midwest building if ever there was one, smokestack and all. Inside, a giant hearth with a blazing fire more or less welcomed them along with the directress. She didn't use a cane. The directress knew her way around. Mother Martha Mary was the only nun Palma saw there in the old-fashioned coronet and ten pounds of wool habit, she stretched out her wrinkled hands to each. Yes, they were four. Come, she said, and led them to the visitors' area. I'll tell Claire you're all here. She'd be so happy to see you, Mother Martha Mary said, and went out the door.

Palma wanted Claire to look just like Randall, tall and slender. Her big, blue, sightless eyes would stare right past her as they held hands, the undeclared saint telling Palma that no matter what, God loved her. Being blind, her white Mulch perceptions wouldn't want to ask right away was the mysterious woman Winnebago, perhaps? Or, what country did she come from? She'd hear her flawless English and imagine Palma like her except not blind. (Palma's wish wasn't to be taken for Caucasian; she wanted to meet the nun without the instant prejudices of the sighted.)

Randall and his parents were chatting about how the Burks had recently put down the family's decrepit dog, how his dad was forced into retirement (but they had their pensions, at least), and that his mom's last physical had come up with a spot on her lungs. Quit that damn smoking, Randall said (as if he was about to take his own advice any time soon, Palma thought).

She was a stocky lass, short, that Sister Claire. She came in with giant wind claws pushing her through the doors, and she pulled off a wet, crocheted shawl. (Crocheting was one of the nuns' ventures, which were sold in their goods shop.) Unlike Randall, she had not had the benefit of braces, and her eyes, not pushed out by Roman soldiers with cutlery but larger than you expected, were the eyes of a fruit bat. She laughed and grinned like her mother and brother, but otherwise went mum like Papa Burk. Randall's sister was the Mad Hatter without a hat.

Palma was introduced, but the nun never acknowledged she was there, even when she'd throw in a comment into their clipped conversations. (Claire had a three-second attention span.) Are you and the sisters looking forward to your Thanksgiving dinner tonight, darling? (Mrs. Burk.) Don't they always, Mother? (Randall.) Grin, smile, bad teeth, goofy eyes staring through space. (Guess.) What will you have for dinner? Brussells sprouts . . . cranberries? (Palma, for the hell of it. Look at me, look at me.) Claire didn't turn toward Palma at all. What kind of saint was that? She got up and stared an inch away from the nun's face. What are you doing, Palma? Randall said. When the directress came for Sister Claire, she told them that there was to be a Mass shortly. Yes, we'll be attending, Mrs. Burk said. After the nuns left, Randall said, I'm going out for a cigarette. His father followed. The mother looked resentful, face screwed in a knot, yearning for a smoke herself, no doubt. Her Midwest Mulch upbringing wouldn't allow her to leave Palma there by herself. It wasn't Mrs. Burk's responsibility or her home, but since they were there visiting with her barmy child, Catholic guilt went into high gear. She plopped her beige, vinyl purse on her lap.

They were alone. The ticktock of a wall cuckoo clock made the only sound in the place. So, dear, Mrs. Burk said, are you and Randall planning on ever starting a family? Palma jumped up. Damn him. She went to the window. He was out there shaking in the cold. He wasn't smoking. His father wasn't either. They preferred coagulation to the mother. Palma turned and looked at that figure which they feared and loved most. What would such a woman want more than life itself? A grandchild. Surely before that black spot grew and ravaged her whole body. She wanted to lie to make the woman feel better, jump on board and add to whatever fictions Randall had told his parents. She sat down next to her. They looked at each other.

Then Mrs. Burk gave that ticklish laugh, touched Palma's shoulder, and said, I know Randall's a homosexual, dear. I know you both are, she said. I just thought you two might get

144

together like God meant when he created each of you, man and woman, and have a child to bring you comfort in your old age.

The door in the next room opened, letting in a gush of cold wind and flurries. Randall and Mr. Burk were back. I'm not *homosexual*, Palma said to Mrs. Burk. She was about to say more but the woman put her finger to her lips to shut her up. They were either not to have that discussion in front of Randall, Mr. Burk, both, or before God. It was moments like that when Palma was glad she was an orphan. Or as she had thought of herself her whole life until that she discovered the letters from Abuela's haunted house. Palma hadn't contacted Angela and Mariano, Jr. in Los Angeles, so she still had the option.

10

A novice in a plain, hand-stitched habit came to escort cracked Claire's people to the chapel for Mass. Palma kept up with her rapid pace while the Burks walked together behind. Palma had the feeling the girl could see, especially when she stepped around a slush puddle. She waved her hand over the nun's face. The novice smiled. I'm not there yet, she said. She was a dark, young woman with an accent. Jordan. That was where she was from. My sight is down to 20 percent, she said. She had been born with a degenerative disease. First went the eyesight. It had been her idea to join the order of the blind sisters.

And you ended up in bumfuck Wisconsin, Palma muttered.

Oh, it's splendid here, the novice said, letting go of her flimsy shawl to wave at the glory of her refuge. It fell on the snowy ground, and picking it up, Palma helped get it around her shoulders again. When they reached the top landing that led into the church, the girl asked, You'll stay for tea afterward, won't you? Guests always stay for tea before they get back on the road. Palma Piedras was about to say she didn't know what the Burks had planned when she had the feeling that the tea tradition for the blind nuns was like cats for single Mulch women. They would stay, yes.

146

The white stucco church was so sparse it almost seemed Protestant were it not for the stations of the cross along the sidewalls. The stained-glass windows of saints were the most elaborate decor. The Mass took Palma back to her last Mass. It was on Pepito's confirmation day. He was thirteen and Abuela had bought him his first suit since he made his Holy Communion when he was seven. Abuela wasn't Catholic anymore but she made them Catholic. Palma speculated that it connected her grandmother with her defunct marido or her Mexican culture. (Most of the people in Abuela's church were Puerto Rican.) Going up the aisle at St. Francis of Assisi with his lit white candle, Pepito was a seraph, a coming-of-age angel in his dark blue suit. It was the last time the three would be in Mass together. Abuela, spent woman that she was, raising two broken children (after she had broken her own two), was out of her element in the big city in El Norte entering the twenty-first century. As soon as Pepito hit his teens, just as Palma had, he left.

Palma looked up at the near-bare altar of the blind nuns, at the bloody life-size statue of Christ on the cross. Jesus had been dealt quite a hand. Some might say good, others said bad. Pepito and she were nobody's victims and nobody's saviors. Remembering their childhoods, Palma couldn't wait to see him in Chicago over the weekend. Randall had persuaded her to get ahold of him via text as they rode the train. Can you just treat him like a cousin? her friend asked. Stop thinking you have to fuck everyone you spend time with. You're worse than Mick Jagger, he said. (Yeah, like Randall would have passed on *that* opportunity, if he'd had it.)

Palma sent a text and Pepito responded ASAP: <3 2 c u, *prima*. Of course, she'd bang him brainless. Palma would love him like the mother he never had and make him love her like the father she never knew. They'd be everything to each other. Tell each other everything in bed (the cum-drenched bed she imagined he now had with putas jumping in and out of it like pinches chinches). Then she'd catch a train with Randall and go back to Albuquerque and pick up where the devil had dropped her off.

After the Mass she lined up with parishioners to say hello to the priest who was at the door. The Burks exited the church after polite greetings and Palma fell behind. It's been a while, she said to him once they had privacy. Oh? He smiled. How long? Since my abortion at fifteen, she said, when I was in high school. A look of concern went over his face. But that was no reason to stay away from the church so long, my child, he said. Have you ever asked the Lord's forgiveness? He put his vein-strewn hand out but didn't quite reach for hers. I've been hoping the Lord might have a word with *you,* she said. He looked confused. If men could get pregnant I'm sure you'd hand out the Pill instead of the Eucharist in Mass. (It was women's studies 101 rhetoric. So what?)

THE NOVICE came and led the quartet to the large dining hall. In the kitchen there were cook-sisters banging pots and pans around preparing their holiday dinner in the dark. The directress and a couple of nuns also joined the Burks and Palma at a picnic-style table, bringing out a pot of tea and bland biscuits. The lights were turned on for the visitors' benefit. When they were done Mrs. Burk said, My husband and I are going to visit with our daughter in her room. Family conference, she added. Randall nodded and joined them. Oh, okay, Palma said, watching them go off, escorted by a Sister of Santa Lucia. When they were gone, the resonating sound of their footsteps faded, the directress said, You seem troubled, dear. Can we be of any help?

Palma was taken off guard for a moment. Uncanny how the woman had picked up on her anxieties. Maybe she made up for not having sight by developing high frequency sensitivity. Actually, Palma cleared her throat, I was robbed blind recently. Her hand went to her mouth. There was a pause, then the group commenced to giggling, one sightless woman after the next, shoulders shaking. (At last, Palma thought, she had found the audience for her loose-canon humor. Of all people. Cloistered virgins.) No, but seriously, she said, everything I own was taken from my home.

Oh, so sorry. That is unfortunate, the directress said (stifled giggles). Well, the problem is, Palma said, I invited in the thieves. I'm pretty sure they were part of Satan's crew. She looked around. The high rafters, drafty building, and ghostly darkness on a snowy night out there in the Wisconsin woods, Satan could find his way there, too, she thought.

Sister Martha Mary pursed her mouth. In the Book of Wisdom, she said, the Lord spoke to us through Solomon, the wisest king known. The wicked are so because they reject immortality and justice. Sister Martha Mary placed her folded hands on the wooden table. The nuns drew near. Palma, too. The pressure was on the directress. She fell back on a familiar quote: *For we brought nothing into this world, and it is certain we can carry nothing out.* The nuns turned their sightless heads toward her. Palma nodded. Well, I did hate a lot of my crap, she said. My ex-husband picked most of it out. Sister Martha Mary nodded, self-satisfied that she had done her job, and the nuns let out the soft sighs of the chaste.

I'll sit with you, the novice from Jordan said when Palma

thanked everyone, rose from the table, and announced that she'd wait for the Burks in the reception area. The girl was around thirty and with the kind of skin that never tanned and had a lot of moles. Her brown hair was pulled back with a barrette. She gave Palma a timid smile but her occluded eyes were fixed on her. Come to my room, she said as soon as they were outside.

Straights wonder if such a thing as gaydar exists and Palma could only say about that and whatever else they contemplated that everything depends on everything else. The novice was no novice. Enough said. In her room they sat on a cot and made random chitchat. It was dormlike, not at all the thick-walled cell you'd have imagined, or at least Palma did on that long train ride believing the blind nuns would save her. I must tell you, she said, I'm a highly sexually charged woman. Well, the other woman said, going under her pillow. She pulled out a ripe zucchini.

The two plus zucchini were entwined to the umpteenth degree when Palma heard the steeple bells go off. In six months the Holy Order of the Blind Sisters of Saint Lucia would be offering a funeral Mass for Mrs. Burk. Shortly after, for Mr. Burk. That Thanksgiving, however, the snow was coming down like bullets while the Burks' dry turkey waited at their home for them to partake of in the all-American family ritual of gorging and living with lies.

11 Randall was saying that he'd forgotten how cold it got in Chicago as they came out of the train station on Canal Street where Palma spotted Pepito leaning against a car. He was in a camel-hair coat, with a wool-blend scarf tucked inside. Her lil cous' had his gloved hands up to his ears to keep them warm. Randall stopped mid-sentence watching her make a quick dash, pulling the carry-on toward her good-looking cousin. Good-looking with a capital *GQ*. Working at the Silverman Brothers or for the Silverman sons had cranked up his style fo' sho',' she thought, gleefully landing in his arms. He kissed her where her head landed near his shoulder, on the hood of her faux shearling. Randall caught up, and after quick introductions and handshakes between the guys, Pepito said, Let's catch a cab.

The traffic was thick with Black Friday rush on the biggest shopping day of the year. They might have gotten to their destination faster, she figured, but it was too cold to walk the distance from the train station to what they soon learned was Pepito's new bachelor pad on Dearborn Street. He waved at the doorman like he owned the whole building and they went up to the twenty-ninth floor. She knew Randall well enough and long enough to know his silence was attributed to being impressed with her cousin. Hell, *she* was impressed when they got in the door of his one bedroom apartment and from the view of the tall windows Palma could see most of the city's famous skyline. Make yourselves comfortable, he said. Pepito as yuppie host. Now she had seen everything.

You guys hungry? He asked, getting to work in his open kitchen. Randall took a seat on the couch where he could easily take in the view. Pepito pointed to the small bar against the wall. Fix yourself whatever you like, he told her friend. Palma was proud of her relation (ho!) offering his hospitality and being ever the gentleman in front of the other man. No French kisses or lewd embraces in the elevator, in other words. She threw off her coat and took a seat at the granite counter dividing the kitchenette and living room. I hope you two like pasta, Pepito said.

Sure, sure, whatever, Randall called from the bar. He'd poured himself a Bourbon and Coke. After the intense visit with the Burks and Claire, Palma couldn't blame him for needing a drink, maybe a few. He glanced over to the balcony and pulled out his smokes. I'm going out, he told Pepito. No problem, Pepito said, retrieving a contraption from a cabinet. It was a pasta maker. He went about his preparation with the ease of tying his tie. Randall came back in just as Pepito was cutting the dough ball he'd pulled out of the fridge. It had been left to harden, wrapped in cellophane while he went to get them at the train station. Seriously, Joe? Randall said when he was back. You are making the pasta from scratch? Pepito rolled out the pieces and smiled as he ran each through the maker. When that was done, he put them through the cutter thingamajig and made linguini. He had his own pesto in the fridge. Palma la prima primavera finally got her speech back to ask: When in God's name did you learn to cook, Chi-Town Joe? He gave her a look that said why are you asking me such a question, oh ye of little recollection? Pepito's cousin recalled then that cooking was what he had done in the joint (where she was sure they weren't using pasta makers). Randall came over to marvel. He was in love. Her friend fell in love at the sight of such savory handsomeness, which was to say it was more about appreciation than meant to be deep and lasting. Palma smiled.

Where *did* you learn to cook like this? Randall asked. I took a cooking course, Pepito said. Down on LaSalle. I saw a sign and thought, I'd like to try that. His cousin looked at him. If there was anything she would have guessed Pepito was doing in his spare time when he wasn't doing things Palma didn't want to know about and making money to afford a luxury apartment, it was not taking a cooking class for fun.

She looked around. Can I freshen up? Right through that door, Pepito said, hurrying around, the pasta in the boiling water, setting out black and white dinnerware (def not Corelle or Crate & Barrel), and (real) silverware and cloth napkins. Host much? Palma heard Randall say as she went into Pepito's bedroom, a.k.a the other side of the looking glass. What if she found a fishnet stocking lying on the bed or a framed picture on the nightstand of a young gorgeousity with perky everything? Would she stay? What if there were long blond hairs caught up in the bathtub drain in his private bath? (She looked. There weren't.) There were books by the bedside. *Notes of a Dirty Old Man* and *The Most Beautiful Woman in Town* by Charles Bukowski. The bed was made with a plush comforter with a tan silk cover. It smelled of lavender. The place was so minimalist and muted in color it seemed like he'd brought in a feng shui expert.

While the trio ate, Pepito said he had plans for them. Plans? Yeah, he said, at the House of Blues down the street.

Cool, man, thanks, Randall said. Who are we seeing? Pepito's adjustment to the outside after a ten-year incarceration was stunning. He was like the god Ra at sunrise grabbing hold of the world. B.B. King, he said. B.B. King? Palma said. He's still alive? Oh, yeah, Randall said, he's like eighty or ninety. But the impresario still gives concerts, Pepito said, smiling, dabbing his mouth with the napkin and pouring them each a little more wine from the bottle of pinot noir he served without asking. She liked it. Palma would like anything from that moment on, she decided, that was issuing forth from the sun god. She liked the gold ID bracelet that dangled from his dark wrist and the modest way he was treating his guests like royalty. Palma liked the lock of hair that kept falling forward no matter how often he pushed it away.

Do you remember when Abuela taught you to make rice? He asked her. Spanish or Mexican rice, the kind with peas and in tomato sauce, with garlic and cumin, he meant. Yes, his cous' remembered. (She was twelve.) The first time she burned the rice at the bottom. The second time it was soggy. When Abuela came home from her church and found she ruined it again, she hit the girl with the hot pan, chased her around until she ran under the old woman's brass bed to the furthest end by the wall where she couldn't reach her granddaughter. Since then Palma's rice had always been nothing short of perfect. Yes, she said, and looked at him the way he glanced at her when she had asked him earlier about cooking. There were things not to mention in front of others. One of them was anything related to their upbringing.

His cousin knew Pepito caught the eyeball message but without a beat he said, Do you remember fixing breakfast before I went to school? Palma nodded. I made what there was to make. Oatmeal with raisins, or I served you an egg and a tortilla. Palma always kept milk in the house for Pepito. You know, Pepito said to Randall, at three years of age my big cousin here taught me how to read. Four, she said. No, I was three, prima, he said, putting up three fingers. By four I was reading. Recalling their growing-up years at home over the elegant meal was their (Pepito's and Palma's) impromptu Thanksgiving, his first since getting out of the joint, she realized as he went to make cappuccinos and serve homemade (!) flan.

My prima here pretended she was a schoolteacher, Pepito said. She'd put on a pair of our grandmother's old seeing glasses down on her nose and use a blackboard . . . Where'd you get that blackboard anyway, Palma? The Salvation Army, she said. In her early teens it was where she bought Pepito's toys and books for her. (*The Hardy Boys* and *Nancy Drew*— which, now that she recalled that early reading, it was what set off the investigation fanaticism. It came as a relief that she wasn't obsessed with killing sprees but with the judicial system. Whom it worked for and mostly, for whom it didn't.)

Anyway, Pepito said, that was how I started reading before I even went to school. He smiled at Palma and gave her hand a pat. Palma didn't think she'd seen her cousin smile so much since he got out of prison. Excuse me, she said and ran to the bedroom. She didn't come out until Pepito called, It's time to go to the concert, prima.

PEOPLE WERE lined up trying to get tickets and inside the crowd was already gathering. Pepito had pre-arranged a table upstairs, and Randall had already figured out, like she had, not to ask how. Soon the blues king himself was onstage down below yowling how his angel spread her wings. He gave her a nickel. She gave him a twenty-dollar bill. Pepito started singing under his breath the rapper T.I.'s tune, "I Need Dollas

. . ." Randall joined in, If I tell you my story, will you give me dollas? He didn't have it right but Palma sang along—*yeah*.

The throngs were wild and the three couldn't be getting along better when Pepito asked Randall to get the next round of drinks at the bar. Of course, Joe, Randall said, giving a friendly slap on her cousin's back. I want you to order from that guy, Pepito pointed to a young man behind the bar with shocks of red hair, lively. Adorable. No problem, Randall said, going right over.

What are you up to? She asked Pepito. Instead of answering, he stood up, put on his coat, and then helped her with hers. They were soon out in the cold, down the street, and back at Pepito's love nest. She knew it was a love nest. Palma hadn't found any evidence of it but he surely couldn't have gone through all the trouble of setting up an *Elle Décor* apartment for the sake of impressing no one. She asked him. I have to entertain sometimes, he said. Business. Right, monkey business, she said. (Abuela said that all the time.)

He turned on the gas fireplace, got the music going which seemed to be coming through the walls but was actually from hidden speakers, and they sat down to share a cognac. Where the hell else besides cooking class had her lil cous' been apprenticing to become an international player? A series of boleros began. Oh no, Palma groaned. She snuggled closer to him but if things got any sappier she'd have to leave. The boleros were instrumental and Pepito stood up and put his hand out. He was wearing a long-sleeved Italian knit that highlighted his buffed-out physique so it didn't take much to persuade her to get up to dance.

La Mentira. There were no vocals but Pepito's cousin knew the words. She heard boleros ad nauseam in Colombia in her former mother-in-law's home. That's all they played on the radio station that that sick woman liked. Boleros, she now realized, because of Rodrigo's brother's lifestyle, had become synonymous in her subconscious with the unspeakable. No one mentioned anything about anything in that home with its armed bodyguards and trained Doberman pinschers loose on the premises. Palma knew the sons were successful but never asked questions. The family had long meals around the dining room table every day (prepared and served by kitchen help) that went into the evenings until one by one a brother, nephew, someone had *business* to tend to and excused himself.

Pepito held her close and the whiff of his aftershave or cologne went straight to her head faster than the Courvoisier. They moved slowly in a circle. He whispered the lyrics in her ear, half singing in Spanish. *You forget that you love me despite what you say. Well, we carry scars on the soul impossible to erase. You forget that I could even do you wrong if I decide . . . I'm not in your class and you almost forget we have a pact . . . Don't feel remorse. The pact is not made with God's consent . . . No es con Dios.* Palma pulled away. It was always back to that irrefutable fact. The conflict of the blood between them was directly out of a telenovela like those Palma's mother-in-law watched five days a week. So one day you'll get married, she said, sounding like a soap opera diva. ("La Jodida Nunca Llora.") She should have been yelling in Spanish for heightened effect, but Pepito and his cousin only spoke that language to each other in half sentences and single words that couldn't be translated, like beso and desamor. Yeah, he said, one day I will get married. ¿Y?

Palma went to his fridge and got out a bottle of water. Y . . . you'll live happily ever after, she said, twisting the bottle cap like she was ripping someone's head off. The water from the tap is filtered, Pepito said. He looked confused. Maybe sad.

For all she knew, angry. Of course it is, she said about his filtered water and fridge with a glass door, her eyebrow raised. She looked at the pasta maker. Who in Christ's name was he? Agent 007? Who do you work for really? She asked. Pepito sat and crossed an ankle over the other knee. I'm a businessman, Palma. She sat down next to him. Albuquerque fights? His cousin asked. An investment in a boxer? Selling her naked picture to a pervert? (She didn't bring up how she had accepted the money.) Their eyes met. His dark eyes were scandalous. Penetrating. She gulped. You honestly think I sold those pictures I took with my cell phone? Pepito said. With that changa face of yours? He laughed. I sent you that check to replace the couch I messed up, Pepito said. Man, Palma, he took her hand.

I did, she said. Entonces, ¿Qué?

You, of all people, Pepito said, should know not to believe all you hear and only half of what you see. He gazed at the fireplace. She watched the electric frames too. Palma thought about what he was sharing with Randall earlier, how she had been such a good big cous'. *You know I cried when you moved out*, he had said in front of Randall. He would have been eight and she just out of high school, almost eighteen. Palma knew the boy had cried. She didn't let him see her tearful eyes when she went out the door with her clothes in trash bags and Abuela waving her rolling pin, warning not to come back. (Jim-Bo sat watching TV, acting like he couldn't care less what happened in that household because he didn't.) Little Pepito stood by the entrance of his bedroom clutching the Ninja Turtle she'd bought him. His lower lip trembled. Don't go, Palma, he said in a child's voice made tiny by a tightening throat. I'll come visit you, she had promised.

Pepito's stories earlier had driven her to the bedroom where she sat on the bed paralyzed by every molecule of memory floating in the air that he'd released. Palma realized then how deliberate his immaculate home stood in contrast to the bedlam of their childhoods. Pepito had landed in prison for ten years, and she had sent herself to her own. Now, he turned his evocative gaze toward the woman to whom, in their long ago past, he'd uttered, Don't go. All grown, a man's eyes, what did they say? Go or stay? She had escaped back then, it was true, but Palma had also kept her promise to the boy and stayed in touch. Another woman might have cried at that moment, but she wasn't that woman.

Ven, Palma said, instead, and led him to the bedroom. Pepito used not one but two condoms. She knew it was for protection but the second one Palma took personally. They had kissed only a little with clothes being ripped off quickly on the bed and Pepito came right after he entered her in his lined raincoat. She didn't want to ruin another visit by starting a fight. Then he held her, which in some ways made up for everything. The truth was she had fallen in love sometime between the first frustrating meetings when he was all thugged out and the homemade pasta. They were going to be part of each other's lives forever, until death do them part. He'd marry someone and they'd have children and she'd be the older tía who came on visits for holidays and his procreating wife would feel sorry for Palma. And meanwhile, wifey would never know that when she wasn't home Pepito and she would fuck on their bed. That's who she was and that was who he was. No apologies, mundo cruel. They weren't just family but cut from the same brutal cloth of inequities. Life wasn't fair and they made it work.

Palma was asleep when his cell phone rang. It was being charged and he unplugged it and answered. Yeah, yeah, he said. She could hear a man on the other end. Yeah, Pepito said again. Make that two, yeah, two. Palma is visiting for the holiday. Yeah, Palma. I'll text over her information. And just like that Pepito and his cousin were on the first plane out of Midway Airport the next morning. The manager would let Randall into the apartment. He could stay or go back by train to Albuquerque, but they were headed for Palm Beach.

THE PAIR entered The Breakers and after registering and getting room keys, Pepito said he had to go. Business. The Breakers was a famous and Randal-ly fabulous resort that had hosted presidents and celebrities. Go to the shops, get yourself a swimsuit, Pepito said, whatever you want, baby. Pepito had her leave most of her things behind because Palma had traveled with winter clothes. He gave her a scrumptious kiss on the lips, the bellhop a generous tip to take their one bag up to the room, and left. He'd been there before. I'll meet you by the pool, later, prima, he said, as he took off.

Palma didn't know what to do with herself. She was overheated in her wool sweater and jeans and fit in the place like Castro at a White House Inauguration Ball. Palma did what Pepito suggested. She needed a new swimsuit. And a dip. She hadn't swum since before Colombia, where she was taking care of an aging woman and never left her home as she morphed into a fearful wife in a fearful life. In the middle of such a day, no one could have convinced Palma Piedras that in the future she'd be at a five-star resort with Pepito headed for one of the pools in an Agua Bendita bikini.

She went to the south pool because one of the staff said it faced the sea. A couple was getting up and vacated their white lounge chairs. She quickly grabbed them. Pool boys brought towels and Palma threw her stuff on the other lounge chair and said, My husband is on a conference call.

He'll be right down. She ordered a piña colada. Piña coladas were emblematic of vacay time and she pretended to sip on the fruity alcoholic drink. She decided to take a dunk in the pool, then came out, asked for another towel, ordered a bottle of San Pellegrino, and signed away. It hadn't taken her any time to get used to la dolce vita.

A Latina had taken the other lounge chair. It's reserved, Palma told the woman who wasn't the least bit dressed or rather undressed for the pool. Sorry, she said, I'm just waiting for my friend. Palma lay back to wait her out. Pepito had to show up sooner than later, and she was pumped to see him in trunks. The crasher acted like Palma wasn't staring her down. She was in rolled-up jeans like someone who hadn't expected to find herself in tropical weather and wore wrap-around reflector sunglasses (tacky), and a post-mullet haircut (tackier). Palma would have put money on it that the friend was a femme. Five minutes later it was a good thing she had no one to bet with because she would have lost.

The friend was no femme and Palma could say that with authority because after she heard the Chilanga accent telling the other woman she thought the staff suspected they weren't staying there and maybe they shouldn't stick around, she uttered, *Dani*? Holy Hell, her ex-lover acted like they were the best of long lost friends instead of the reality: Palma had left her on the floor of her shabby Mexico City apartment with a sprained arm nearly a year before. ¡Mujer! Dani squealed the second she recognized her ex, opening her arms wide for a hug. Palma didn't reciprocate. Yes, she was staying there, she said, acting like she was on top of the world (which was where you wanted to be when you ran into an ex). Wanna drink? she asked the women. Palma flagged over a waitperson and invited them to a couple of beers. After they swilled down the first beers lickety-split she ordered two more. You really have a room here? the other one asked. Palma waved her room card. Well, why don't you take us up? Dani said. It had been about ninety minutes since Pepito took off and if he didn't find her by the pool he'd know she was in the room. Of course! Palma said, all too ready and willing to show off.

They no sooner got into the lovely (although small) accommodations with double beds and balcony facing the ocean when Dani and her friend asked if they could take a shower. Yeah, I guess, Palma said, obviously irritated by such a bodacious request but to Chilangas being bodacious was a way of life. She remained in her bikini with nothing appropriate to change into in any case, trying to be calm. Palma was waiting on the balcony when they both came out in towels and joined her, leaving wet foot tracks in their trail. You don't have another swimsuit? Dani asked. No, Palma said. Can I get a beer from the minibar? The friend asked, wangas chichis spilling out from the towel. She went back in without a reply. Dani came up to collect a kiss, standing on tip-toes. Palma gently pushed her away and went inside. Come on, Dani said, following. You used to like me, remember? The other woman let go of her towel and got hold of her. Ándale, Don't be like that, Palmita, she said, following. We're all friends here, Dani said, putting her arms around her from behind. In front her friend was embracing her or trying to when Palma heard a cardkey go into the door lock. In the background, the tide rushed in.

12 When Palma la Rocky was back in Albuquerque the lights were on in the house on the cul-de-sac. (The trip back had taken twenty-four hours by express bus from Florida.) Now what? She wondered, walking up to the door with no carry-on or pride left. If Lucrecia and her wicked band had come to take over the place entirely, Palma would put it on wheels for them to roll back to the trailer park. She pushed the key in the door and prepared for the worse: something outrageous and unimaginable. Presto.

There was Rodrigo standing in the middle of the room eating a peanut butter and jelly sandwich, in a pair of paisley pajamas. (He knew damn well how she hated paisley.) In the living room was an inflatable mattress, a newspaper strewn on the carpet, his reading glasses, a hand mirror, a blanket, and a reading lamp she didn't recognize. Palma Piedras's ex-husband had aged in the year since she had last seen him. His temples had gone gray, a distinct line went from nose to below the lip on the right side of his face, and he had a deep forehead crease. It looked good on him in the way that some men matured with distinction. He was still in shape too, with just the slightest paunch from those long meals at his mother's, no doubt. After the initial surprise of her barging into her own house, he smiled. Rodrigo had the best smile of anyone she knew. It instantly made him simpático. (Correction: Made him *appear simpático*.)

Palmi, he said, coming over, arms out. ¿Cómo estás? She gave him her cheek. She could hardly wait to hear why he was back in the country. I thought you had moved out, Rodrigo said, getting over the fright her abrupt arrival gave him. I thought *you* had moved out, his ex said, going to the kitchen. The fridge had a stock of food and she pulled out a carton of Rice Dream. (Rodrigo was lactose intolerant.) I tried to call you, he said. (Of course, there had been no answer. The rat-movers took the phones although the line was still connected.) Where are all my things? he asked. My shot glass collection? Obviously, Palma had some explaining to do, but it was late. On top of fatigue, her heart dragged from yet another debacle with Pepito. (He would talk to his prima again, she was fairly certain, but the likelihood of something happening between them beyond them talking about the piss-poor upbringing they shared, seemed less likely with each meeting.)

How's your mother? Palma asked.

Mamá passed away, Rodrigo said, It was for the best.

Have you moved back then? She asked.

Yes, he said. Well, for now, he added. Apparently, the family was having some troubles and the brother thought it would be wise that Rodrigo leave Medellín. By *troubles* Palma took Rodrigo to mean, in Cartel-speak, that he was now on the lam. He decided to lay low at her house. Lovely. Half expecting a rain of *Scarface* machine-gun fire to come through the windows, she said she was going up to bed. You look tired, querida, Rodrigo said, as if he had never left that abode of marital boredom. She went upstairs.

PALMA WOULD never forget Pepito's look of revulsion at The Breakers. Her not-so-lil cous' had walked back out of that hotel room faster than a speeding mullet. Aw, hell no, was all he said. Then he was gone again. Palma Piedras turned and said something to Dani and her girlfriend. Who knew what? Get out, par de viboras, probably. She ran to find Pepito. He was nowhere.

Rodrigo came up as subtle as carbon monoxide. Palma was drying her hair with a towel in the bathroom and he bent over and kissed her the way he did before their lives came apart in Colombia. He propped her on the long vanity counter. It was just at the right height. They both knew it. He didn't like talking when they had sex. Palma suspected that talking and even her moans distracted his concentration and he put a hand over her mouth. *Shh,* he said, pounding inside her. Calla. He had her legs around his neck.

Rodrigo was tanned from living near the equator. A tan line below his navel showed his light brown color. Palma kept her eyes open, checking him out. He was still in good shape being an amateur soccer player, but there was something new and not so good. It was a jagged scar that went right above his heart. The skin had puckered from healing without stitches. They went a long while. At last, the spray they both knew spurted out and ran down the front cabinet. Palma tried to bite his hand over her mouth as Rodrigo twisted one nipple while sucking the other. Rodrigo was hurting her. It was new, not like him, and she didn't like it. She began to wriggle away. He stopped, acted regretful, picked her up and took her to the bedroom where he laid her on the carpet where the bed used to be. Gradually, they started kissing again. Something had changed. As a married couple they had sex two, maybe

three times a week. It was always predictable. Mutually satisfying in its way. This was a steeled Rodrigo. On the floor he
moved up and stuck his hard dick in his ex-wife's mouth. She
didn't feel like doing it for several reasons. (For uno, Palma
didn't know where that dick had been in the past year. And
dos, although she slept with *strangers*, an ex-husband now a
stranger belonged to a new category.) He pushed it into Palma's mouth. She dug her fingernails in his thighs and but-
tocks. He pried her hands away from his flesh and held Palma's
wrists back. She felt his penis swell and when she tried to pull
her head away he pushed in further. She started to gag and he
didn't care. Who was this man? Was he pissed that his wife left
him—and the way she did, leaving him to face his family with
the humiliation of her escape? Took the house in the divorce?
The missing shot glasses . . . ? He got off her and she spit on
the carpet. Pinche mierda. He was breathing heavily. The pair
fell asleep. Some time in the middle of the night she woke with
Rodrigo fucking her in the missionary position, tenderly, the
way they once had. Palma dozed off and woke up and he was
still at it.

THAT COLOMBIAN'S strung out on his own blow, Randall
informed Palma when she went to his bar the next evening
and told him about the miraculous apparition of San Rodrigo
of the Intrusive Dick. Puh-lease, girl, Randall said. Spare me
the sordid details for once, will you? They were enough, however, for her friend to insist that Palma stay at his place while
Rodrigo figured out his next move. How naïve can you be,
woman? Palma Piedras was back to square one, except that she
wasn't even living out of a suitcase now, but the Gucci purse.

They were having late morning coffee chased with vitamins and fresh OJ when she brought out the letters. (For some

reason she had started carrying them around.) Palma would have to make a decision some time as to what to do with the information. As Randall read his jaw dropped. I had no idea, he said. *I* had no idea, she said, leaning back on the kitchen chair. He pulled one after the other out, speed-reading, engrossed. Listen to this, he said: *She is ours, not yours, mami. One day she will come looking for us . . .* Randall pulled off his Greek-chic, Wayfarer reading glasses. He looked smart in them. (He was smart, obviously, but it wasn't the same as looking it.) He stared. She stared back. Well? He said. Well, what? Well, have you gone looking for your parents? (Of course, she hadn't.) There you have it, sweet pea, he said. Have what? She said, going to the window. He had a narrow backyard enclosed by a cinder-block wall, like the other backyard walls on his street. Institutional-style Mulch developments. Randall was content. He always said he should have been dead by fifty. He wasn't. Mulchdom therefore, at any level, was a triumph.

That morning Randall and Palma both knew she was going to Los Angeles. It'll give your ex-hubby time to sort out what he's gonna do, Randall said. You know the cartel will catch up to him sooner than later. He probably was using too much of his own merchandise or stole from his brother or some other unforgiveable thing that will cost him dearly now. Randall groaned. Yes, she said. You'd better stay away for while, he said. Yes, Palma said. Then he came over and put his hands on her shoulders. We'll pick up some lighter clothes for you this time, he said. Yes, Palma said. Aren't you glad you shop at Walmart now? he asked. You're living a disposable life-style, girl. Get you a disposable camera and some disposable panties while you're at it.

After a few days, she left Randall's and went back home. First Palma rang the neighbors' bell. Hank answered. Hey, he said. I have to go away on family business, she said. Take care of the kitty, will you? No problem, he said. Do you want to come in? No, she said. Did you hear Lucrecia got picked up with my Mercedes? Yeah, Hank said, back in Gallup. At the Giddy Yup Lounge. They nodded, said nothing. The Mercedes was being sent back to her. Lucrecia was going up the river for grand theft auto. No sign of the others or her stuff. Poof. Palma refused to ask after Hank's wife. He volunteered. Patricia's not here, he said. She took the kids, too, he added. Now Palma knew why he looked like the Man Without a Country. Come to think of it, just like Rodrigo.

13 When Abuela's granddaughter was in Colombia, she became pregnant. No one knew about it. She waited for the right time to tell Rodrigo, which never came before she realized the mild-mannered school administrator had been pulled into the Dead Sea. Alarmed over his safety, having no one, not even him to discuss any of what she suspected, she caused a miscarriage. The pair had one marriage in the States and a different relationship in Colombia. They used to talk. They were friends. Now the couple existed in the shadows. Palma, in his mother's house, and he, under his brother's rule. She ended up in a hospital where they took all her female parts without asking her. They had different rules there about consent. Apparently they got it from Rodrigo, who said later he was afraid for her well-being so he gave it to them. *They* being white-coat-wearing, white-masked troglodytes. Rodrigo and she never discussed her being left barren. Palma was Penelope taken for a long, dark winter.

One day, she agreed to import something to Mexico. Not in her entrails the way poor mule girls did. This was in an emerald-filled statue of Michelangelo's David, hand carried. It looked bronze and solid but wasn't bronze or solid. No one will stop you, Rodrigo promised. All the officials from there to Mexico were on the dole. You'll leave it at the desk of the hotel when you check in. The next day you come home, he said. As they promised, no one stopped Palma, although her heart was in her throat the whole way. Yerba Santa para la garganta, Abuela would have recommended. The only deviation from the plan was that she did not return the next day. Palma didn't stay at the hotel. She asked a cab driver to take her to a women's bar. It was way off in a shady neighborhood. Ricardo's people in El De Efe could search up and down La Zona Rosa, nightclubs and shops, and no one would find her sleeping in the backroom of a women's bar in a perilous district. Palma told the managers that her husband was looking to kill her because he found out she was lesbian. By the time she came out of that place she was, more or less. Palma met Dani there.

Her new lover, officially two inches taller than a dwarf, was like a mythical character. Dani was crazy with a capital C for Chilanga. They partied for a month. When Palma went to live with her, she lacked for nothing. The dwarfish dyke's place was located in what seemed the rubbles of post-World War II Europe, but life with her was a smog-ridden blast. One night the two went to hear the mariachis at Plaza Garibaldi and they slipped into a dancehall where they danced the quebradita and drank tequila and Squirt drinks until four in the morning. Or rather, Dani did. After the first tequila and spin on the floor Palma threw up on someone's shoes. She sat the rest of the night out, re-routing sent-over drinks to Dani who was such a spectacular dancer, she was the most popular girl in town at that humongous joint. Hobbit legs and all.

Dani had no favorite poets but she loved above all artists, Dalí. Being in a constant state of anamorphous was her ideal. When she said she was an aficionado of the surrealist Palma said, You know he bought his wife a castle. He could not enter it without her consent, she added, as if the dwarf could afford anything more than a seedy pensión if she was trying to impress anyone. Yeah, Palma said. Gala was ten years older than he. Did you know that? No, Dani said, lining up her sports shoes against a wall like prisoners of war ready for execution.

Well, he was.

The other made a so-what face. Or maybe it was her normal face. Anyway, she said, he was un-gay so it didn't matter. It was an example of their exchanges. Society was one big gay cover-up to Dani. Palma stayed with her in her apartment on Colonia Guerrero and worked at the bar waiting tables. One day the boss asked about the emeralds she had for sale. (Just a hopefully undetected handful.) She wanted to make a pendant for her new amorcito. At last Palma Piedras had the cash to return to Albuquerque. And then some.

14 When she returned from Randall's, Rodrigo was still in the house dressed to go out, maybe to vacate. He did not look high this time but like his ol' neurotic self. Seeing that Palma hadn't returned to pummel him, he invited her to lunch at one of their haunts. In his Lexus rental they drove to Sandia Peak and took the tramway riding slowly over the Cibola Forest to the mountaintop. The High Finance Restaurant gave a glorious view of Albuquerque, but mostly its infinite skies. There hadn't been much snow and the place was scarce of skiers. It was a clear day and you could in fact, see forever. In the restaurant Gershwin's "The Man I Love" was playing when Palma's green chili stew and Rodrigo's club sandwich arrived. I haven't had one of these in a long time, he said. No, his ex-wife didn't guess he had lived in a home where fried plantains were a daily staple. He crunched on a chip and leaned back. What is it? Palma asked. Long after you divorced you still knew each other. His most innocuous flinches and flaws still made her want to pluck out his eyes. Send him to serve Santa Lucia in the afterlife in Wisconsin.

I'm moving to Canada, he announced. Good, she thought. The further, the better. Then he dropped a shoe. I've met someone, Palmi, he said. She hadn't asked. It wasn't any of her business, but there it was. They met when she was visiting family in Medellín, her ex-husband said, but she lives in Vancouver. Palma lifted her glass of iced tea to feign a toast. He lifted his coffee. He figured she took that bit of news well and then dropped the other shoe. It hit her on the head. We had a baby together, he said. (Silence.) She's a month old. (Dead silence.) Well, he said, it just happened, Palmi. (Catatonia.)

Rodrigo and Palma returned to their former home without much more to say. Look, Palmi, he said, as soon as they were inside and he collected his things to leave. He pulled out a wad of dollars wrapped in a rubber band. They were all hundreds. She turned away. No, he said, look, I can't leave you much but I want to thank you for caring for my mother. Now she was insulted. Palma started walking away and Rodrigo caught up. He stuck a bunch of paper money in her hand. She had told him that she was going to LA to check out the parents Palma had never met. He now said, Use this for your trip. Maybe not all families have to be as deadly as mine.

15 Los Angeles was delineated with palm trees up and down avenues and boulevards. Mariano Jr.'s people followed the harvest when they arrived in California, to work garlic in Watsonville and oranges in Sacramento. Angela fell in love with the tall palm. She called her baby Palma. This was the most of what Palma knew about herself and her mother—how she got her name. She was staying at the Westin Bonaventure. Austin fetched her that first evening and took her to dinner. He was by far the best-looking man she had seen in a long time, hands down (aside from Pepito, but Pepito was Pepito). Palma Piedras and Austin White walked along Venice Boulevard to the restaurant. She thought of her cousin's about-face at the doorway of their would/should/could have been love nest at The Breakers and heard a distinct crunch way inside. It sounded like an acorn. What is it? Austin asked, seeing her so pensive. Palma shook her head as he held the restaurant door open for her.

Zabumba's was Brazilian. They were seated at a table on the enclosed patio. It was early for dinner, but they were starved. The musicians were starting to set up inside. An Amazon dressed for carnival with a great plumage headdress and a couple of sequined straps covering her privates came out and said, We'll be giving a samba lesson shortly if you two want to join us. The two did not, they replied, preferring to start ordering. The sun was setting on the smog-saturated city. Austin blabbed nonstop about his over-the-rainbow life in Hollywood, dropping names and stringing anecdotes involving celebrities of all kinds like Christmas lights. He was working on a film with Cameron Diaz and also as a stylist on a Nicki Minaj video. She's the king's jester, Palma said, mostly because Austin was showing off, partly because it was her opinion, and finally, because Palma was jealous of how Austin got all giddy over the rapper. Pink wigs, all ass, she said, Barnum & Bailey had better, with big, floppy shoes. Hey now, Austin said. Don't be a hater. You know you're my dawg. Palma of the Los Angeles palmeras looked at him. Your what? He wasn't dazzling anyone with brilliance but the bullshit went down smoother with the caipirinha he ordered for her. (Considering how she hated fruit drinks, it wasn't bad.) He had his customary scotch. Cami—Cameron is redoing that old show *Cagney & Lacey* on the big screen, Austin said. She's playing the pretty one, naturally. (Uh huh, Palma kept saying. Like Austin's glitterati lifestyle was going to affect her.) The waitperson brought out a plate of mardioca frita and another of bedinho de bacalhau. Austin had given up red meat. He was now a Buddhist.

Just like that? Palma said.

No, he said. It takes work. Muito trabalho, he said in Portuguese in the spirit of their dining experience. The white V-neck tee he wore under a thin leather jacket set off Austin's dark mahogany shade.

Are you Brazilian? she asked.

He took a bite of codfish, shaking his head. Why, because I'm so dark? Palma nodded. Oh, he said, I come from slave stock in Virginia. We were just lucky not to have any founding-father night creepers. Well, at least none that are evident, he said, putting out a black hand as proof. Rio is as amazing as you'd imagine, he said. *Sim*, Palma agreed, although she'd only seen it in movies. People were starting to fill up the patio and she detected a growing waiting list. For five minutes Austin shut up while he polished off the appetizers and quickly ordered grilled shrimp. We'll be full before we order entrees, Palma said. I won't, he said. He was wearing Carrera aviator sunglasses with golden-tinted lenses. Austin in a word: Fly.

Los Angeles air was heavy. Where are the mountains? She asked. He pointed with his fork. Palma turned. There was nothing; they were enshrouded by contamination. Still, there was the salt. The sea might be a good change. Maybe Brazil was the place.

Tell me about your folks, Austin said. You say they reside in LA? Have you seen them yet? Whoa, she said, still warming up to the idea. Palma pulled out her favorite letter from Angela. It was the best way to set up *The Situation Room* like Wolf Blitzer. Austin looked at the envelope she placed next to his plate. It was stained from the oil from her fingers, crinkled from handling. Palma's mother's childish handwriting glared up at him. He picked it up. *Dear Mami* (Austin was going to read it aloud). He stopped. Oh, I love the way she spells mammy. Palma looked at him. It's not mammy, Austin, it's mommy in Spanish. Oh, he said, as if he suddenly realized Angela might be smarter than he assumed. Or he, less.

She got pregnant by a boy when they were in their mid-teens, Palma said. Mere babes in the woods. (More like the tomato fields of Indiana, where they went to pick at sixty cents a bushel after dropping out of high school, Palma thought. What a life her young mother had. No wonder she couldn't keep her. Or at least Palma found herself thinking that was why.)

Dear Mami, Austin began again. *How are you? Me and Mariano, Jr. are good except we miss our little girl very much. Mami, we live in California now. Please let us know if we can go get are dauhter. Whenever I see a palm tree I cry. And there are a lot of palm trees out here, Mami. Please stop being mad. Love you, your dauhter, Angela. P.S. Will you send my clothes? I need them. P.S. Give Palma a big kiss from her mom and dad. We will come get her next summer when we work the tomatos in Indiana. Don't be mad, Ma.* Austin had taken off his shades to read the letter. He cleared his throat. So, he said, did they come back for you the next summer?

Palma shrugged. How would she have known? All she knew was that Palma Piedras had no memory of parents.

Well, you must go see them, baby girl, Austin said.

She knew that already. It was why she was in LA and had dropped them a letter that very morning, to the return address on Angela's one-sided correspondence, and included her cell number. She suspected they still lived there with his family. If Angela and Mariano, Jr. were gone, someone had to be around to give a lead. But she'd wait. Palma wasn't about to show up like the ghost of Christmas past.

PALMA SPENT the next couple of days in the vacuum generated by a room at the Bonaventure. She was on the fifteenth floor. She prayed for no earthquake and purchased water and snacks at a convenience shop to stay alive. Among other eyeball anesthetics, she watched a reality show marathon about celebrity drug addicts. (Review: The sniveling famous weren't any more compelling than the sniveling crackheads.) Occasionally, she'd wander out to the ice machine in a pair of girl boxers and tank top. The maids handed Palma towels and handfuls of little shampoo bottles and soaps.

177

One afternoon she ran into the couple in the next room. Literally. Excuse me. Oh no, excuse *me*. Shall we dance? He was on his way to the pool or the spa. She was not. They laughed and wished each other a good day. He alone came back and she ran into him again. He stopped and watched the petite woman, who didn't bother to throw on a robe, fill the small plastic bucket with ice. You use a lot of ice, he said. Palma nodded and hit the button for more ice. You ever watch *Nip/ Tuck*? he asked about an old series set in LA. Maybe, she said. In fact, Palma had seen an episode for the first time that day. It was about two Alta Mulch plastic surgeons suffering from *Jesus Christ Superstar* complex. The ice spilled over the flimsy plastic bag hotels provided to line the ever-diminishing ice pails. The neighbor continued: They had an episode about this woman who one of the doctors went to see in a hotel. She was lying unconscious in a tub of ice. He revived her by fucking her. The man smiled like it was how doctors were supposed to revive their almost-dead patients. Interesting. Palma started back with her little bucket.

Call me Bob, the man said. He had an after-five shadow at three p.m. Bob was around five feet ten and weighed in at about two-fifty if he weighed a gram. He was in a white ter-rycloth bathrobe and bedroom slippers. The robe said Westin. Keeping up he pulled out a joint. She shook her head. He was more entertaining than any TV show. What d' you think? He said when they reached her door. She left her keycard tucked in the back of her boxers. (No pockets, plus no need to have Mr. Loco Rogers push his way in.) How much? He asked.

What about your wife? she said.

Oh, she isn't my wife, he said. Palma rolled her eyes.

She was just a girl, he said.

Okay, Billy Jean, she said. See you later. Back off or I'll call security.

All right, all right, he said, like they were haggling over the price of provolone. Okay, he said, I called for her. They said she'd be up for it. She wasn't. How much? He asked again.

PALMA'S CELL phone rang. It was Austin. What are you doing, Palma? He asked. Not much, she said. Have you heard from your folks? Austin asked.

No, Palma said.

That's rough, he said.

Yes, she said, going to the minibar. She selected a canister of macadamia nuts. No sound from Bob. Palma peeked in. He was in the life-sized, compression-molded ice bucket, a.k.a the bathtub. He looked miserable and yet, at peace. Eyes shut, he gave a thumbs-up. Listen, sweetheart, Austin said, if you want to stay in LA until you hear from them, come to my place. Mishu is here. I'll come by for you.

All right, Palma said, popping open the nuts can. It gave a small exhale sound. It had easily been the most painless hotel stay she'd had.

16

She used to read Anaïs Nin. Palma read all of her diaries and novels. (She didn't think much of *Delta of Venus* in view of how "decadent" no longer meant anything.) She used to do a lot of things when she studied at the Art Institute that she didn't do anymore. Eat red apples. (Her teeth couldn't take them now.) Draw. (Palma toted black notebooks around and sketched everything as if she were Toulouse-Lautrec.) Anaïs Nin launched writers off into the world like Henry Miller and Lawrence Durrell. She knew Gore Vidal when he could hardly wipe his nose. The diarist used her banker husband's money to publish Miller, whose own abuela wouldn't have financed his writing.

Nin slept with women, as Simone de Beauvoir and Colette had, although the former was loathe to admit it, and all three in the end paid homage to the almighty dick. Behind the scenes, along with capitalism and cockroaches, the dick ruled. Those divas of the first half of the twentieth century, with their turbans, stunning talents, and peg legs, loved them some va-j-j. Frida had a penchant for muffs, but popular myth maintained she was all about a larger-than-life lascivious toad. The portraitist slept with María Felix—the most beautiful woman in the world, according to *Paris Vogue*—and María and Dolores del Rio also bedded each other. There were all kinds of hushed bedding in Hollywood back then. Gays had to keep mum, too. You could not let it be known that you took it in the ass. Only the female, the inferior, was penetrated (i.e., violated). Some men felt guilty about their dicks being American Express "Black Cards" in a world where dick cache had everything to do with everything.

Palma Piedras couldn't pull Bob out of the tub. They had come to a mutually agreed-upon price. What neither had thought to pre-arrange was how she was going to get him out of the tub in order to revive him. Fucker was drifting off to the Antarctic. She started digging out the ice. Then she pushed his bowling ball head aside and turned on the shower. Water sprayed down hot. Caliente. He started gasping.

17 Austin didn't pull up to the Bonaventure until around half past two in the morning. Palma got a call from the lobby, went down, and checked out. He was out there waiting in his Boxster. It was a cool night with streamers of neon lights going by as they drove to his place. He was having trouble with Mishu, who was crashing there. (Crashing was not an expression.) In the case of the youngish man who came from Albuquerque to get into the "industry," Austin said he was being pulled by the undertow of the harsh reality of Hollywood excesses.

Why would you bring him out here? Palma asked. You know, he's like Bambi in the enchanted forest. She smiled at her analogy of the pretty boy. (And who would Austin be then? Thumper?) He looked like someone who had just carried a friend through the trenches—while blinged out. His chocolate diamond necklace with the face of Jesus caught the reflection from streetlights. You couldn't miss it like you couldn't miss his festering mood. *I* didn't bring him out here, Austin said. He brought himself. Then Austin added, Or more precisely, *Miranda* brought his ass out here over Thanksgiving. All they did was get baked. He started accelerating. His soon-to-be roommate gripped the seat. Miranda's on her way down and fast, Austin said. The scene at Babbaluci had been cut because she couldn't make the other scenes she was in and was replaced. Mishu followed the scent of her stash to LA.

Is he at your place now? Palma asked, wondering what kind of night they had ahead. He was when I left to come get you, he said, shrugged his shoulders, shifted gears. I'm tired of his mooching, Austin added. Maybe you can take him back to New Mexico. She put her hands up: I'm nobody's babysitter.

They were on Sunset Boulevard and pulled up to what looked like a modern castle emanating the ghosts of Jean Harlow and Clark Gable. A vintage neon sign read Chateau Marmont. She'd heard of it. John Belushi was found dead from an overdose there. Now it had become the cool place to stay for a new generation of celebrities and their entourages. Austin pulled up along the driveway. They both got out and a valet took the car. You live *here*? She asked. Austin went ahead, long legs in skinny jeans, carrying her roller carry-on by the handle on the side. She caught up. Only while we work on the film, he said. A few of us are staying here, he added. They went through the funky, faux-gothic lobby and straight up to his suite.

Marlene Dietrich had stayed there. Or somebody. There was a dining room and kitchen, and once—decades before—it was the epitome of modern and style. Class-y. The bathroom was small and all porcelain. Black-and-white checkered tile floor. You can have the bedroom, Austin said. There were still gentlemen left in the world. Palma turned and faced him. She was in the shearling coat over a spandex track outfit that came above the knee. While she waited for Austin earlier she pacified her anxiety by cutting her hair. It was visibly slanted along the back, now at around earlobe level. Look, Austin said, walking over to a Bose CD player and hitting a button. Chopin came on, soft as night. You know it's not like that between us, boo.

Palma went into the bedroom, pulling the carry-on. She

came back out. Austin was pouring himself a scotch. You want something to drink? He asked. No, she said. There's bottled Vitaminwater in the fridge, he said. Considering his hearty ego, she wasn't surprised that Austin thought Palma expected a replay of the Hard Rock Hotel with Mishu. No doubt he had gone through some things since they met and more than likely those things had to do with Mishu the Heartbreaker, but she'd gone through a few herself. The last months had been a season of Lifetime Television movies. Television for Women. As Native red-brown, Palma couldn't get her stories on Lifetime, B.E.T., or Univision, whose heroines normally looked like Croatian beauty contestants with extremely poor acting skills. *If I tell you my story will you give me dollas?*

You're my host, Austin, she said. I don't want to go to bed with you either. She sat down on the art-deco print sofa. Austin came over and sat down. Yeah, baby, he said, Our lives are complicated enough. He crossed his slender legs. He was wearing Messina loafers with no socks. Complicated was an understatement. Palma had not picked up that he was gay-lite when they met at Chana's restaurant. (Or, as she saw now, gay full-tilt?) She had lost her touch. When had the invisible ripping into her sexability started? Abuela always said her granddaughter had a hard head. Cabeza dura. Cabeza de coco. Cabeza de piedra. That's why she hit the girl the way she did, the supposed pounding of sense into a child who never learned.

Let's do it, Palma said to Austin, for old times' sake. (Maybe instead of pounding sense into her it had been pounded out.) He swilled down his drink. You remind me of my ex-wife, he said. She couldn't take it back. Why had she said it, if not just to test, push the parameters? Abuela was right. The lessons in life were hard earned.

Someone put an old-fashioned key in the door. Enter

the irrepressible Mishu. (Formerly Vincent Martinez of the Lower Valley.) He was wearing Austin's clothes. (The sleeves of the ivory shirt were too long and with the top buttons undone, he looked like one of the Musketeers. Austin's jeans created rings around the shorter man's ankles.) His eyes were bloodshot, unfocused. He didn't even recognize the woman from Albuquerque when he came in, or maybe, startled to find someone else there, he said nothing.

Palma is here, Mish, Austin said, and his demeanor changed. They were back on stage. Lights out in the house and spotlight on Mishu. He threw his key on the coffee table and tried walking straight to the kitchen. They heard the refrigerator door open and shut. He came out and went to the bar. Make me a Martinez, he told Austin who got up to do it.

You mean a martini? Palma asked.

No, Mishu said. *I* am Martini. The drink is a Martinez.

LA or Hollywood was where dreams came to die, Palma thought. An old friend of hers, John Rechy, would have agreed. He was beautiful when he wrote his novel *Numbers*. John and she met at a bar at LAX. He was still gorgeous then, too. He didn't drink and neither did she. They weren't watching a sports game on TV but killing time. John would have had a lot to teach Mishu. Why did the young on the planet always think they discovered fire?

Austin made the drink, shook it up, and changed the music to Chet Baker, which put them in the groove. Mishu had his drink out of a Martinez glass with a gilded rim. He had a red string around his wrist. He was still lost. The kid touched his clean-shaven chest. Someone took my chain, he said.

You mean *my* chain, dude, Austin said, disgustedly.

I'll take a drink, Palma said. The men were glaring at each other. Broke-ass fake, Mishu called his lover. I think I'll go to bed, she said and started to get up when Austin put his hand out to make her stay. She'd have given anything to be that color. Or white as his porcelain toilet. Either black or white. The in-between thing hadn't worked out in her most recent incarnation. The brown woman was taken for the chambermaid in hotels or the housekeeper in Alta Mulch homes. Did she speak English? Spanish? Would she *nanny* for them? Did she clean windows? Maybe it was the look of the future owners of the world but not yet.

Palma started to get up again and Austin didn't put his hand out. It was Mishu who said, don't go to bed, Palma. Stay.

Get me a drink, Mishu, she said. I have news about your brother. Mishu got up, zigzagged to the bar. Austin went to do it. My brother? Mishu turned and looked at her. Smiled. Since their near-film debut at Babalucci, his hair was longer and sun streaked. The world had lost out on a memorable face, she thought right then, by not giving that Mexican kid a chance. Unless Palma was mistaken he had a faint line of kohl along his lower eyelids. In that perturbing place he was Ramón Navarro, Ceasar Romero, and Valentino rolled into one. Maybe Johnny Depp, stirred and served. The drink in his shaky hand spilled. He took a sip. I told you, I like Appletinis, he reprimanded Austin. Then a flighty laugh. Phony baloney and full of macaroni. He didn't give a shit. Neither did she. Maybe Austin did.

Palma stood and pulled off the Spandex top. Her breasts fell out. She knew they didn't care about tits. The twins were free, breathing, getting air—salty, polluted air. Belushi's ghost brushed over her nipples. Dance with me, she said to Mishu. "My Funny Valentine" was playing. How had Chet Baker died? In a plane crash? The intoxicated man-kid stepped back clumsily. You. He laughed under his breath and pointed a finger. He had a silver band on the index finger. You fucked my brother. My brother is a genius . . . Mishu staggered back. Is this true? Austin asked, jaw dropped. Palma looked at Austin. No, his brother is not a genius, she said, as if that was what he'd meant. Ha! Mishu said, stumbling toward the bedroom.

Palma is staying there, Austin told him. The other came back and stood right up to Austin. I don't love you, he said.

Of course you don't, Austin said. You don't love anyone.

Yes, I do, Mishu said. I loved my sister, he said. Bernice. He glared at the woman. You remind Hector of her, too. She was killed—murdered—by her old man. My mother is raising her kids. We loved her, he said, and falling back, he landed sitting on a chair.

You loved her before or after she died? Palma said. That was how it was with dysfunctional families, meaning everybody. They spouted eulogies for the dead, but while alive, relations were mercilessly put down for how they raised their kids, the gifts they gave or didn't, or borrowing rent money and neglecting to pay it back. Whatever. It was nearly daybreak. Palma headed to the bedroom, throwing her arms up, no stranger to drama but not about to be the last diva standing. She woke about thirty minutes later. Austin and Mishu were going at it—not fighting but fucking. Who had come up with the story of Narcissus? Now *he* was a genius.

18 Austin took Palma to the set. Maybe he was a fake as Mishu accused, but his gig was real. No celebrity sightings but they had plenty of work. I'm telling people you are my assistant, he said. On practical terms, she was. Austin sent her running for this, getting that, and soon, she was fed up with him (despite the tempting incentive that if Palma did well or someone liked her or approved of her extraordinary skill as the gofer of a stylist, one day she might move up in the Austin White World of Costume Design). He paid his assistant in room and board at the famous Marmont.

It was five days since Palma sent the letter to the parents-who-never-were. She'd give it another week. Or until Mishu told Austin to throw her out because she reminded him too much of his dead sister, or what Palma suspected was more likely the truth: he had no use for a woman he couldn't charm. Meanwhile one afternoon she took her malfunctioning cell phone to the dealership.

It's possible I'm not getting my calls, she said. No one's called me in a week.

Yes, that is peculiar, the guy behind the counter said. Who doesn't get calls?

Me, Palma said. The clerk fiddled with the mobile and got it working. Well, you do have messages, he said. Oh? She looked at the texts. Yep. She listened to the voicemails. There was Pepito. Like Jimmy Stewart at the top of the light tower before a pristine sky, she got vertigo. He whom Palma had almost loved singularly and purely had returned.

In a Psych 101 class way back she heard that unconditional love in humans seemed to be taught, not innate. The maternal instinct was debatable. (Surely, so far in Palma's case.) There was no guidebook to teach a person how to give of herself unconditionally. Who had taught Palma and Pepito that kind of love? Now it was obvious that he didn't need anything from her. On the contrary. Pepito's texts were brief— *Hey*. Until she met the people who left her behind as a baby, Palma Piedras wasn't ready to revisit the doubts she had about love and its variations. Delete, delete, delete.

19 Lying by the pool at the Marmont in the Agua Bendita bikini, the sun was out but the air was hostile. It gave Palma goose bumps. She put a beach towel around herself. Mishu came by. He was in shorts and a *Married to the Mob* tank. It had King Tut's face. Let's go for cigarettes, Mishu said. All right. She threw on a sweaterdress and slipped into open-toe wedgies and the pair went walking. Past fruitless lemon trees, flowerless bougainvillea, and scentless eucalyptus trees, they found a convenience store. Why is it so tense between you and Austin? Palma took the opportunity to pry.

Mishu shrugged his shoulders, looked straight ahead, and then said, He made a lot of promises he knew he couldn't keep. She nodded as if she understood but the fact was that Mishu was trying to use Austin and Palma didn't like it. No one owed him anything, like he tried to pretend just because he was a papi chulo. Austin was good-looking too, and shrewd. She knew he could handle himself. The way Palma looked at it, the small-time hustler had met up with the big-city hustler and was getting his due, which, as Palma saw it, would be zero. Still, Austin, growing older, whether mellowing or letting Mr. *Young & the Restless* into his core, was becoming a toxic hazard. She was preparing to witness spontaneous combustion due to his unrequited feelings for the The Mish. Raja of Men's Hearts and Dicks.

However, there was something more than love that would be Austin's demise. Being splendiferous was an intoxicant, and the façade of his success and extent of his grandiosity was dissolving like an Alka-Seltzer antacid tablet in water. *Plop, plop, fizz, fizz.* That very morning she had picked up an eviction notice left under the door. She put the notice back in the envelope on the floor for Austin to find. King of the Wannabe was about to get thrown out. The recession had driven him and his ilk out of the woodwork. (Ilk, i.e., Palma?) Mishu, on the other hand, was not any kind of Mulch. He was in his own category. You wouldn't find him in a souvenir shop in a box packed with straw and a label that said Made in Malaysia, China, Taiwan, India, or Mexico. He was an alpha and omega, a survivor, although he lacked an essential ingredient, one that Austin and Palma learned a long time ago. That of being a chameleon. Stand out or blend in, but adapt to the circumstances. Side by side, the misfit wasn't much taller than she, an ethereal figure of a man. He lit up a cigarette right away and smoked it like he was waiting to be called to an audition. In the stark light of day, he was thirty-seven all right. Palma and Mishu didn't hate each other. They didn't have use for one another. She could have used a friend in LA. He would do. But Mishu was not the friend type. Not hers, not anybody's, and scarcely one to himself. They strolled back in silence like a funeral cortege of two.

THAT NIGHT Palma went to the club where Mishu gigged. It was mambo night. Not mambo as in one chick walking around recruiting customers out to the dance floor to pick up a few steps before the DJ started playing Pérez Prado tunes. It was MAMBO NIGHT, baby. Austin had sent over costumes. He'd have to meet them there after work. Mishu was the emcee for the drag show. His outfit would be a high-waisted pair of flared pants and a ribbed T-shirt. (Some people called them wife-beaters, maybe thinking of Stanley in *A Streetcar Named Desire*.) Suspenders. Austin's "assistant" was given something spec-tac-u-lar—a black, lacy, button-up blouse with short-cuffed sleeves. Strips of black lace worked around creating a *Kiss of the Spiderwoman* effect. The black bra would be evident. It went with a tiny, stretchy, shimmery, tight skirt and high heels with straps. She wasn't a mambo dancer but a good follower on the dance floor. It was going to be a razzle dazzle night. Sábado Gigante and *La Cage aux Folles* rolled into one. At least for Palma Piedras. She had a surprise for Mishu behind curtain number one. Clearly, he wanted her out. And she was going—when the trois of the ménage was ready. But Mishu was on his way back home sooner than he knew. It would be for his own good.

They carried their costumes by bus to the club in Melrose. Tom, Dick, or Harry's Cabaret was an exclusive men's club in a different sense of the term. She was allowed backstage by the manager as Mishu's personal stylist. They went to his dressing room. It was everybody's dressing room. There were at least a dozen performers getting ready in front of mirrors at a long counter that took up one wall. Enough makeup, wigs, and prosthetics to stock Broadway. No one raised any verbal objections but she got the hint. The sooner she got out of the way of their creating magic by disappearing dicks and pumping up pompis the better.

Mishu, you've got some stray hairs there, she said pointing to his chest. You missed a patch or two when depilating.

What? He said, looking down. Oh, not to worry, she said. I have wax strips in case of emergency in my bag. Hey, someone called, Can I get a couple of those, honey? Sure. She saved a few for Mishu's maintenance and passed the box around. Friends for life. Meanwhile, Palma pressed and yanked around Mishu's nipples (much to his agony and ecstasy). The things we do for beauty, she said loudly. Right on, sister, someone agreed. It turned out she had all kinds of life-saving items—gauze, cotton balls, loose face powder, clear lacquer polish, Q-tips, Dr. Scholl's foot pads, Band-Aids, anti-oil face wipes, safety pins in all sizes, needle and thread, underarm sweat pads for men, throat lozenges, ad infinitum. Much of it came from Austin's list of the basics for a fashion stylist. She had three potential clients' digits before Palma finished getting the emcee ready. Love your hair, girl, one of them said. It's so asymmetrical.

Yeah, Palma said. I did it after I nearly froze a guy to death in a hotel who wanted to be revived with fucking. Everyone stopped. It was like being in a wax museum. There was Barbra, Tina Turner, Marilyn, Madonna, and Cher. Among the younger ones, Lady Gaga and Beyoncé, who had been practicing her number "If I Was a Boy." They were all frozen statues. Marble eyes with glitter eye shadow all on her. That was when and how Palma Piedras knew it was getting near time to cut out her antics. After shocking a room full of drag queens, Celia Cruz broke the spell, "You crazy, chica!"

Yes, yes, she was.

Celia started singing "Babalu," her number for the occasion of the night's theme. BABALUA! She had on a big pink wig but did not look like a Barnum & Bailey clown. Celia Cruz could sing, gente. And that Celia Cruz started to rock it, too, in that back storage room. The others broke up and went back to their anamorphous. Here, Palma said to Mishu, who had scarcely thanked her for being there to dress him, Let me help you get these on. Palma meant the tight pants that required he wear a jock strap or some kind of dick compressor. (Palma's new job had a lot to teach her.) She was wearing a pair of gloves. No one asked why. Wow, she said to Beyoncé as Palma put on the final touches to his ensemble. Mishu turned quickly to see whom she was admiring. Just then the take-no-prisoners stylist slipped in a couple of twigs with fresh leaves of stinging nettle into the crotch of Mishu's costume. Earlier that day the gardeners at the Marmont were cutting away the treacherous weed. Ramón, their boss, was reluctant when she asked for some. I don't know, señora, he said. Oh, she said, it's so hot today. It's why I'm going out to the pool, Palma said. She pulled off the wool dress. In her bikini she was freezing. The Marmont stowaway reached into her top and drew out a twenty. A nipple peeped out. I'll be careful, she said to Ramón, I promise.

Now, for good measure she quickly brushed the stinging nettle inside the jock strap, withdrew it fast and got it out of the way. Hey, Mishu said, watch it. Sorry, Palma said, I was just trying to straighten out your junk in the flimsy pants. A few of the others nearby nodded. She packed up and skedaddled. Good luck, ladies!

The host gave her a table near the stage. The place was packed with mamberos. Austin arrived. He came as Benny Moré. (He had to explain since a Cuban conductor and lead singer from the height of Havana wasn't the easiest person to identify, even on MAMBO NIGHT at Tom, Dick, or Harry's.) He looked good with his hair oiled back, drawn-in, pencil-thin mustache, and a forties, double-breasted suit with wide shoulders. Even better was Austin's date.

It was Cameron Diaz. Or a dead ringer. Hi, Cami, Palma

said. Hi-ee, the actress said and gave her a quick handshake. They sat and ordered a bottle of Piper's. It was going to be a grand night. "Cachao" was playing over the speakers and Celia Cruz was warming up the audience with dance lessons. She approached their table and pulled Palma out to the dance floor. The performer was at least six feet tall in platforms. They shimmied until Palma thought she'd thrown out a shoulder. Celia had a strong grip. They finished the number and she took Palma's hand. They went back stage where it was dark. Bésame, preciosa, Celia Cruz said. Palma felt her hard-on. Mama mia. She pushed her against the wall. Ay, preciosa, Celia kept mumbling, as they kissed madly. Palma started lifting up her dress as the drag queen helped her get the thick fabric over generous hips. No padded undergarments. Palma pulled down the spaghetti straps and her breasts were—real? What kind of wondrous creature was this? Her eyes wide, Palma touched one lightly like she had just discovered the Great Barrier Reef. Worth every penny, Celia said. Oil of Olay smooth. (If it wasn't for Austin's Nivea in the shared bathroom, Palma's own flesh would have felt like a plucked ostrich's.) She commenced to suck one implanted mammary facsimile then the other while Celia had her hand up in her like Giovanni had done way back in grammar school, searching for who knew what. She was the quintessential dykedog and Palma was ready to turn around and have her give it to her when she heard Austin's voice. Palma? Get out here, girl. *Now.*

Reluctantly, she returned to the table and Cami leaned over and said, You dance swell. I'm half Cuban but I'm all white girl when it comes to rhythm. She smiled big. Cami was in a rumba blouse with long ruffled sleeves. Tall. Taller in the platform wedgies with straps going up around the ankles. (Palma had peeked under the table. You could tell a lot about a woman by her shoes. Men, too.) You're much prettier in person than in your movies, Palma said, because she was.

The show was about to start, the DJ quit, and lights went down. A semi-hush went around the place and a disembodied voice introduced Mishu Martini. Drum roll. A big, round spotlight hit the empty stage and then he appeared from behind the curtains. She glanced at Austin who was biting his bottom lip at the sight of his creation. Mishu *was* bangin' in his costume, all right. How's everybody doing? Keep those drinks coming, damas y caballeros. You'll need 'em. He was saying things like that over the hand-held mic. Everyone was doing just fine. There were a lot of customers in mambo outfits or what they thought were mambo outfits, male and female versions. Unwarranted ruffles and exposed innies, outies, and in-betweens. The bar was packed and Mishu was evidently flushed, dabbing his forehead and upper lip with a hankie. Is he nervous? Palma asked Austin, leaning across Cami who sat between them. The star looked concerned, too. Well, even the best of us can come undone in front of a live audience, Cami whispered. Austin shook his head. Something was wrong. Mishu looked almost feverish. His hand kept going over to his crotch—trying not to scratch.

Our first diosa de la noche, ladies and . . . he said, evidently losing concentration.

What's the matter? Cami asked Austin.

Maybe we should do something, Palma suggested, putting her hand on the personal stylist/medical bag. Just then Mishu let out a girl scream, clutched his goods with both hands and went running off stage. Austin jumped up and the three hurried back stage. In the dressing room the delirious lad had already thrown off shoes, pants, and jockstrap. His thing looked like a boiled crayfish. What the . . . ? Austin said helping Mishu lay down on a divan. A few of the performers were already inspecting. There were tsk-tsks and speculations about what form of STD Mishu had managed to contract when someone said, it looks like poison ivy. It was Cami. The manager noticed her. Cameron Diaz? His eyes popped. The statuesque celebrity batted her eyes down at him and gave her famous wide smile. He grabbed her hand. No better way to save the show, he said leading her out toward the stage to entertain the troops. I gotta see *this*, Palma said, and was about to follow when Austin grabbed hold of her elbow. *Do you have anything for a rash in your bag?* Perhaps she did. Palma took out baking powder but first, came the slices of cucumber from the ziplock bag to soothe the "affected area." She also had some antihistamine tablets. You really are prepared for everything! Celia Cruz said, who had pulled herself back together. Yeah, Austin said, not as convinced that it was by chance. A miserable Mishu, who was lying flat, reached out and put his hand at Palma's throat. *You're going down*, he whispered. She pushed it away and finished applying first aid. Maybe, she whispered. But *you'll* never see it.

THE NEXT evening when Palma came home, the once amor among Austin's *amores* was curled in a fetal position on the Murphy bed he and Austin shared in the living room. A sheet was over him but she could tell he was cupping his burned ding-a-ling. It turned out that Mishu was one of those people who reacted severely to weed rash, so Austin and Cameron Diaz had ended up taking him to an emergency room.

I just feel sorry for him, Austin told her, that's why I haven't kicked him out. It was left to Palma. She was hoping Austin wouldn't come back early or at all that night. Palma got her wish. Operation Eject Mishu was wrapped with a Draconian bow. While she heard him in the kitchen she left the bedroom calling out that she was stepping out for the evening. All right, he responded. It was only to let her know he had heard her. Otherwise, they were no longer speaking. The night before when they got in he called her a cunt under his breath. That was the last word he spoke before taking a couple of Valiums and passing out.

She slammed the front door, locked it, and snuck into the hall closet. It was old fashioned with room to move around and a real wooden door. Palma changed, waited until everything was still, and sensed that Mishu was back in bed and hopefully asleep. The place was dark when she peeked out and tiptoed to the kitchen. Thanks to one of the staff at the studio, Palma had gotten hold of what she needed. In a long satin robe with padded shoulders and wearing an auburn Rita Hayworth wig, she began a clatter with the dirty dishes, faucets running high. Palma heard Mishu tossing about in bed, mumbling, and finally what sounded like him getting up. What's going on in there? Austin, man? He muttered, standing groggily at the doorway.

He hit the light switch on the wall and Palma turned around, face powdered chicken-frying white. The front of the exquisite robe was covered with phony blood. Across her neck was a fake gash prop stuck on. The pièce de résistance was the eye contacts. She could see out (almost) but they looked like she had no pupils. She smiled at Mishu and he went pallid. It looked like he wanted to run, but couldn't will it. His mouth opened and nothing came out. Finally an *aghhhhhhh,* and as it grew, it propelled Mishu, who took off to the front door and tried to yank it open a couple of times before realizing he had to unlock it first. He swung the door open and ran out into the hall with his baked goods exposed.

Palma locked up and got ready for bed. She didn't expect Mishu back, but a while later there was a knock. It's the police, a man's voice said. They found her in pajamas. It was two police officers in uniform with a raw Mishu. He ran in as soon as she opened the door. This is the woman who locked me out of my room, Mishu said, and got the sheet off the Murphy to wrap around himself.

Who's registered for this room? One of the cops asked. My boyfriend, Palma replied. She said Austin was working late and added that the couple had been allowing Mishu to stay as their guest. He's crashing in our living room, she said, until he recovers. (From the messy sight it wasn't hard to imagine that *something* required recovering.)

When Palma got up the next morning she was alone in the suite. She made coffee, looked around, and verified what she suspected. His things gone, Mishu had cleared out.

20 The two's-company-three's-gone-back-to-New-Mexico pair were having a celebratory lunch (or, at least Palma was) in West Hollywood. Austin was on his second scotch when the guaca with salsa and chips came. They were sitting on a patio that opened out to the street. The waitperson gave her recommendations. She was apple-pie white and the place was about as Mexican as Taco Bell.

Palma Piedras suspected Austin was privately relieved that she had eliminated the weapon of his mass destruction. He was quiet but in good spirits, humming to the piped out music and apparently enjoying people watching. No word from your folks-at-large? he asked. His device in hand, he started to GPS. Maybe we should take a ride to see if anyone still lives at that address. Where is it? He nodded after she told him, stretching out his legs toward the street as if somewhere there was the answer to what they should decide about the matter. It was chilly and Palma hunched over as she sipped a virgin margarita (LA code for an expensive lemonade) through a straw. Austin looked as if he was waiting to be discovered by Oliver Stone and she looked okay but her dress was smashing. It was flared, overstated, and very fifties, with a gold lamé, Aztec motif. (Abuela would have sold a kidney to wear it to la iglesia.) The stylist at the studio let Palma borrow it. They had become chummy based on their mutual love for gold lamé and anything cut on the bias. The stylist, Alicia, said one of the actors on *The L Word* wore it in the "Livin' La Vida Loca" episode where she meets and fucks a Mexican beauty who they dressed up to look like Stanley Kowalski (or society's idea of a player).

The pair noticed a woman go by with a child, a boy of about four. She was olive skinned, thin boned—graceful. There was something about her that radiated from her pores one-day-I'm-going-to-be-famous (more than with most in LA). She was of average height with two long plaits, red lipstick, and rouged, prominent cheekbones. Her natural breasts jiggled beneath an acrylic sweater with one sleeve, the other shoulder bare. The boy jumped along holding his mom's hand. Another day in his life. Mom looked bored. Then she saw Austin. He saw her and stood up. Venus, he said. Venus? Palma said. Venus dashed toward them, pulling along the kid. He too, was slight, dark, and had spiky hair. Wow, what are you doing here? The slender woman asked Austin, man-all-about-town. She joined them while the kid, who immediately took out Captain America and Hulk action figures from his backpack, entertained himself. Palma and she were introduced and when she said Venus, as Austin had, she corrected her: Veh-noose. Venus de la Vega. What she was doing there was coming from the wine bar next door, which offered live music for a listening crowd. We're playing there tonight, she said. I had to make sure the sound was okay. Tonight? Austin asked. He had the quality of making anyone feel instantly that they were important. Yes, tonight, Venus said. She had long fingers, smelled of a Bach oil blend, and the second time she snuck a glance at the other woman, she in turn smiled at her.

Austin and Venus were in an acting class together. Palma

didn't know he had any aspirations to be an actor, and he didn't know Venus was a musician—cello, piano, violin, and bandeleon. (All at once? No. She was, however, the director of the Mi Buenos Aires Quartet.) I'll be on the piano this night, Vehnoose said. Tonight? (Palma.) Yes, this one. And we will also have a guest tango singer. It'll be fun, Venus said. Why don't you stick around? She gave Palma a smooch on each cheek to say goodbye then jumped up, went around the table, and did the same with Austin except *la tanguista* left her hand on one of his biceps. Maybe she liked men. Maybe she liked women. (The question was, did she like Palma?) The kid wrapped up his Avengers battle and was ready to go. I have to get him home before I can come back. Venus left them to their faux Mexican meal. Austin watched her hurry off. Too bad I have plans later, Austin said. He couldn't wait to wash that Mishu out of his hair, she figured. Afterward, as they rose to leave the restaurant, Palma let him know she had plans of her own. The wine bar? He guessed with a chin pointing next door. Uh-huh, she said. You so crazy, he said.

THE WINE bar was a franchise. Bogus Tuscan memorabilia on the walls and bunches of plastic grapes hanging from the track lights. Carlos Gardel was coming through the speakers. The day you love me, he sang in a voice that permeated with nostalgia even while he was alive. Just one? The hostess said, eyeballs giving Palma the woman-of-color to woman-of-color once-over. Not exactly the evil eye but something like it. In the spectrum of women of color giving killer looks to each other in public, African Americans were least interested, Latinas were bad but Asians—forget about it. Worst of all. From India to Vietnam. Nothing like Filipinas and Koreans, however, to each other. The hostess, young, svelte, breathlessly gorgeous in a slinky dress, dropped the menu on the table, sauntered off in platform heels, and two minutes later was back. You can give me your order. Palma hadn't even touched the menu yet. What? Tell me what you want.

Waiting for her to drink, the new tango aficionado sat staring in this direction or that and thought about how many famous people had died in small plane crashes like Gardel. More recently the rising singer/actress star, Jenni Rivera. There'd been Chet Baker, Patsy Cline, Richie Valens, Roberto Clemente, Buddy Holly, John Kennedy, Jr. as pilot. She pulled out her journal and began to jot. The vino arrived and the girl, annoyed that she had to hold the tray a nanosecond more for Palma to move her journal out of the way said, You a screenwriter? You look like you work in Hollywood. Palma shook her head. She was about to explain the borrowed dress, the rhinestone earrings right out of a Joan Crawford collection, also borrowed, but shrugged instead. No, she said. I'm working on a book—*The Cuntalogs*.

What? Oh you mean like *The Vagina Monologues*? the girl asked.

No, Palma said, shoving the journal back in her bag, pen in a side pocket. It's actually a travelogue for cunts. You might like it.

Cool, the hostess said and swished away.

The cell dinged. It was a text from Pepito. *Do u Tango?* He was not asking her to dance but inviting his unforgettable prima to communicate with him through the app that allowed people to also see each other on their devices. Synchronicity. Palma thought. Tangoing with Pepito through cyberspace while hearing Gardel. Instead of a tango from el Sr. Pepito however, she got another text. *I have a customer. Call you later.* He loves me. He loves me not. He loves . . . Palma looked up.

There was a gypsy with a handful of roses. She'd walked off the stage from the opera *Carmen*. Long skirt, scarf around the head. Fake gold hoop earrings. Should I buy one for myself? No, la gitana said, but I'll tell your fortune. She took Palma's hand and traced the lines with a dirty fingernail. Be careful, she said, someone close to you will try to hurt you. Palma nodded. That was vague enough to hold truth. She pulled out some bills, which the fortune-teller promptly stuffed inside the front of her blouse and moved on. Customers drifted in and then one musician carrying her instrument case, then two, and then there was Venus.

Palma felt she was bordering stalker when the other woman smiled but did not come over. Instead, Venus waved at the manager, greeted a couple of people, and headed to the back. In her venue Venus de la Vega was the star. Tinseltown they called it; the place where dreams came to die. You could keep dreams alive perhaps, in small niches. A teeny flicker of a birthday candle you might write home about. She could have someone in Argentina who awaited such dispatches. If not and even if so, she had Palma, this Venus, with her slender calves and pleasant rear upholstery. And she def had the other woman when a roomful applauded for the four poised women who walked out in 1930s style outfits, each taking her place. Venus at the piano gave the signal and they began their set with (but of course) "Mi Buenos Aires querido." It wasn't until the third number that the guest vocalist came on stage. Some clapped. Most ignored the concert.

They went on guzzling or nursing their alcohol, going in and out to smoke or getting on mobiles, texting, or tweeting; orders were taken and delivered. Palma got a way overpriced fruit and cheese plate which consisted of four red grapes, two diced strawberries, three thin apple slices, three slivers of Manchego, same for the other cheese, and a condiment bowl with a black olive, Spanish olive, and two generics which she nibbled on while observing the rude Thirty-Something Aspiring Alta Mulch crowd. She didn't envy them, with their credit card debts and animal instinct for outlet malls. Her own thirties were rough years. Your true youth gone forever and you know it but hope no one else notices—not your boss, lovers, or so-called best friend, who is the first to point out when you lose your waistline. By forty, if you hadn't gotten in the game, you never would. What game? The game of beating the rest at whatever you did best. What had Palma Piedras ever done best? Nothing that could be mentioned in polite company.

These Thirty-Somethings, like Mulches all over the world, were def in the game. Little Mulch mice in a maze, rushing toward parenthood, taking care of aging parents, obtaining mortgages, starting businesses, or getting promotions and establishing pensions. Fighting the good futile fight against the inevitability of their mortality.

Now she was stumbling through her forties like a shot, bewildered deer. Or better yet an aardvark that had once been content feeding off ants, not special ants, just whatever came along her path, and now the ants were in revolt. If she had fought for dreams, goals, or aspirations in her thirties, she couldn't remember them now. When she thought about the future it looked like the surface of Mars or the moon or a Walmart parking lot. Hostile and non-trekable. Holy Cow. Her problem wasn't being forty plus. She had become a Nihilist Mulch.

Maybe it was the tango music.

The quartet finished the set. Not many noticed. Palma settled the tab and then hung around outside. At last the directress came out. The violinist and she were talking,

205

then parted ways. She knew Palma was waiting. Thanks for coming, Venus said. There were shy smiles and coy miradas that swallowed the other whole. With Christmas nearing, the thirty-something Veh-noose said she was very busy with family obligations, auditions, rehearsals, and whatnot, but they were playing again the next night if Palma wanted to come. We're doing Latin fusion tomorrow. Instead of cello we'll have a bass. She looked at Palma, maybe waiting to see if she had any questions. She didn't. I'll be here, she said, instead, not knowing if she would or not. Venus asked where Palma had parked. Albuquerque. You're funny, Venus said. The truth often is, Palma said. Venus offered a ride.

There was a child's seat in the back of the Hyundai and kid crap all over. It was a ride full of self-conscious silences and enough body heat to steam up the windows. When she pulled up at the Marmont, Palma shooed away the valet. Okay, she said, I'll see you tomorrow, and leaned over to give Venus a doble paso beso. Venus turned her cheek so that the second kiss landed on her lips. Palma stopped and stared at her eyeball to eyeball. *This is the moment you decide,* the look said. Venus had the best skin, poreless. Her hand came over as if to touch Palma's arm or try to go around her waist and instead landed on her breast. Venus left it there as they gave each other a real kiss. When they broke away Palma asked, Are you married? (And this was when henceforth she would detest adverbs.) Not *really*, Venus said, huskily in Palma's ear. That night it was a good enough answer.

She saw the Argentine the next night and for the next eight nights and knew that whatever Venus had said that first night would have made no difference. Palma bought her a vintage bangle by Monet. Venus gave, in turn, a Sweet Scandal cuff. They were BFFs. The pair didn't talk about going to bed, but desire hung over their heads, threatening to drop and knock each of them out. They didn't look up or ahead but took it, as it were, un jour at a time.

SHE'S MARRIED, you know, Austin said one morning before going to work. I didn't know, Palma lied. As long as she didn't see him or hear of her husband, Venus and she were in a Sapphic bubble. The same with the kids—they were not yet on the Isle of Denial where their mother played the lute while Palma composed songs à la Fierce H. (I love you. You love me. Always through eternity. Yeah.) One day the children of Venus would also be hers. Palma would pack their lunches and take them to school or pick them up from football practice or chess meets while their mother pursued Andy Warhol's ghost to fame. One day the two would buy a home in the Hollywood Hills with a pool, and Ramón would come and plant rose bushes. While Venus and she were with the quartet on tour la nanny from Ensenada would teach the kids Spanish like in *Babel* before she disappeared in the desert.

One night the star Palma wished upon spent the night at the Chateau Marmont. There was nothing about her in bed that spoke I've never done this before. She was a natural.

Or, in love.

Palma, too.

Synchronicity had a sharp aftertaste. She was not the only one falling in love. One day Palma got a different kind of text from Pepito: *I want you to hear it from me. Her name is Stephanie.* Wow. Really? Really, you bastard? You couldn't give it to me but you could give it to a Stephanie? Palma worked herself up throughout that day as she picked up Venus in her lover's car and took her to this appointment and that one and who then dropped Palma off at the Marmont. Don't come up,

Palma said. I need some time to myself. She didn't think her lover was staying anyway because her kids were a priority and on the Venus totem pole Palma Piedras wasn't anywhere near the top.

She went to the Safeway and asked the butcher for a heart. I don't care if it's a pig's heart or a chicken heart, she said. Just make it a heart. He handed a white package over the counter and she went straight to a private mail business. Palma packaged it and had it shipped overnight in care of the Silverman Brothers. It wasn't Voodoo. He'd figure it out.

Palma spent the evening ahead throwing darts. Austin didn't have a dartboard. She used the steak knives on a magazine picture of a Covergirl model taped to the wall. It was Queen Latifah. She named her Stephanie. When Austin walked in he startled her. Hey, he said. Hey, Palma said, and lowered her hand. He hardly came home. She'd stopped going to the set. They'd become a couple of dinghies passing in the night. She chugged from a bottle of Cutty Sark. Hey now, he said, when he saw she was trying to tie one on. In a Canali blue shirt he looked celestial, an angelito negro coming to gently take the bottle from her hand. In the background La Lupe was belting out a torch song on one of his LPs. *According to you, I am the bad one. The She-Vampire of your novel.* La Lupe was one crazy Cuban woman. But she was good. Austin, an inch from Palma's face, pressed against her, his mouth came down on hers as he reached a hand around and went inside the back of her shorts. He jabbed in a finger. Palma lifted a leg around his torso. While she believed he was glad to be rid of Mishu, you could tell in the way he now looked at her, he resented her. He pulled away and sauntered off. I gotta shower, he said. People are waiting on me. Cami? Palma said. Yeah, he said. Give me a break! We know that's not Cameron Diaz! If it looks like a duck and walks like a duck . . . Austin called. IT'S STILL NOT CAMERON DIAZ! She screamed and threw the Cutty Sark against the far wall. In a few minutes Palma heard the shower running. Hey, baby girl, he called. She dropped her clothes on the way. In the hot shower Austin glistened beneath the spray. The water was on so high she thought she'd drown. She'd be an obituary the next day in the *LA Times*. Survived by no one. Austin lifted Palma by the waist. It was payback time in the Dirty Boys Social Club and she was its honorary member. He turned off the faucet. Bent in half Palma reached between her legs and grabbed hold of his pair. Squeezed hard until he pulled out.

VENUS DROPPED by later. She looked like a woman on the run. Out of breath, head sweated. No overnight bag. Guts in tow. Palma was alone. They had a spinach salad with walnuts and dried cranberries that Palma prepared. By then she was sober. Later, they were tongue-deep in sixty-nine when Venus's cell dinged. A text. She broke away and with her nimble body was on the cell phone like a frog on a fly, talking fast. It was practically a stage whisper. Palma heard everything. Yes, yes. I'll be right there, she said, clutching the device and getting off the bed, away from her lover so she wouldn't hear what was being said on the other end, she moved to the bathroom to wash up. As soon as she was off Palma followed her.

I have to pick up the kids, Venus said. She didn't look at the other woman as she ran the sink faucet. They caught each other's gazes in the mirror. What? she said. *I have to pick up my children*. Palma stood next to her to see her face. You're going to him, aren't you? Huge glaciers were melting. A nuclear disaster had occurred. They stared. No reply. Venus washed hastily and went to put her clothes on, Diesel jeans, a segunda sweater, and jean jacket. She'd come that evening looking as if she had dressed as hastily as she was now leaving. You two are separated, Palma said. No response. *You two are separated*, she repeated. Venus stopped for a second as she tied her shoelaces. Yeah. It didn't sound convincing. With Stanislavski method practice, she said it again, Yeah. Palma's head grew light. Since when? She asked and threw on Austin's PJ top. She couldn't stand fighting with a lover with her titties all over the place.

Venus looked put off. (Great plan of defense—act offended.) She rummaged through her purse, produced a brush, and ran it through her long hair. (It was outstanding hair. Obsidian shiny.) She gave a deep sigh. Look, Palma—she started to say something. Palma stared at her. Okay, Venus said, he left after the night I didn't come home. When I spent it with you. She threw the brush back in the bag and started for the door. She was leaving. Going back to him. He wants to come home, she said.

Palma, feeling herself about to be dumped, prayed to the god that sat in her heart, like where Oprah said she saw her god. Palma's god looked like one of those Tahitian ceramic drinking glasses in Tiki bars. It was green with big lips and slits for eyes. He never said much but listened plenty. I thought you loved me, she said. (Corny, but true.) Venus swung open the door. I do, Venus said. Her eyes were wide and red. I do, she said again and left. When Austin came back hours later he found his roommate bawling. She'd hoped he would take pity upon the wreck of her former self and rock Palma to sleep and he did. He smelled of Cami's perfume.

21 The next morning Palma and Austin went out for breakfast. Lattes, bagels, huevos rancheros. This is the day, he said. Palma looked up. She didn't like the sound of it. We can't stay at the Marmont indefinitely. Let's go meet your peeps, boo. He checked the time on his cell. Fuck it. I'm not going to work. She got the feeling the plans had to do with his own reasons. Palma took a deep breath. The address was in her purse. Let's do it, she said.

They left the restaurant and headed near downtown. Maybe the area was called Central. The city was a puzzle made up of many small pieces or hamlets, Palma didn't know. You couldn't see anything a mile ahead that day. To make herself feel better that morning after the rejection from a would-be star or planet that Palma Piedras let get too close, she put on a Phillip Lim silk and cotton coat picked up in the Fashion District. It was multo Asian and fit like she was born to wear it. Underneath she wore Kill City pleather leggings for which she fought tug-a-war with an Iranian sales tracker at the store. While she hadn't planned the outfit, it was important to make a decent impression, even on strangers she'd been waiting to hear from for over forty years.

In Austin's Boxster they were there in an ozone-permeated flash. Zooming onto a street lined with Edwardians. Tall, looming frame buildings. Some with groomed front lawns and sprays of sunflowers, tuberoses, or gardenia bushes. Others were shabby. There were those freshly painted and a few suffering from neglect. The house Palma was looking for was ambiguous. It might have been disregard or lack of resources why the steps were crooked, the awning hung slightly off balance, and the front door didn't match. (Modern, made of steel.) All the windows had incongruous black wrought iron. (For security, to be sure.) Austin pulled into the driveway. Here you are.

There was a woman outside pruning the hedges. Straw hat and a sweatshirt over a long sweater over a button down apron. She stopped, sheers in hand. The first glimpse Palma had of her mother was her curious look at the Porsche and the man behind the wheel. Angela's frown. She was not the ghost of the future Palma. There was a resemblance but her daughter was yet to know it and it wasn't in the face, hands, or feet. They were blood, tied by Abuela, with razor sharp self-preservation. None of this could she know or yet guess as she stepped out of the car, hearing Austin say, I'll come back for you. Just text me. Palma of the palmas of Los Angeles swaying in the late autumn's breeze hesitated at hearing he wasn't planning on staying. It wasn't his duty. It was no one's duty to be at her side.

She went steadily toward the gate.

Angela watched her approach, said nothing, and did not smile. (She also didn't run.) The hour had come. By the look of dread on the woman's face as Palma neared, however, she felt like La Bruja. (Mexicans' idea of the Grim Reaper.) She was fiddling with the lock on the gate when out of nowhere a woman and a teenage girl came up behind. They were going to the house, too. They opened the latch and invited her into the yard. Palma heard Austin's Boxster take off with a zoom and all the sounds in the world ceased save for a voice inside that said, *please don't go.*

Angela gave a weak embrace, which nevertheless sent an electro-shock through Palma's body, slighter than her mother's. The woman who arrived with her daughter, she soon discovered, was Genie. (Palma's sister, and as she figured it out later, three years her junior.) She's my daughter, Angela said, each woman looking at the other, not sure to which one she was referring in her introduction. Evidently, an awkward woman with little social grace, Angela looked relieved to not be alone with Palma and from then on made Genie the mediator.

We tried to call you on the number you sent, Genie said. She was a couple of inches taller than Palma and looked like their mother—face, body type, and most of all, her impenetrable attitude. (As for Angela, she had Abuela's arms, hips, and enviable widow's peak.) It was possible they had tried calling when her cell wasn't working right. (Then again, maybe Genie was a liar.) Palma nodded, noting her brand new sister was sizing her up, too. How long are you staying in Los Angeles? Angela asked. These were among her first words to her daughter. Not long, Palma said. It was a safe answer. How is my mother? Angela asked next. Your mother, madam, is dead, Palma thought but did not say. My grandmother passed last year, she said. Angela nodded. Genie nodded. Palma smiled at the teen who smiled back while she snapped her gum. Crack, crack, crack. Do you want to come inside? Genie asked. If you have time, Angela added. (Yeah, she had time, Palma thought, like the last four decades.) They went up the creaky steps and Genie's daughter stepped ahead to open the door. All the while until they got inside Angela was talking to Genie about her rose bushes and being out of fertilizer. In turn the daughter said tomatoes were on sale at the market. Palma followed along feeling like a Jehovah's Witness who had only been invited in to be tolerated for a Christian minute.

The house was divided into apartments. The girl explained: Angela and husband were on the first floor. Genie and her family lived upstairs. In the back, Palma soon learned. The whole gang was there. (Minus one. Have you heard the Good Word?) They sat in the living room. Well-worn couches, photographs of all the stages of children and grandchildren everywhere, a big flat screen TV against one wall, cluttered coffee table, X-Box, remote controls, and whatever else Baja Mulches needed to escape their lackluster lives. You could hear the noise of the outside traffic and sunlight filtered through synthetic lace curtains. There was an old touch-tone landline on an end table. (They'd been a simple phone call away from her all Palma's life?) Kids toys lay around on the ugly green carpet and for some reason the children's absence affected her.

Do you want coffee? Angela asked as soon as they sat down. No, I want a mother, she thought, but did not say. A father with two gonads, if you have one available, would be excellent. Palma had recovered from the initial meeting and now snuck a glance at the daughter her mother and father kept. How do you like LA? Genie asked, as if Palma just happened to be passing through. Palma felt something ugly and welling inside wanting to bust out, not like a tumor but *The Alien* and she didn't answer.

Are you going to be around for my *quinceañera*? Genie's daughter asked Palma. Her curly locks were saturated with gel. She had acrylic or gel nails, zebra print (Genie, who said she worked at Home Depot, had hers clipped). What? Palma asked. Oh, it's just a family party, Angela said. Yes, Genie said, come. Okay, she said to the fourteen-year-old MAP—Mexican American Princess—with a muffin top over her skinny jeans and a middle-aged woman's bosom (most likely due to an unholy consumption of fast-food fries and nachos with Cheez Wiz.) My cousins, uncle, and grandpa will be playing, the girl said.

What? Palma said.

Yeah, the girl said, they have their own mariachi group. (Palma's father was a mariachi?) My husband is in Mexico right now, Angela said. *(Her husband—not Palma's father.)* His mother is very sick, the woman added. She's dying. (What was she doing there? Whose "peeps" had she intruded upon, who were celebrating festive occasions and preparing for mourning? Damn that Austin.) From the recesses of her entrails she conjured Pepito. A single thread of spit connected the pair but he was *her family.* Jim . . . Yimmy's son, Palma told Angela, sends his regards. (It wasn't true.) Angela's simple face went blank. My brother had a son? She sounded only vaguely curious. I don't know, Palma said. His name is Pepito. Angela and Genie looked at each other. No, they knew nothing about such a person. My mother never wrote to me about that, Angela said. (They wrote to each other? Abuela and Angela? It wasn't one sided?)

Palma had heard enough. She jumped up and texted Austin. Angela stood, too. She seemed relieved. Okay, Palma. She had not spoken her daughter's name until then. Why did you call me that—? Palma asked. Angela went flushed. Genie's face grew red, too. Why did you call me Palma? She said, again. Abuela's ward wanted the mother to say what she'd written in those letters. It was her wish for her first born to see those angular trees and to perhaps one day pick dates or coconuts or whatever fruit they bore.

Angela looked paralyzed.

For the palms, remember? Palma said. After you left the freezing winters of Chicago and your widowed mother, who only wanted to keep you near? Palma's own eyes glazed like two tiny cups of crème brûlée. Angela gave a sad vibrato sigh. Then Genie seemed to regroup and her tattooed eyebrows relaxed as she went to put a protective arm around her mother. Taylor will give you the details of her party, Genie said. (Yeah, Palma thought, being invited to a quinceañera should make up for keeping me out of the family all my life.)

Go feed the dogs out back, Taylor. Angela had gotten her voice back. Her tone was right out of Abuela's Guide to Tough Love. Taylor, Angela's granddaughter, wasn't fazed. She got up, asked for Palma's digits to put in her cell, and rolled her eyes at both mother and grandmother before exiting. Pop, pop, snap, snap went the gum. Palma left, then, too. Austin caught up in his car on the next block.

22 The two went back to the hotel. The desk clerk called Austin to have a word. Palma waited on the side. Her friend leaned, hands in his trousers, smiling his irresistible smile, and in a couple of minutes he and the guy were both smiling. Nevertheless, she knew. The unpaid bills piling up on the dining table, the fast lifestyle—it was all catching up to the bluesome twosome, and it was nearing time for Palma to hit the Red Road, Jack. Austin hooked his arm with hers and they took the elevator up to the suite as if all they had to worry about was why everybody didn't love them.

He soon went out and Palma Piedras pulled out Angela's letters and spread them on the bed. As she looked at them again, reading the youthful thoughts of the woman she met earlier, all sentimentality was vanquished. God gave and the Devil took away, Mother Martha Mary of the Blind Sisters might have said. What she had discovered that afternoon left no doubt that she was indeed Angela's daughter. They were both equally selfish. But what about Mariano, Jr.? Palma's *father*? Had he wanted her or not?

The cell dinged. A tango from Pepito. He had most likely received the stinking heart. Not a pig or a chicken's but a goat's. She clicked the green button and he came up on the little screen. If she had the guts she'd have beseeched him to come to LA and save her from herself. Instead she heard herself say, how's Stephanie? Pepito winced. For a woman who doesn't like to be judged, you can be very non-accepting, he said. He held up the opened box. What happened to you, Palma? He said. You used to be my hero.

I met my mother, she blurted.

Palma, he cut in, what did Abuela do to you to make you so bitter?

What?

The old woman put a roof over our heads, he said, food on the table—and we weren't her responsibility.

She beat the shit out of me, Palma said. Pepito lowered his gaze. Well, maybe she thought you needed it. He offered a cheer-up smile. Maybe it made you the woman that you are. Or maybe, he said, that was just how she was raised. Old school. You gotta let it go, Palma. Before she could reply the call dropped. She stared at the device while she was left with the question as primal as birth: What *had* Abuela done so terrible when it was her mother and father who were answerable to Palma? And maybe not even them.

A WHILE later Austin was back. He came into the bedroom and found his roommate lying flat on the bed like she was about to be tarred and feathered by the villagers. I'm going to the Zen Buddhist Center. He sat by her and stroked her head. Why don't you come?

They drove to Pasadena. Palma went as she was, a mess with a box of Kleenex. Austin said he felt the need to meditate. It's better than horse tranquilizer, he said. Palma gave him a look. Just sayin', he said. They pulled up to a clean stucco building. It was modest and would hardly have stood out except that on that day there seemed to be a lot of commotion out front. A flurry of Chinese monks in yellow robes, police cars, TV-station vans, and a gathering of mostly hemp Mulch spectators. The pair drove around the corner, parked, and came back on foot. Himalayan incense filled the air. As Palma and Austin moved through the crowd they realized much of the excitement surrounded one individual in particular. He stood by the door in red robes and a red silk sun visor. He smiled incessantly and it looked like, despite his rimless glasses, he couldn't see a lick.

Wha . . . ? Austin said, under his breath. What is it? Palma asked. You know who that is? He said. It's the Dalai Lama, she said. Austin gave her a double take, as if he couldn't imagine how the heathen had guessed. (Maybe he also wondered why she was nonchalant about the spiritual head of Tibetan Buddhism, reincarnation of the bodhisattva of compassion being right there before them.)

Siddhartha was a prince who went out among the people, Austin said. He saw the suffering, poverty, and cruelty brought on by human greed, aging, and finally, discovered the existence of death.

Well, Jesus was born among the people, Palma said. Basically, when it comes to spirituality, she concluded, you have to keep it real. Austin cut his eyes. *You* have to keep it real. No, you.

There were several news media people with mics in the people's monk's face. He put his hands up to gesture that he was done with answering questions and they reluctantly put down their cameras and microphones but didn't leave. He looked around at the crowd and gave everyone a wave. Palma was in the back, pulling out tissues from the box to blow her nose and wipe swollen eyes. She heard whispering like a small brushfire catching on until it reached her. Please, a young monk in yellow robes stretched out his hand toward her, he wants a word. Austin White, who was black, went white. He gulped. What in the world would the Dalai Lama say to Palma? Worse. What would *she* say to the Dalai Lama. *Watch your cussin,'* he whispered as Palma was led away by the monk. She reached out for Austin but the monk said, no. When she approached the Dalai Lama he bowed. Clueless, she imitated his bow. Come, the Dalai Lama said, and they went inside the center. The place with tall windows, white walls, and blond wooden floors was all light. Palma had stopped crying. She offered the Dalai Lama a Kleenex. No, thank you, he said, ever smiling. Why were you crying? Were those tears of joy perhaps? He asked. He placed his hands behind his back and held them there.

She shook her head. I think lama means mother, Palma said, right?

He nodded.

I'm not mad at you but I am so pi... put off by *my* mother, she blurted. I think she has always been angry with her own mother, too. Look, Your Highness, I don't blame my mother. I grew up with my fu . . . funny grandmother, so I understand. The point is, she said, my mother hasn't apologized for abandoning me to the old wretch. (Palma was about to start crying again.) Then, my ex-husband signed away my rights where they took out my womb. I'll never know now what it is to be a mother. (This last admittance surprised her.) The Dalai Lama nodded. He took in the rant, then said, We all come to this life with a biological lineage. We also bring our own spiritual lineage. Everything we feel and think, how we perceive the world, comes through one of these lineages. You know your biological lineage but do you know your spiritual lineage? He looked at the bloated-faced woman with his black brushlike eyebrows raised. Of course, she didn't. We came, Palma told him, my friend and I, to meditate.

Yes, the Dalai Lama said, meditation is one way to understand our existence, by looking inward.

Honestly, she said, I'm not sure how looking inward is going to fix my mother or even my dead grandmother in purgatory.

Let me share this, the Dalai Lama said, If you wish to heal your sadness or anger, seek to heal the sadness or anger of others. They are looking to you for guidance, help, courage, strength, understanding, and for assurance. Most of all, they are looking to you for love. He smiled.

I'm not Buddhist, Palma said. I'm not anything.

My religion is very simple, the Dalai Lama said. My religion is kindness.

Palma looked down. She was wearing a pair of Mishu's flip-flops that he left behind. (She hadn't even realized it until then.) The monk sensed her inability to forgive. Or reluctance. The Buddha told us—the Dalai Lama continued to spout his wisdom like a golden fish fountain in the middle of Nirvana Plaza—that holding on to anger is like grasping a hot coal with the intent of throwing it at someone else; you are the one who gets burned. Palma looked at him. She was burned, all right. Crisp.

You know, he said, healing may not be so much about getting better as it is about letting go of everything that isn't you—all of the expectations, all of the beliefs—and becoming who you are meant to be.

Palma started weeping again. She put her hands to her face. The door opened and it was Austin. He was pale. He'd probably talked his way past the monks and security dreading that she might say the most wrong thing that had ever been said to a holy person, but the Dalai Lama, like the Great Spirit of the Sweat Lodge, knew her heart even if she couldn't put her desires into words. He waved in her friend and pointed toward the meditation room. We will meditate together. Then he said to both: **everyone has the right to achieve happiness.**

23 Happiness came to Palma Piedras that very evening. Venus returned. Her new lover showed up at the hotel unannounced. She was on a life-changing roller coaster and had gotten an all-day pass for her lover to ride along. Venus was in a warm-up suit and brought an overnight bag. Her husband had the kids. He would move in with his mother to let their children stay in the home with her and keep their routines. I have to go back and resume my duties as a mom, Venus said, even if not as a wife. She looked at Palma, who nodded. I'll help. I mean, if you need my help and want it. Yes, her lover said. She and her kids were a package deal. Take it or leave it, she told Palma. Well, *mi reina*, the other said, I ain't leaving. So you're stuck with me. Venus laughed. (It was good to see her laugh considering how upset she was when Palma last saw her.) You're stuck with me too, now, she said. She meant now that Venus had thrown out the husband or he voluntarily withdrew and someone had to catch her free fall.

The lovers decided to prepare a late supper. Venus wasn't a cook. She went out and came back with a box of frozen crab cakes, fresh snow peas, and a box of Riceland Rice. My favorite, Venus said. Mine too, Palma said and imagined how many thousands of meals they were going to have, how many boxes of Riceland Rice and bushels of steamed peas and crabs would die to nourish their love.

This has been a mind-blowing day, she told Venus as they sat at the table, ready to dine by candlelight. Do you know whom I met? Venus took a sip from the Dragon's Gold gluten-free beer she was having and lifted her chin, as if to ask whom. Her hair was in braids like the first time Palma saw her. She thought about how talented her lover was musically and one-by-one mentally went down a list of praises of Venus de la Vega, her new honey.

Austin and I met the Dalai Lama at the Buddhist center where we went to meditate, she said. Venus didn't look impressed. I don't think that was the Dalai Lama, she said. What was she talking about? Venus replied that she had seen on the local news earlier that an eminent Buddhist monk had been in town that day but not the Dalai Lama.

No, Palma said, it was his Highness. The other shook her head. She speared a snow pea with a fork, picked it off the tines, and began to nibble. The monk who visited LA, Venus said, has written all kinds of books on compassion. Very popular. Thich Nhat something I think they said his name was. Venus stuck another pea with her fork and nibbled on that one, too. Palma gave a sigh. He said some wonderful things to me, she said. Venus nodded. He told me to forgive my mother and my grandmother and the universe in general, Palma said.

Well, he is a best-selling author, her lover said.

Poof.

Palma lost her joy.

She got up, went over to the bar, poured a scotch neat, and came back with it. (Without yet knowing why, that evening, she was drinking on Austin's behalf.) She thought of the text from Taylor earlier inviting Palma to the quinceañera. My niece, Palma said aloud. She never had one before and was about to try her out. The girl gave her the information about the coming-out party traditional for Latina girls whose parents gave a shit. You have to go, Venus said. Yes, she was right.

That night Palma's lover and she had an idyllic time with the exception that Palma couldn't get it out of her head that she hadn't met with the Dalai Lama. Instead of killing the messenger after dinner Palma sucked, kissed, and fondled Venus in bed with ditto reciprocation. After the lovers went to sleep Palma got a call from Austin. Twisted and noble cavalier. He'd been arrested. He wasn't calling to be bailed out. It wasn't a DUI or a weed charge. He hadn't been in an altercation or talked back to a cop after running a light. He wasn't caught fucking a Mishu substitute in Echo Park. Austin was picked up for so many outrageous charges it set Palma's head spinning like the Wheel of Fortune. Where would they stop? Embezzlement, extortion, all kinds of fancy, white-collar crimes. Can you get ahold of my lawyer? he asked, calling her because the Chateau Marmont was the only number he could get at that hour. He also asked Palma to call his mama in Virginia. She had money of his. Mishu's involved, isn't he? Palma asked. She knew in her gut the bad boy should be in jail, too. (Who you gonna call when they come for you?) Don't blame him, Austin said, aware that their talk was very well being recorded. Austin's arrest was the start of her own *First 48 Hours* episode. It was to last seventy-two.

24 Austin's lawyer called back. Palma gave him the info and requested to keep her updated. She called the mother in Virginia. Oh, Lord, the lady said, when she relayed the message. Venus helped Palma vacate the Chateau Marmont. The husband was moving out as Palma was being forced to vacate her quarters. Such was the nature of chaos but it was all clear as night to her as they took Austin's things and went to the house in Montebello. It's a rental, Venus said. Her husband lost his job in sales. They lost their home six months later. He started working with a brother-in-law in construction. He's not very good at it, she said. Her music gigs were helping keep up with bills. Three bedrooms. Unkempt yard. They pulled up into the driveway, Venus jumped out, opened the gate, drove the Hyundai in, and Palma left most of the cargo in the garage.

As they were going through the back door with her bags they heard the front door slam. It was the thirteen-year-old daughter's way of saying, Screw you. Ten minutes later the dad pulled up in front and took her away. Palma never saw the girl face-to-face. Her pictures were around, atop the old-fashioned piano in the living room and the non-working fireplace mantle. A cheerleader. By the size of her she was going to be a bigger woman than her mother.

The girl had her own bedroom. Justin Bieberverse. You

can leave your things in there, Venus said. What? Well, they won't fit in my room, she explained. There was hardly space to step into the girl's room, with unmade bed, desk, computer, dresser, bureau, bike, a mountain of stuffed animals, and scattered shoes. Enough clothes in the closet—sliding doors open—to start a vintage shop (although Palma hadn't yet considered the 2000s vintage years). Plates of half-eaten pizza, open chip bags, plastic tumblers with unidentified leftover liquids. Palma hesitated to step in. As teens went, she was sure her mother's lover was the last person the girl would want in her domain. Between sleeping in the daughter's bed, however, or Venus' matrimonial one, with its well-worn bedspread, a pile of cushions, pictures on the dresser with her husband, closets with his broken tennis racket, funky sports shoes, and dirty socks on the floor, it wasn't a tough call. Palma's love and she could have conjugal visits in her daughter's room, she figured. (That thought, however, was thrown out later, when she realized the youngest still slept with his mom.)

Next came the eleven-year-old who went from school to soccer practice to doing homework at a classmate's house and thereby avoided anything remotely involving the family-life catastrophe. Instead of coming home, he had his father pick him up and take him for the weekend.

The little kid Palma met when she first saw Venus didn't ask questions. In fact, he refused to speak altogether.

They were all off to a good start.

The first morning the three castaways were in the kitchen. His mother served a breakfast of a strawberry Pop-Tart and Captain Crunch cereal. He watched Palma—head low over the bowl, scooping up cereal, with the eyes of a shark pup as she stood near the sink sipping a cup of coffee. That's my grandma's cup, he said. I could use another one, she said. The kid shrugged. Venus took him off to school. She came back in twenty minutes, and they went back to bed. Palma's new amor was convinced it was all a matter of everyone adjusting. We'll sort it out by next week, she said. Sure, Palma said, right after I help the secretary of state sort things out in the Middle East.

On Saturday, the little kid began to wail for his dad who rescued him from the jaws of their Vagina Dialogue within an hour of the call. It was honeymoon time. The women had sex on the living room floor. Palma's head ended up beneath the Christmas tree. There was a small manger of mismatched pieces beneath it but no presents. Venus said she kept them in the garage until Christmas. Do you think that's weird? She asked. Los Yankees tell me I'm being mean. Palma shook her head. I grew up in a house devoid of Christmas cheer and we were as American as chimichangas.

They reheated spinach empanadas (apparently the one thing Venus did know how to make) and got dressed for the quinceañera. The lovers showered together, shared a razor, and gave opinions on what shoes to wear. Palma was in the mambo outfit from Tom, Dick, or Harry's. (For some reason it spoke Mexican party time to her.) Venus was going to wear a regular dress, a conservative frock, very Angelina Jolie in *The Changling,* and a pair of black pumps. When she saw Palma in the risqué get-up, she said, Wait, and ran into her bedroom and closed the door. When she came out Venus looked like a delicate Carlos Gardel, pinstriped suit, silk ascot tucked inside the white shirt, and fedora. She had a cigarette holder in hand. The Mi Buenos Aires quartet always dressed for performances. Tango, mambo, 1930s, or 1940s—only the discriminating eye of an Austin could have told the difference. Carlitos gave Palma her arm and they went out the door.

THE PAIR was early. Actually on time but the rest arrived whenever they arrived. In the church lot Venus and Palma stood by the beat-up Hyundai in bad need of a wash, watching in silence. Our Lady of Perpetual Sorrows was in Angela's neighborhood. People parked and waited in the church lot. Cars decorated with crêpe flowers and streamers began to fill it up. Taylor's big ass family was LOUD. Their cars gleamed, some bounced. Most blasted something they called music. They all had the gift of satisfaction with their lots as Baja Mulch. Today, they went to the fiesta. Tonight, they would eat leftovers and cake and go back to worrying about their rents, cholesterol, and the gunshots that rang out at night in the neighborhood. Abuelos with their oxygen tanks and walkers were helped along and little kids ran around like cottontails in a carrot patch. The girls in the quinceañera were a bouquet of pudgy posies with big-armed tattoos and hair piled high in Selena curls. Taylor in a white, bell-shaped dress with hot pink sashes stepped out of a rented Hummer limo with several of her party and of course, Genie, Angela, and the men in their lives. Mariano, Jr. among them.

Venus leaned over and asked, Is that your dad? *Palma's dad?* Her dad. Her father. No matter how you put it, no. But yes, there he was. Not very tall, paunchy, and so somber you'd think he was a pallbearer. She could have picked him out in a line-up. Until then Palma Piedras only had Abuela as a point of reference for her Lama biological lineage. Mariano, Jr. as a young man may have been a short Luis Miguel with black hair. His aquiline nose and deep set eyes explained her own genome departure from Abuela's (and Angela's) indigenous looks. Realizing the resemblance left her with goldfish mouth, open, shut. Maybe a little bubble went into the air. She felt

Venus's hand reach out for hers, a slight caress of Palma's fingers. Maybe she could see it, too.

Taylor's grandfather took her gloved hand. Genie, the Home Depot manager with a royal wedding butterfly hat pinned to the side of her head, yelled instructions at everybody. The three led everyone to the church. Venus and Palma brought up the rear like an invisible guard. They all started up the steps and when Mariano, Jr., Genie, and Taylor reached the entrance they turned around. Genie, signaling to this one and that one to get in formation. Angela was in a beige synthetic outfit and Payless heels and nothing coordinated. She is a non-fit like me, her non-daughter, Palma whispered to Venus. Stop it, her lover said.

After the Mass, the cotillion army charged toward the church hall. The group was herded up to pose for the hired photographer and videographer while the rest rushed to get the fiesta started. Tables filled while Venus and Palma stood around like hired security. Let's just find a couple of empty seats and see if they let us join them, Venus suggested. Palma followed. She could tell her lover wasn't thrilled to be ignored, not out of vanity but because her plus one thought she was coming to a family function and Palma had yet to be acknowledged. The couple sat down at a long series of fold-out tables covered with paper tablecloths. I'm going for a margarita, Venus said, spotting the automatic margarita machine. There was a line. She eventually returned with two frozen drinks in short plastic glasses. Angela was sitting at the family table. Palma's and her eyes met. The woman gave her a Queen Mother wave and then looked away. Venus noticed. Do you think we should go over? She asked. Palma didn't know. Taylor had seen her and smiled. The girl went over to her grandfather, whispered something, and he looked toward Palma's table. They did not come over. Venus left the envelope they bought at the gift table and went to Taylor to wish the girl a happy birthday. Their meeting lasted about a second. A feeling Palma recognized as unmitigated terror screwed her down to the seat. Her hands were cold. A DJ set up and a microphone system was put in place. The buffet table was made ready and the throngs got in lines in each direction to load up on catered rice, beans, tamales, and pasta. Food they had at home. There wasn't a day without beans in Abuela's house. (Mexicans liked Mexican as much as everyone else. More.) There was the traditional waltz danced by all the kids in the quinceañera party and the girl's dance with her father. The dance started with the father and ended with the escort. Taylor's escort was a seven-foot future NBAer. Do you think we should go say hello to your family? Venus kept urging.

Mariano, Jr. was gone. He reappeared in a charro suit, holding a violin. Oh, Venus said, as if pleasantly surprised. Yes, Palma thought. Someday they would all be at a family gathering and her musician lover and he would play duets. On that day, the president would also have restored the economy single handedly and there would be peace in the world. The mariachis warmed up and went over to perform "Las Mañanitas" for Taylor and her party as the rambunctious group chowed down at their long-ass dais. Around the third song they played "La Mentira." Palma felt sick. Funny about the *bolero*. It wasn't Pepito's song now but had morphed into Angela's and hers. Palma fixed her gaze on the plastic margarita glass. *You forget I could do you harm if I chose . . .*

The crowd was invited to the dance floor by one of the mariachis. When Palma heard "Si Nos Dejan" she took her sweetheart's hand to the dance floor. She was shorter than Palma even with the fedora. The pair danced the number like they were the ideal couple. (When you were in love, you thought you were.) Slowly they went around, as Pepito and she had, but now with an audience. Venus rested her head against Palma's shoulder. The mariachis played. Taylor was on the dance floor dancing with another kid, not her escort, probably her real boyfriend. Stumpy like her. People kept going up to dance and soon Venus and Palma were lost in the crowd. The song finished and a fast one began. Mariano, Jr. stopped playing. He went over by his wife and Genie. There were others with them but of course, they were unknown to Palma Piedras—lone acorn dropped in a far away land long ago. They could have been brothers, sisters-in-law, cousins, nephews, and nieces.

I think they're talking about us, Venus said, as Palma held her hand back to their seats. The women should have left then. Venus looked like she wanted the ground to swallow her and her second-hand hat. She took it off, let her hair down, shook it loose, and looked around in her purse for her red lipstick. It wasn't easy being a dyke. It wasn't a Mi Buenos Aires Quartet performance or Tom, Dick, or Harry's drag show. It was life on the heterosexual half shell. Palma could have concluded instead that it wasn't easy just being her. Abuela had left her with the distinct feeling that it was harder for those around the girl. Let's leave, Venus nudged her elbow. We should say goodbye first, Palma said. Her eyes watered and she picked up a birthday napkin to dab them and keep the mascara from running. (Tears were familiar lately but they were quickly losing their novelty.) Palma counted one, two, three, held her breath, and took Venus's hand.

They began the march across the dance floor to the tribal council. Just then, the DJ started out with The Wanted's "Glad You Came." Everyone under thirty hit the dance floor. It was the longest walk of her life and not just because now they had to go around the dancers. (Correction: it would be the second longest. The longest was the Trail of Held Back Tears a few minutes later, marching across the hall, pairs of watchful eyes as they went out the door.)

This is Palma, Genie told Mariano, Jr. He gave her a weak handshake but his light-colored eyes drew her in like the nozzle of a vacuum cleaner. In seconds Palma was inside a dark place, suffocating. She started a coughing fit. Get her some water, someone said. Palma thought she saw Angela look up. A stranger (maybe her brother?) brought a filled glass. Genie was looking at Venus, a quick all-telling, who-are-you once over. This is . . . Palma started saying, half-choked. I'm her partner, Venus said. (Really, Venus? And what about your husband?) Partner? Mariano, Jr. said. What kind of business are you in? (Old joke. Ha-ha, we forgot to laugh.) Now Palma knew where she got the humor that was less humor than acid sprinkles. Genie smiled, looked away, and pretended to be preoccupied by other matters. Palma searched Angela's face for her gaze to meet hers but she was pretending to be distracted with wiping a child's mocos. Nowhere else to turn, Palma looked inward as the (possibly) Dalai Lama taught her. He had urged her to heal the ignorant. (He hadn't called Palma's relatives ignorant. She did.)

This is a family party, Genie said to Venus, who didn't catch the insinuation. She was new to homophobia. (It wasn't homophobia when it was directed at women but no one pointed out gynophobia because society was in the thick of it.) I'm here with Palma, she said. She thought Genie had meant they were party crashers, not perverts. It's nice to meet you, Mariano, Jr. said to her. Genie went off to give people orders. (It was her thing.) Angela and her husband looked away, pretending to enjoy watching everyone on the dance floor. They wanted Palma *gone baby, gone.*

Then came the worst part. The mariachi snuck a glance her way. His hazel eyes went up and down Palma like a set of windshield wipers. Here was what they said: *You are one fuckable woman.* She couldn't breathe. She's hyperventilating, Venus said, who then ran off. Palma plunked down on the nearest foldout chair gasping for her last breaths when her lover returned with a paper bag from the catered food table and she started breathing into it. Palma, being with a woman lover, spelled sex to Mariano, Jr. What a marimacha needed in such men's minds was a penis to cure her depravity—made evident by her attire. At the quinceañera, Venus and Palma had found no shortage of slinky, skimpy, and generally inappropriate outfits for any occasion on women, guys, and children. The objection to the two women's looks wasn't that you could see Palma's bra. (Maybe it was, but that wouldn't have been the main reason.) She alone in a mambo get-up screamed Forty and Sexy. (Okay, maybe, Forty and Slutty.) And Venus in a man's pinstriped getup said simply eccentric. (The pope, after all, was Argentine.)

No, the scandal Venus and Palma managed to cause had to do with their combination. The couple hadn't remotely been aware when they left Venus's house that they were being scandalous. (Yes, okay, Palma had some idea but hadn't anticipated the lethal results of girls just wanting to have fun.) Venus and she returned to the shabby house in Montebello, threw off their clothes, and went to bed without talking. Their last night together, as it turned out.

Once upon a time, a baby was born and nearly ruined a boy's mariachi ambitions. Why he had stayed with Angela only he could say. Probably what was expected by his God-fearing mother. And why did Angela go along? As a girl she may have been his biggest fan. Or the best tomato, garlic, and orange picker in the family. Why did anyone stay with anyone?

When Venus and Palma had gotten up to make their exit, Mariano, Jr. snuck another look her way. Their eyes met again. If she'd found him in a bar or at a fiesta, neither the wiser about the blood they shared, Palma would have fucked him. She was his daughter, all right.

★ PART THREE ★

1 The following days did not require the gypsy fortune-teller to warn Palma Piedras that life had its regrets. Christmas was around the corner. In LA it didn't look like Christmas but there was plenty of tinsel in Tinseltown, bulbous-nosed Santas at the malls and shop windows, peddling their wares amid fake snow.

The day after the quinceañera Venus and she hardly spoke to each other. Her kids refused to return home (as long as the other woman was there). They were with their father at his mother's home. Venus and she had just gotten together and already they were two wrecking balls for each other's families. (Palma's, not so much, but nice to think she might have one to wreck.) Venus's mother-in-law was no longer speaking to her. She went to the woman's house to try to persuade her children home but returned alone. It's going to take time, she said, as the couple sat in silence, having tuna fish salad with crackers. (Of all the lovely things Palma would remember her for, a culinary dare would not be among them.)

Yes, she said.

Maybe, Venus said, if we—you and me—try again, let's say, in six months, by then, everyone will have gotten used to the idea. Palma stared at her. What idea? she asked. Venus avoided her eyes. It made Palma already miss her. Look at me, she said. If her lover was going to tell her to leave she had best say it to her face. Venus usually wore contacts but had on a pair of generic-framed glasses. She pushed them back at the nose and brought her gaze to Palma's. She had no right to be there, it said. I'm going to pick up my kids later, she said. (Read: Get the fuck out.) In six months, Palma's lover said, if you come back to LA my domestic situation will be worked out. (Domestic situation? Was that what they were calling marriage these days?) Venus had already sent her away. Palma stood part-way up from the seat and leaned over to kiss the other woman on the mouth. Her lover kissed back the way people did when they were mad and didn't want to admit it. Palma sat down. The kiss of Judas said a lot. But the bags Palma already packed, lined up inside the daughter's bedroom door, and the cab scheduled to pick her up—right after the flatbread, bottled water, and the sea animals who lost the viscous struggle for their lives became the couple's last meal together—had the final word.

Palma Piedras had been saying goodbye since she left Abuela's with trash-bag luggage, turning away from Pepito's Orphan Annie button eyes. Saying goodbye was her thing. Angela and Mariano, Jr. never said goodbye, or if they ever did, their first-born didn't hear about it, and they surely hadn't said it at the *quinceañera* when they had the chance. Instead, they'd looked away. Palma should learn from people like that, the hardcore deserters.

She suddenly felt Venus trying to get her attention and she turned away. Her lover wanted her to make her feel all right. Venus's decision was hers to make. It wasn't right or wrong. (Well, it felt, somewhere at Palma's gritty solar plexus, more right—because of the kids—but she couldn't get herself to admit it that afternoon.) The sun was hinting that it was on its way to China or Australia or wherever it headed every day at dusk. Palma's cell phone rang. The cab was waiting outside. She didn't know what to say. Rocky Piedras was a champ at exits but a changa when it came to saying goodbye.

Pepito must have most likely learned about walking out from his big cous'. It was funny the things people taught kids—their own and others—without trying. Without wanting it. Do as I say not as I do. Don't lie. Don't steal. Don't covet your neighbor's wife. The next thing the neighbor is petitioning for a divorce, thanks to you. (In Palma's case, thanks to Ursula.) You told them honor thy mother and thy father while they heard you complain to others about your own. You ordered don't worship false gods and then put up a statue of the Hare Krishna and made wishes on it as if he were your fairy godmother. No wonder kids turned to drugs. Palma got up and made her way across the small house to the girl's room. Venus seemed confused. She thought she was calling the shots. What's going on? She asked, following. Palma said she'd get Austin's belongings picked up ASAP, and made her way to the door with her bags. I thought later we'd go out for dinner, someplace nice, Venus said. (And then drop Palma off at the Greyhound and leave her there like the stray dog the little girl brought home and was firmly told she could not keep?) The cabby got out and helped Palma load up his trunk. There was loud reggae blasting from his car. Venus stood a few yards away like she had stepped into quicksand. Her lover waved adios and got in the vehicle. Where to, Madam? The driver asked, strapping on his seat belt. She'd booked the same room at the Westin Bonaventure. It held maudlin memories. And if not, she most certainly brought a few back from the fiefdom of Nuestra Señora de los Angeles.

2 Palma Piedras returned to Albuquerque on Christmas Eve. Azucar was playing with her new catnip toy. She had three white paws, a white mouth, and the tip of her tail was white. The rest was black. She took to her madrina. More than likely it was the stench of sardines on Palma's hands from the can she opened. She had gotten the Mercedes back from the cops and went shopping for a few food items. She put up a miniature fake tree—with red chili lights and presents. A cat stocking filled with more catnip, balls, bells, and kitty toys, a gift from Austin, and of course, the Silverman Brothers box from Pepito. The gift from Austin was actually his shades. Palma took the ones he'd been wearing last as a souvenir of the man who put the swag in swagger. She'd wanted to visit him in jail but his lawyer said it wasn't a good idea. Palma gave the attorney Venus's address, and he assured Palma he'd get her friend's possessions put away in the storage space where apparently all the rest of Austin's mugrero was since his condo had gone into foreclosure months earlier—way before Babalucci. Austin, it turned out, was homeless when they met in Albuquerque. A homeless Buddhist hustler with a taste for la vida Alta Mulch. He showed Palma how to live splendidly from the inside out.

Azucar and her godmother were having eggnog. The

cat, out of her new Color Me Happy signature housewares cat bowl, and Palma, out of the plastic tumbler Rodrigo left behind. If it wasn't for items like that, the Rice Dream carton in the fridge, a nose-hair clipper in the medicine cabinet, and what Palma swore was the lingering aura of their defunct marriage, she'd have doubted his fleeting return. She was watching *It's a Wonderful Life*, which she uploaded for free on the MacBook Pro, when Azucar's big ears went up. The cat jumped up and went to the door. It was her daddy coming up the walk. It had snowed just enough to make it a Holy Night as she heard the crunch of boots on the fresh snow. Next came the doorbell ring. Hank had a plate with homemade sugar cookies and gingerbread men. He also brought over a six-pack of beer. Hank, Palma said, you shouldn't have. (Really, he shouldn't have.) The neighbor came in, removed his boots, brushed off the wet from his coat, and took it off. Wow, he said, picking up the kitty and checking out her bling collar. He read the tag with her new name and laughed. His hostess had bought a ready-made dinner at Albertson's. Baked ham and fixings. Hank and she were like Will Smith and his dog in *I Am Legend*. The last two beings on earth. No one was out in the streets. They fixed their plates and sat on the rug. Still no furniture. Rodrigo's air mattress stayed like a homicide victim in the corner waiting for the cops. She wasn't going near it and Hank avoided it like he had decided he no longer had use for beds.

It was going to be one of the best Christmases of Palma's life. For one, she wasn't alone. For two, she had just formalized her online brand as a startup company. The stylist who worked at the studio with Austin and she were now partners. La Rocky accessories—from handbags to fluffy handcuffs—a brand without borders. Don't worry about designs; there are computer programs for that. Each client, in every shape and size, will get her clothes to fit like a pleather glove—Alicia told her.

A pleather glove . . . Palma had repeated at that meeting. Fuschia silk lining? Tiny dots or herringbone pattern? Yeah, yeah, Alicia said. Wanna see my designs, Rocky? (She was artsy-fartsy from New York. Everyone at the studio hated her. Not Palma. They were both in love with the same thing—color and materials.) Give it to me, she said. Natural dyes and recycled fabrics? The MBA-slash-stylist Alicia tested her. No problem. Local talent and manufacturers? Yes, again. Their startup company was already in the works. Most of their collaboration could be done online. Alicia in Tinseltown and Palma on land, air, or sea.

If you want to come with me tomorrow, Hank said, my ma's making posole and tamales. She shook her head. Palma regretted passing up homemade tamales but she could live without posole. In any case, she had a ticket to fly out to Chicago the next day. What? Hank said. Yes, she said, I got a cheap fare because it was a holiday.

Palma had accepted an offer on Abuela's house, or she wanted to but needed Jim-Bo's consent. You'll have to keep Azucar, she told Hank. No problem. He sat cross-legged, looking around at the empty walls with lines where frames once hung, while he munched green beans.

How are the boys getting along with Ursula? Palma asked about his stepchildren. Hank's face went blank. Isn't Patricia in Houston with her boys and Ursula? she asked. Why would Patricia be in Houston with the boys? He asked. *You* said, Palma said. No, I didn't. They did a Who's-on-First Abbot and Costello exchange for a few minutes before they stopped and started over. That was when and how Palma found out that

Patricia and Ursula had never become lovers. They did a you-show-me-yours-and I'll-show-you-mine with their you-know, Hank said, indicating the chest area.

That's all? Palma said. She put her plate on the carpet and Azucar took her ham without apologies. Listen, he said, I wouldn't have liked it if she was doing that with a guy. It's improper for a married woman. After a few minutes Hank said, I'm just old fashioned. Yes, maybe he was. Or maybe he was just committed to the relationship. You should call Ursula, he said. Palma shook her head. Unlike comedy routines, life got away from a person with bad timing. There were exceptions for the lucky ones. Anyway, she had not heard from Ursula lately. She had most likely moved on.

Palma, however, had heard from someone else, her niece, Taylor. Merry X-Mas, Tía Palma, the text read. Love you. She'd keep it forever. Or until her stupid mobile erased it. No one had ever called her tía. Palma texted back, <3 u 2.

Randall's man-cave bar was decorated with early nineties string lights, silver tinsel, and plastic mistletoe. The clientele that night too, what there was, looked like they'd been coming around since then. Randall had on a shabby Santa hat and his business partner wore the red suit. Randall held up plastic mistletoe over their heads. Palma leaned over the bar and they did a mwah-mwah on each cheek. She bought a present. A little known fact about her friend was how much he loved to read. He opened it. *Peel My Love like an Onion?* he said, reading off the title. Never heard of it. Well, it's got a Chicago setting, she said. Cool, he said. He gave her a gift, too, the gift of knowing he was content. Randall and the redhead from the House of Blues in Chicago were meeting after Christmas to ski together in Santa Fe. Why don't you come along? He invited.

I've got plans, she said. With the door opening and shutting every few minutes Palma kept on her new coat. The big surprise. Pepito's present. A Silverman Brothers' design. Vintage three-quarter mink, sleeves removed and replaced with thick sweater sleeves. She loved it. No card. (Didn't like that.) Palma texted a Merry Christmas and thank you to Pepito with no reply. You know who rolled by here one night, lovie? Randall said. None other than Mishu Martini. He came to say goodbye, her friend relayed. He's moving to Canada. What was it about Canada? she wondered. The new sanctuary for outlaws? Maybe he left with Rodrigo, Palma said. Good riddance to both! Randall said. It's going to be a new year, he said, with new beginnings.

3 Chicago was colder than Abuela's heart had been. Sometimes. Coming from a long line of Totonacas patas rajadas who had survived the conquest. Or so she liked to say. Or maybe, in the end, the religious fervor was all due to the dread of meeting her Maker. And maybe she hadn't raised Pepito and Palma out of compassion for humanity, but fearing the pangs of eternal damnation. Palma would never know, she decided, when checking into the James Hotel downtown. She called her lawyer. Maybe he was of the Scrooge persuasion. He answered on Christmas and reported that there was no word from Jim-Bo. Big shocker. His client left several messages on the outdated answering machine on Abuela's landline. She imagined the old woman's son staring at it while listening to his niece's voice coming over it like the harbinger of doom. Jim-Bo would get his share of the money for the property but it'd be like moving a desert rat out of its barrel-cactus shelter. She hadn't received any replies from Pepito either.

The next day Palma took a cab to the Silverman Brother's shop on Halsted. It was a large store. Tailors available. Personable salespeople on hand. It looked like athletes favored the place from the appearance of a few customers. She didn't know sports teams, but they were big men with cash to spend getting measurements taken or checking themselves out in mirrors, matching hats and shoes to new suits. There was a striking woman with long, salt-and-pepper hair in a wheelchair, watching her lover admire himself in his new duds. He had a ponytail almost as long as his cockiness. She was in a long skirt to hide her legs and her lap was covered with a fur throw. If I didn't know better, Palma said, I'd think you two stepped out of the novel I just read, Palma said. The woman flicked something from one of her fingernails, considered her reply then said, I'm real enough. Yes, her companion called, just like that coat! He gave a whistle at Palma that nearly rang through the store.

That's one of ours! A woman called coming over. She had a pair of reading glasses dangling from a chain around her neck and reeked of Alta Mulch. Palma checked out the wedding finger. French doorknob proportions. Nails done, natural and old school, filed like little shovels nearly to a point. Her wavy coif shouted same-neighborhood-beauty-shop-for-the-last–thirty-years-kiss-my-ass. She was on the fence between sixty and *never more*. I got it for Christmas, Palma said. Is Joe here?

Joe? The woman said. Nooooo. Are you . . . ?

Palma wasn't sure if she was, but before she heard whom she might be she said, I'm Joe's cousin. *His cousin?* The woman said. Yes, Palma said. You know? Palma Piedras? She folded her arms, turned to look at the woman in the chair and her flamenco lover and they were gone. Well, who are *you?* She asked the woman.

I'm Karla, the woman said, my husband owns the store. They were curious about one another. Karla said her husband was John Silverman, son of one of the original owners who was now retired in Palm Beach. In a home there. Joe's like a son to us, she said. A few more exchanges and Palma found out it wasn't that Karla didn't know much about her but a lot. Joe has the week off, she told Palma, who then didn't ask where she thought he might be. (If he himself couldn't be bothered to tell Palma, there was no point.) How 'bout some lunch? The woman invited, looking at her watch. You like corned beef?

They left and got in Karla's Jag to drive the three blocks to Manny's. A valet took the car. The place was slammed to the gefilte gills. The manager came over, kissed Karla on the cheek, and materialized a table. It was all small talk confined to complaints about the recession and how business had slowed down at Silverman Brothers and then Karla brought up Pepito. He's done so much for the family, she said, taking trips to look into our investments and visiting my father-in-law in Florida to make sure he was all right. Oh, that old man gripes about everything, Karla said, even though my husband John makes sure his father has the best. If it wasn't for Joe, who goes to check on things in Palm Beach, and all the rest of what he's done for the family, well, we don't know what we'd have done, Karla said. You need a guy for such things, she said. She and her husband had two daughters, both married and not interested in the family business. One married a lawyer, the other a doctor. A mother's dream. My daughters studied at Vassar, she said, as if that was where a girl went to ensure she married well. (Like Palma would know.) Well, Karla continued, it's admirable how Joe has cleaned up his act since his release. He was always basically a good kid, the woman said, but frankly, he was on the wrong track before, you know.

Yes, Palma "knew." He had allegedly killed a man. Not a gangbanger but someone high up in crooked, white businessdom. Palma figured it had been a hired hit. Back then, Karla said, Joe was using . . . (She leaned forward and whispered) you know . . . *drugs? Cocaine.* (Then louder) Prison probably saved his life.

If that's what you want to think, Palma said. The prison system wasn't exactly known for rehabilitating anyone, but she didn't feel like having that discussion with Joe's boss. He's fine now, she said.

Yes! Karla said. He's doing great, just amazing! After the sandwiches arrived, Karla said, I must say, that's a marvelous coat of ours Joe picked out for you. I would have done something else with the sleeves, Palma said. Heh, the woman said. Let's see the lining. Palma opened both sides. (She hadn't taken it off since Christmas Eve midnight except to shower.) As she showed Karla the lining she noticed her initials sewn inside. She hated her initials. (She would always hate them.) Right next to them was an inside pocket. The corner of a paper stuck out. Karla spotted it, too. Maybe it was the card Palma sorely found missing with his gift. She pulled it out. It was a legal size envelope, folded in half. She opened it and found a photocopy of Pepito's birth certificate. He was born in Chicago. He came to the world at the county hospital on the very date and year Palma knew was his birthday. What glared at her, however, were his parents' names. All his life Pepito had used Abuela's surname. It was how she first registered him in kindergarten. Who were these people on his birth certificate?

Karla watched Palma's face. What is it, dear? Palma handed over the document. The woman put on her reading glasses and examined it. Yeah, she said. Joe's folks were from Mexico. She handed it back and Palma stared at it again. It's a shame that they were forced to leave their little boy behind, the woman said, but thank God, the woman he called his grandmother took him in. Apparently, she was truly God-fearing, Karla said with authority, the way she said everything else, and went back to her lunch as she talked about Abuela. Joe told us how his parents were deported and left the little boy at the church day care. Instead of the lady he came to call his grandma taking him to immigration, where they would have sent the child back to Mexico, she took him home. What a saint, Karla said about Abuela.

Palma pushed the coleslaw around on the plate. She hated anything cabbage—on principal. Gastritis only made her more antisocial than she might be already. Anyway, she couldn't eat. She was reeling from the news. Pepito and she were not related at all and he knew it. Abuela had left him all her stories. He never referred to me as his cousin? she asked Karla, who shook her head. Well, you're not cousins. Then, as if the woman thought the fact might upset her, she added, He was always in love with you, you know.

After lunch, Karla and Palma were about to part ways at the restaurant entrance when the woman took hold of her shoulders and looked her dead in the eye. My family and I are eternally grateful to that young man, she said.

How's that? Palma asked, a little rattled from Karla's eyeball-to-eyeball directness. You must know? Karla said. Her eyes darted into Palma's. Joe protected my husband, she said. The eyeball penetration continued for an infinitesimal second longer, then Dame Karla walked off. Palma was stunned, Chi-Town Joe's story unfolding before her was like an ancient codex, part indecipherable glyphs, part precious truth, and part do what you will with it. Once a story was given, it was in the hands of the receiver. He'd been just a kid trying to stay out of trouble, working for the Alta Mulch. Someone thought it clever to string him out on coke. Anybody could get money for crack but coke was another class. (Hadn't Whitney made that point to Diane Sawyer back in the day?) He started living in the fast lane, per se. Her lil cous' gave up a decade of freedom to protect a rich man. In exchange for what? Forty grand for starters.

PALMA TOOK a cab to Jim-Bo's. It had snowed over Christmas. The streets were clear but the icy temperatures left frozen clumps of snow along curbs, against the chain-link fences that divided the front yards in Abuela's neighborhood, and against the façades of buildings where in summer there were hedges. She rang the bell like it was an emergency alarm. No one answered. Maybe Jim-Bo had gone to work. He was a clerk at a paint store. Thirty years and his mark of success had been not getting fired. The snow was freshly shoveled and there was salt on the steps. She rang again. Someone peeked through the front window blinds. You'd think she was the census taker. Mexicans hated census takers and not just the gente without documents. It was a sunny day with clear skies. You could see your own breath. Palma pulled her cashmere scarf up to her chin. The longer they kept her out there, the firmer her conviction was to throw them out. She rang again and kept her thumb on the doorbell. Abuela's doorbell sounded like the kind they had on small businesses for backdoor deliveries.

At last, Jim-Bo opened the door. He pushed back the storm door so they could talk. Instead, she let herself in. You two are going to have to move, Jim-Bo, she said. We've accepted the offer on the house. It's fair. And you have no choice. You'll get your half. Palma waited. Jim-Bo was in a short-sleeved, high-collared, white T-shirt as always, crinkled khaki pants from Kmart. (He got everything at Kmart.) He let out a loud belch in lieu of an answer. His old lady in the kitchen doorway got a kick of it. Heh-heh. You, too, Palma said to her, then pointed to the floor indicating that whoever she kept down there had also better scat. She put her hand on the doorknob, pulled it, and pushed open the screen. You'll get the paperwork from the lawyer, she said.

As Palma was coming down the steps she saw Pepito. With residents at home for the holidays there was no street parking so he'd left his car further down. He was in the camel-hair coat, taking deliberate strides. At first she was surprised to see him, then remembered Karla. The Silvermans were his peeps. If you can't help your family, who can you help? The first Mayor Daley famously said after it was revealed that he intervened in his son's "passing" the bar after failing it four times. Palma stopped and tried to smile but he was moving fast, took two steps at a time up the steps, nodded, and went passed her. He didn't ring the bell, but with his leather-gloved hand yanked open the storm door, turned the doorknob, and let himself in their childhood home. She followed. Whatever was about to happen, Palma would have a ringside seat. She nearly tripped on the doorstep.

Jim-Bo, in his easy chair watching TV, never had the chance to get up. At least not by his own volition. Pepito pulled the stout man from underneath his armpits and tossed him to the floor. Standing over him, breathing hard, Pepito did a come on gesture with both hands. Jim-Bo stayed down. The woman gasped. Who are you? she demanded. Pepito pointed a gloved finger at Jim-Bo and then at her. Palma wants you out. The house is sold. Either you do it today or I'll come back and get you both out. The guitar noise coming from the base ment stopped. Pepito looked at the floor. He started toward the basement door and Jim-Bo's old lady jumped in front of him. No, please. He motioned to Palma and they left.

Outside, she steadied herself. Pumped with adrenaline, Pepito went down the steps with his long legs as if in flight, while she tried to catch up. Are you okay? he asked, slowing down and offering his hand. Palma didn't know if she was. He stopped. Aw, for God's sake, he said, and led her back to the stoop where he sat her down on one of the top steps. He put a foot on the third step, leaned forward on the raised knee, and reaching, put his hands out. Gloved hands held gloved hands. How are you? he asked. His voice was unusually soft. She was wearing Austin's glasses. They were too big. Palma pulled them off. She wanted to say something, many things. Everything. It wasn't her little cousin anymore. Or her big and tough grown cousin. He looked up at the sky. Why did people always search the heavens with such intent? Not just people in her life story, but from the beginning of time. The skies brought rain, sunshine, and moonlight. They enabled harvests to grow or let them dry. Pepito leaned over, kissed her on the cheek, and straightened up, his departure imminent. He wanted Palma's blessing, his official dismissal. We'll always have Tango, she said, holding up her mobile. He nodded and she stood up. I have a plane to catch tonight out of O'Hare, she announced and kissed him on the cheek. Here, she said, taking off the fabuloso fur. PETA advocates might throw eggs if they catch sight of this, she said. You know how much I hate eggs. (Just because she didn't care much for pets didn't mean she couldn't care after they were dead.) Her lil cous' looked like maybe he had her wrong all those years. Maybe he had. She took a last look at Abuela's house. Chi-Town Joe accepted the return of the gift and turning around slowly started to walk off. Stopped. His head half-turned. The profile—strong chin, Apache nose—magnificent, man. Want a ride? He asked over his shoulder. No thanks. Palma gazed up at the dark skies. It was summer in Rio.

ALELUYA.